Bernie looked makeup.

She had faint freckles spattered across her nose, he noticed for the first time. In that moment under the fluorescent bathroom light, Liam found himself wishing that he could close the distance between them. It would be the most natural thing in the world to slide an arm around her waist and kiss the top of her head. He pulled his thoughts away from the precipice.

Bernie was a part of the cutthroat world he was trying to protect Ike from. One word from her would bring her family's legal team down on him, and Ike could very quickly be swept away. Attraction shouldn't factor into this, and entertaining these feelings would only blur his perspective. He needed to be careful. Having the Morgan family's undivided attention could be a dangerous thing.

Except that he *was* feeling something for this woman—something he hadn't felt in a good many years. Was it just that he was lonely, or was it their combined effort in sorting out Ike's scrapes? Whatever it was, he needed to keep it in check.

Dear Reader,

This book began with an image I had in my mind of a bedraggled bride driving up to a service station in Small Town, USA, in a classic Rolls-Royce. Her makeup would be smeared. Her hair would be a mess. Her dress would be dusty and possibly even a little torn. She'd get out of the car, walk up to the stunned mechanic and say "I can't believe I made it. It stopped twice on the highway on the way here. Can you take a look?"

But who was she? And what was she doing in Small Town, USA? And if that stunned mechanic happened to marry that bedraggled bride, what a fantastic "how we met" story! A novel was born.

I hope that you enjoy this story as much as I loved writing it. And if you like sweet romance that tugs at the heartstrings, come check out my other novels in Love Inspired and Harlequin Western Romance. All of my books are wholesome, so you can trust them, no matter which line they are published under.

If you'd like to connect with me, you can find me at my blog, patriciajohnsromance.com, or on Facebook. I'd love to hear from you!

Patricia Johns

HEARTWARMING

The Runaway Bride

Patricia Johns

⟡ **HARLEQUIN**® HEARTWARMING™

Recycling programs
for this product may
not exist in your area.

ISBN-13: 978-0-373-36839-6

The Runaway Bride

Copyright © 2017 by Patty Froese Ntihemuka

Printed in U.S.A.

Patricia Johns writes from Alberta, Canada. She has her honors BA in English literature and currently writes for Harlequin's Love Inspired, Western Romance and Heartwarming lines. You can find her at patriciajohnsromance.com.

Books by Patricia Johns

Harlequin Heartwarming

A Baxter's Redemption

Harlequin Western Romance

Hope, Montana

Safe in the Lawman's Arms
Her Stubborn Cowboy
The Cowboy's Christmas Bride
The Cowboy's Valentine Bride
The Triplets' Cowboy Daddy

Love Inspired

His Unexpected Family
The Rancher's City Girl
A Firefighter's Promise
The Lawman's Surprise Family

Visit the Author Profile page at Harlequin.com for more titles.

To my husband, who inspires the romantic in me. And to our little boy, who once upon a time was a toddler who liked to share cookies.

CHAPTER ONE

BERNADETTE "BUNNY" MORGAN could hear the murmur of voices from the Manhattan cathedral where her family and friends already waited. Ten minutes from now, she'd be walking down that aisle on her father's arm to the traditional wedding march. She'd imagined this moment a thousand times since they'd booked the cathedral two years ago. Weddings of this caliber didn't come together in a heartbeat. Everything from the choice of the groom to the color of the scented beads in the dressing rooms took careful planning.

Each element of this wedding was traditional. It had to be perfect, as her mother so kindly pointed out, since the media would be picking it apart. This wedding would be on all the society pages and blogs…but her mother, Kitty, had taken care of most of those details for her from the flowers adorning the church to the Rolls-Royce they would drive away in. Her father had been less inclined to hand over his antique Rolls, but what Kitty wanted, Kitty got. And Kitty demanded perfection for her daughter's wedding.

Thankfully.

Bernadette loved that car, and she liked the idea of driving off with Calvin toward the Four Seasons Hotel, their security entourage flanking them. It would be the first glorious foray of Mr. and Mrs. Calvin McMann.

"We want them to think of the Kennedys when you drive off," her mother had told her. "Regal. American royalty. We might not be there yet, but we can put a picture in their minds. I want them to think Jackie Kennedy. So remember, sweet, demure and classic. Always classic!"

Bernadette twisted her engagement ring on her finger—a princess-cut diamond in a cloud of smaller stones, all set in platinum. It was beautiful, eye-catching and fabric-catching, too. She tugged it free of her gauzy skirt, wincing as she noticed the tiny snag.

Calvin was just down the hall. They'd agreed to have a few moments of private contemplation before the wedding began to calm their nerves, but Bernadette was regretting that now. Her stomach flipped as she paused to look in the mirror one last time. The face that stared back at her, framed in glossy dark waves, looked ashen.

What would Calvin be doing with his "contemplation" time? Practicing his golf swing, no doubt. Calvin McMann was unflappable. Tall, chiseled, tanned—he was perfection in a suit, and whenever she felt doubts nagging, all she had to do was look at him, and she'd remember their carefully orchestrated plans for a successful life together. Calvin McMann was a senator, and the position had settled a certain comfortable confidence onto his shoulders. What she needed right now was to see her fiancé—have him give one of those trademark winks that made him so electable.

"Sweet, demure, classic," she reminded herself aloud.

Kitty would kill her if she snuck into Calvin's dressing room. Brides stayed put until they went down the aisle… And heaven help the bride who let her groom see the dress a second too early.

This was stupid! Who really cared if Calvin saw her dress? That was superstition, and this marriage wouldn't be built on something so flimsy. They were a political team, a financial powerhouse. Love on these levels was 80 percent choice, and she'd made the right one in Calvin McMann…hadn't she?

Her stomach twisted again. Logically, marrying Calvin made sense. She knew that, but…

Bernadette eased open the door and peeked into the hallway. No one. The bridesmaids were with the photographer out in the church foyer—she could hear the photographer's instructions. Her mother's voice could be heard over his, telling Courtney, Bernadette's maid of honor, to stop "standing there like a common tart," whatever that meant.

Bernadette's dress rustled when she moved, so she gathered it in her arms and crept down the hallway toward the room Calvin was using. She'd have knocked if she weren't afraid of drawing everyone's attention, so she turned the handle as silently as possible and peeked inside.

It took a moment to make sense of what she saw. She'd been expecting to see Calvin standing alone, fiddling with cuff links or something. Instead, it was a mess of black suit and pink tulle. There was a flash of tanned skin, a swath of blond hair... There were some grunts, a sigh, then she made out Calvin's tanned hand moving up a white thigh. And suddenly, the whole scene came into focus.

Vivid, ugly focus.

She didn't feel rage, just numbing shock, and then the sickening sensation that she might vomit. And she saw the truth as clear as day: this was what her married life would look like—a handsome groom satisfying his carnal desires with another woman in the next room.

Bernadette recognized the woman in her fiancé's arms—it was Calvin's ex-girlfriend, who was supposed to be in the distant past, or so he claimed. Would Kimberly be a fixture in their marriage, or was this going to be a revolving door? One thing would be expected: she, the dutiful wife, would have to stand there with the grace and dignity of Jackie Kennedy, *taking it*.

No. That was the first word to pop into her mind as the shock began to fade. *No!*

She paused for a moment, waiting for hysterics to set in, but they didn't. She didn't feel frightened or panicked. She didn't feel uncontrollable fury. A strange, eerie calm settled over her, and she eased the door shut once more, gathered up her skirts and crept down the back stairs.

"Bunny?" Lanie was one of the junior bridesmaids and one of her second cousins. She stood by the back door, a cigarette in one hand, apparently sneaking a quick smoke before the ceremony began. Bernadette hated that stupid nickname. Her parents had set her up for a lifetime of country clubs and golf courses with that name.

"Hi, sweetie," Bernadette crooned. "I'm just going to get something from the car." She put her fingers to her lips in an exaggerated display of secrecy, and her young cousin giggled.

"I'll hold the door!" Lanie whispered after her.

The car was parked close to the church, ready for their big exit, and Bernadette fished around in her little satin bag for the car key, and pulled it out. Her father might have hand-picked her groom, but he wouldn't trust Calvin with the keys to his favorite car until the vows were final.

She popped the trunk, and looked down at the two suitcases. One was hers, packed with such attention to detail over the past few days, and the other Calvin's.

"Miss Morgan?" It was the security guard, and he looked suddenly disconcerted. "Or should I say Mrs. McMann?"

He apparently didn't know if the wedding had happened yet.

"Bunny is fine." She shot him a reassuring smile, then she paused. "Actually, no. I hate that name. Call me Bernie."

"Yes, ma'am. Can I help you with anything... Bernie?"

"Yes!" She smiled brilliantly and hauled Calvin's suitcase out of the trunk. "Be a doll and hold this for me, would you?"

The young man stepped forward and took the proffered suitcase, then she slammed the trunk shut and beelined over to the driver's side. She let herself in, piling her voluminous skirt into her lap, then slammed the door shut and started the car.

"Ma'am?" The security guard started around the car just as she stepped on the gas. "Wait! Miss Morgan! I mean—"

She didn't hear the rest of what he said, because she was driving at full speed toward the security checkpoint. Uniformed guards scattered like bowling pins as she sailed through and took a squealing turn onto the Manhattan street, narrowly missing a yellow cab. The driver leaned out his window and let out a string of curses that faded away as she accelerated.

She had no idea where she was going—just away. Far away! She'd think this through later. She might have the classic, dark-haired beauty, and she might come from wealth, but she was no Jackie Kennedy.

LIAM WILSON WIPED his greasy hands on a cloth and tossed it onto his workbench next to the pickup he was working on. It needed another part, and he'd have to order it in. The front garage door was rolled up, allowing a breeze to move through, but the air was still thick with heat. June had warmed up fast, and they looked like they were in for a drought after a winter of not enough snow and a spring with too little rain. That was bad news for surrounding farmers and ranchers, and it would affect everyone. If only the bad news had stopped with the weather.

Liam was trying to keep things "normal" at Runt River Auto—he still had vehicles to fix, after all—but last month normal had taken a backseat when a two-year-old boy with big brown eyes and a mop of dark curls had been delivered to his home by a police cruiser. The officers had said his name was Ike Wilson; the little guy wouldn't answer any questions. With eyes welling with tears, the boy had simply whispered, "I want Mommy."

Liam was Ike's closest relative, even though that situation was about as complicated as it could get. This was his estranged wife's child—not his. Leanne had been working on Senator Morgan's campaign when the affair started. Liam had been blind to it all, trying to convince her that they should try adoption since an incredibly rare childhood episode of mumps had left him sterile. The vaccination hadn't taken for him, and he'd suffered more than the painful illness—he'd also lost his ability to produce children. Leanne had desperately wanted to be pregnant and have a baby of her own. He couldn't exactly provide that, but he'd wanted a baby just as badly as she did—he was just willing to adopt to make that happen. So when she'd told him that she was pregnant, there'd been no doubt about what that meant.

That was almost three years ago. Liam knew they should have divorced, but there hadn't seemed to be any urgency, and she'd still been his legal wife at the time of her death in the car accident last month. He was her closest living relative, so Ike came to him—the baby his wife had with Senator Vince Morgan. According to Ohio law, he was Ike's legal parent unless someone could prove otherwise.

Liam took a swig from a water bottle. He still had no idea how he'd sort all of this out. He obviously couldn't keep the kid, but he didn't want to send him off into the child welfare system, either. Liam had grown up in foster care, and he didn't recommend the experience. So he'd done the only thing he could and called up Lucille Neiman, the kind older woman across the street, and she'd agreed to help out with childcare for a while. He'd just needed time to think. A month later, he was still stumped.

The sound of a faltering engine came rumbling up the street—a sputter, a bang. That was the sound of a customer. He stepped outside and shaded his eyes against the glare of the late afternoon sunlight. Runt River Auto sat on a corner just south of the gas station. Travelers with car trouble stopped at the station and got pointed in his direction. About half his business came down that highway.

The car came around the corner, a white antique Rolls-Royce, by the look of it. He blew out a low whistle of appreciation, then squinted to see if he was hallucinating. He could see the driver clearly through the open window—a woman in a wedding dress and a veil, her dark hair disheveled. The car crept up to the sidewalk, let out one last rattling bang, then heaved out a hiss of steam.

Liam headed toward the car just as she pushed open the door and stepped out, jerking a voluminous skirt out after her. Her makeup was streaked from tears, and she batted a curl out of her eyes. The veil was tangled behind her, but it was securely attached to her head by some feminine mystery.

"I can't believe I made it," she said. "It started with a clunking noise, and stalled twice along the highway. Can you take a look?"

"Uh—" Liam swallowed. "Sure. Yeah. Sure."

He didn't know what to say. It wasn't every day a disheveled bride drove up in a Rolls. He angled his head toward the office.

"Come on inside and I'll take down your information."

She crawled back into the car, reaching for something, nothing but that poofy skirt and pale blue shoes visible. Then she emerged again, a small satin purse in her hand, and followed him toward the low, brick building. Liam had worked at this garage since he was a teen, and he'd eventually bought it. And in all the years this place had been in business, Liam was pretty sure this was the first time it had seen a Rolls-Royce and a rumpled bride.

Liam eyed the woman curiously as she passed into the office ahead of him. Her dress had little capped sleeves, and the skirt tumbled around her in waves of rustling fabric. A few stains were visible—a streak of grease, a splotch of dirt. She headed straight for the water cooler.

"I'm so thirsty. I'm starving, too. Is there anything to eat around here?"

Liam looked around helplessly. "Sorry, not really—"

He caught her looking at him with one eyebrow arched incredulously, and he chuckled. "You mean in Runt River. Of course. Yeah. There's a couple of diners and a hotel. Look, you mind if I ask what happened?"

"I ran out on my wedding." She drank a paper cup of water and bent to refill it. "That was in New York, and I just kept driving."

From New York to Ohio—that had been quite the drive. Both of her hands were bare of rings, and the dress was dusty and soiled around the hemline. She drained the second cup of water.

"Do you need to borrow a phone?" he asked.

"No, thanks. I've got a cell phone here." She raised the small purse.

She didn't offer any more information than that, and Liam watched her for a moment, trying to make sense of this. She was obviously in rough shape. She'd been crying, she was a mess and her car was toast. But that car—it was expensive, perfectly detailed and newly refinished. The motor looked original, though. She either came from money or had her own, he was willing to bet on it. Regardless, her affairs were her business.

She was here to have her car fixed, and he wouldn't take advantage of her because she had money. He did quality work for a fair price—always had and always would.

"Could I get your ID?" he asked, pulling up a form on the computer screen.

She opened the purse and pulled out her driver's license and passed it over. He looked down at the card and froze. Bernadette Morgan…as in, *the* Bernadette Morgan of the American political family? Vince Morgan was the senator who'd seduced Leanne, and from what Liam knew, he was Bernadette's cousin. The Morgan money had funded more than one illustrious political career. The wedding between Bunny Morgan and Calvin Mc-Mann had been splashed all over the news for weeks now, and Liam hadn't been able to completely avoid it, much as he tried. The Morgans left a sour taste in his mouth, but then he had personal reasons for his resentment.

"Bunny Morgan?" he asked cautiously.

"Pleasure to meet you. But I prefer Bernie. And I'd appreciate it if you could keep all of this quiet. The reporters are already hunting for me, I'm sure."

He wasn't sure what to think, but while this woman was related to Vince Morgan, she hadn't been the one to tear his marriage apart. What was he supposed to do, kick her out?

"Are you okay?" he asked at last.

"No." Tears welled in her eyes. "Not at all."

Okay, that was fair. He grabbed a box of tissues from under the counter and pushed them in her direction. She took one and wiped her eyes.

"What did he do?" he asked after a moment.

"Who?" she asked.

"What's his name—the McMann fellow you were supposed to marry." Avoiding news about the Morgans wasn't really possible.

"*Senator* McMann," she clarified, as if the title were important. She looked like she wasn't going to say anything more, then she sighed. "I suppose it doesn't matter now. I caught him making out with his ex-girlfriend in the room where he was supposed to be getting dressed for the ceremony."

Ouch. If something were going to end a wedding, that would be it. Looked like *Senator* McMann and old Vince had their philandering in common, even if they weren't officially family.

"I'm sorry," he said.

"Me, too." She smiled weakly. "But I made it here, and that's something. I'm looking for my aunt. She's supposed to live in this town. Her name is Lucille Neiman. Do you know her?"

"Your—" He swallowed. "Lucille is your aunt?"

"Yes…" She cleared her throat. "I don't really know her myself. I just thought…maybe you could give me her phone number or address?"

Liam had known Lucille since he was a kid, and she was a fixture around Runt River.

"She's my neighbor. I'll swing you by when I've got all your information and I get the car into the garage," Liam replied. "I've got to head on over there anyway."

Bernadette Morgan had stumbled into town a month after her two-year-old relative had been left with him. Liam was a practical man, and he didn't believe in coincidences this huge. Had Lucille called her? Maybe the Morgans would acknowledge the kid after all, and Ike would go to his biological family.

An image rose in his mind of that curly-headed boy, his eyes glistening with tears, whispering those plaintive words, "I want Mommy." Leanne had died, leaving behind an innocent kid to whom she was the whole world. He'd had a month to get attached to Ike, and caring for him had awakened his fatherly instinct. When Ike had first arrived, Liam had considered what it would mean for the boy to go live with his biological family, and the thought had left him unsettled. Liam knew just how corrupt the Morgans were, and handing an innocent child over to people he didn't trust—that wasn't right.

Now, Bernadette Morgan was in town, and while she seemed to be here for totally different reasons, Liam's suspicions were piqued. Things had just gotten a whole lot more complicated.

CHAPTER TWO

AFTER THE PAPERWORK had been completed and the mechanic pushed Bernie's car into the garage, he heaved that old door shut again. He stood there in cowboy boots and surprisingly clean blue jeans, squinting slightly in the lowering sun.

"I'll drive you over, if you want," he said.

"Thanks. I appreciate it." Bernie tried to sound confident, but she didn't feel it. She'd never met her aunt before, and all she knew was that Lucille had been part of a big family squabble that had started before Bernie was born and had only grown over the years.

The mechanic opened the door of a rusty, old pickup truck, and gestured for her to get in. It was a far cry from the lambskin seats in the Rolls-Royce. Bernie gathered her skirt, then stepped onto the rail to hoist herself into the truck. Was it a good idea to trust a mechanic driving a wreck? That vintage

Rolls-Royce was from her father's personal collection, and if it didn't come back in mint condition, that vein in his forehead would burst. Mind you, she'd just walked out on the society wedding of the year. That vein had probably already blown.

The mechanic held the door open for her as she clambered up. Her wedding dress was ruined. She plucked at the place where her ring had snagged the gauze. A hole had spread, large enough to poke three fingers through. She'd dreamed about what her wedding day would be like, and nothing like this had ever occurred to her... Right now, if things had unfolded differently, she'd be at her reception, dancing with her handsome groom, making small talk with the who's who of New York, turning toward camera flashes and cutting cake.

The mental image of Calvin and Kimberly entwined in each other's arms was sickening...and she couldn't quite banish it from her head. She'd been numb to the full impact of what she'd seen, but it had slowly hit her as she drove the long stretch between Manhattan and Runt River.

This wasn't the future they'd all planned:

Calvin was going to run for president down the line—he had Bernie's father's financial support, the backing of the Republican party and a boyish grin that charmed even the stoutest Democrats. He'd be the first from the Morgan family in the White House if he were elected, and the Morgans wanted this so badly that they salivated.

They'd been trying to get Vince groomed and ready to run for president, but her cousin wasn't quite clean enough. He'd had too many affairs, hired too many hookers, thinking no one would notice if they left by a back door… Calvin had been a compromise—a senator they could not only get elected, but who could be in the Morgans' debt by virtue of how much they could do to support his rise to power. As his wife, Bernadette could supervise him… Bernadette wasn't interested in running for office, but had she been willing, her father would have made ample use of her, too. But all those political plans mattered very little to her right now. She would never be his First Lady, and she sincerely hoped he never made the White House. And how had she not noticed that he was cheating?

"I'm Liam Wilson, by the way," the mechanic said.

She hadn't asked, she realized belatedly. She shot him an apologetic smile. "Nice to meet you. Thanks for the ride."

"No problem." He slammed the door shut behind her and ambled around to the driver's side. She followed him with her eyes for a few seconds, taking in his relaxed good looks. Where Calvin had been smooth shaven and smooth-talking, this man had stubble on his face and grease-stained hands. The inside of the truck was like a furnace, and sweat sprung up across her forehead. Liam hopped up into the driver's seat and started the engine. She pushed the button to lower the window, the outside air meeting her face to provide some relief.

"How long will it take to fix my car?" she asked as they snapped their seat belts into place.

"I'll have to look at it, see what parts we need and then order them."

That didn't sound quick. "So how long is that?"

He shot her a dry look. "Can't say yet. I'll get started first thing in the morning. If you don't want me to work on it, you can always call for a tow to take you back to New York."

No, she didn't want that in the least.

"I'll wait," she said. But if he thought he was going to drag this out for money, she had lawyers who could end his business in a matter of days.

"You said you've never met your aunt?" he asked as he backed the truck out of the parking space.

"No. She's always been distanced from the family, so I never got the chance."

"So she didn't call you?" he asked.

"Call me?" She frowned. "We've never even spoken. Why?"

"Nothing." He put the truck into Drive and pulled onto the road.

This town was miniscule, and the fact that people actually lived in a place like this was mystifying. Compared to New York's bustle, the three or four cars along this street were kind of eerie—like a *Walking Dead* episode. But even that didn't make her want to head back to New York right away. The big city also held the wedding she'd run from. She closed her eyes, trying to dissipate the anxiety that bubbled up inside her. Her parents were already furious, as the McMann family would be. She'd talked to her parents briefly—long enough to have them order her to return and for her to tell them it wasn't happening—and then she'd turned off her phone. She couldn't deal with their anger right now, especially when it was all aimed at her instead of her cheating fiancé. She didn't much care what Calvin thought; he could go rot somewhere, for all she was concerned.

The newspapers, the magazines, network news channels…they'd have a field day with this. How long had it taken before people figured out the bride was missing? Probably not too long. The security detail would have made sure of that. But thanks to Kitty's tireless PR work, no fewer than four newspapers and two bridal magazines would have been there to record the catastrophe.

New York traffic had been miserable, as it always was, but luckily an angry bride shaking her fist out the window blended right in in New York. She hadn't called her parents until she hit open road, and by that time, Milhouse and Kitty Morgan were beyond tender concern and had gone straight to irate shouting.

Should she call them now? They'd be worried sick. Also furious, and she had no desire to bring her father's security detail over to this tiny town to hustle her back home. She was thirty, not a child…and yet she was plenty old enough to know that her family's power lay in more than simple wealth. Their influence was political, and politics required kid gloves with everything…including cheating fiancés.

"Runt River is pretty small," Liam was saying, and she dragged her attention back to the present. "I think our population is seven hundred now—we hovered at 698 for about three years before some babies were born."

He looked over at her, and she thought she caught some humor in his half smile. He looked kind, and after the day she'd had, she was grateful for a little bit of kindness.

"So why are you here?" she asked.

"I've lived here most of my life." He shrugged. "It's home."

"And you have enough business around here?" she asked dubiously. This was her education in marketing and economics shining through.

"Oh, yeah," he replied. "I'm the only garage in Runt River, and then there are people coming down the highway who have engine trouble. There are garages in nearby towns, but those are far enough away that I do okay."

"That's a good setup," she said with a nod. "A cozy little local monopoly. I like it."

"I can't complain." He glanced in her direction again, and she noticed a new sparkle of respect in his eye. Most people didn't expect her to care about anything beyond fashion and brunch, but she was no vapid socialite. Bernadette was the future owner and CEO of her father's businesses—a responsibility she didn't take lightly.

It was a relief to be so far away from New York and the pressures there, but she was nervous about meeting Lucille. She'd heard the stories. Lucille was her father's sister, and apparently, there had been no love lost between them. She'd married some guy named Arnie Neiman—someone desperately below her—and settled into Nowhere, USA. But there was more to that story—one Bernie had managed to piece together over the years. The whole estrangement had been about a three-carat engagement ring that had belonged to a grandmother. She'd verbally promised the ring to her grandson, Milhouse, after he'd sweet talked her into it. Lucille had already turned down two very charming marriage prospects, and Grandma was planning on proving her displeasure by changing the will, but then died before she had the chance. The will left the ring to Lucille, and Lucille wouldn't part with it. And a feud was born. It was ridiculous. A three-carat ring was a nice size, but it wasn't exactly unattainable. Bernie's own engagement ring was probably worth more. Milhouse had bought Kitty plenty of bigger diamonds over the years, so why let a three-carat ring come between siblings? That was why she'd decided to come out here to find Lucille—she might be the only person who understood her instinct to run like heck. Still, Bernie had never met her aunt, and she was curious…who was this woman who kept a ring and cut out the rest of her family?

"What's my aunt like?" she asked.

Liam was silent for a few beats. "Lucille is kind. A good neighbor. Honest."

"But you didn't know she was a Morgan," she countered. "Are you sure she's that honest?" The mechanic's description didn't match what she'd heard about her aunt.

"I haven't heard her side of it yet," Liam replied. "So I'm reserving judgment."

That was new—who did that these days, reserving judgment on another person's failings? No one she knew personally. Apparently, Aunt Lucille had some loyal friends.

Runt River's downtown consisted of a few stores—a ranch supply store, a burger joint, an ice cream shop, a drugstore—and only one stoplight that Bernie could see. Most vehicles seemed to be pickup trucks that parked in the angled spots in front of stores, their tails hanging out into the road. Downtown came and went in the space of two streets, and then they turned on to a street of houses. These were decent-sized, well-maintained, with large yards and mature trees. In New York, they'd be worth a couple million, but out here in Runt River, Ohio, they would probably sell for pocket change.

"Here we are," he said, pulling into the drive of a large white house. An older woman sat on the porch, a toddler beside her eating crackers out of a box she held in her lap. The little guy was cute—with the biggest brown eyes she'd ever seen.

Was that her aunt?

Bernie couldn't make out any of the Morgan traits in the older woman. She was gray—what woman let herself go gray in their family?—and she carried some extra weight. She wore a flower-patterned summer dress, and her hair was cut in a chin-length bob—just a touch of fashionableness. The older woman squinted when she spotted Bernie in the front seat, then leaned forward.

Liam got out of the truck, and looked back at Bernie. She slowly pushed the door open and raised a hand in a tentative wave.

"Hi, Lucille," Liam said. "I've got someone here who says she knows you."

Lucille stood up and fixed Bernie with a shocked expression. "Aren't you supposed to be getting married?"

Bernie's hand flew up to the veil still affixed to her hair with clips and pins. The stylist had promised that it would stay put, and that was no lie.

"That was the plan," Bernie replied, gathering her skirt up into her arms again. Liam had the decency to come over and offer her a hand as she climbed down so that she didn't land flat on her face.

Lucille came down the steps, the toddler staying on the porch with the box of crackers, and she stopped a couple of feet away from Bernie, looking her over carefully.

"You're Bernadette, aren't you?" Lucille asked softly. She'd called her by her full name, and a place in Bernie's heart warmed at that.

"Yes."

"Did you marry him?"

Bernie blinked. "No. I...didn't."

Lucille nodded twice, then turned and headed back toward the porch.

"Come on in, then," Lucille called over her shoulder. "I imagine you've got lots of questions, and so do I. You, too, Liam. We'd better sort this out."

IKE STOOD ON the porch, a cracker in one hand, crumbs all over his fingers. He wore a new outfit—shorts that were long enough to be pants on him, and a too-small T-shirt. Lucille must have dug them up from somewhere. Liam was grateful for Lucille—she'd stepped in when he was fresh out of ideas—

but even she didn't seem to be enough for the little guy. Ike's eyes were filled with grief, his little mouth pursed into a rosebud. He looked more like a Morgan to Liam. The curls, the eyes...

He misses Leanne.

And Liam couldn't fix that one. He'd spent the last three years missing her, too, on some level or other. He'd known it was over when she left him, but that didn't stop him from thinking about her at the strangest times. They'd been married, after all. That had meant something—to him, at least.

Ike trotted over in Liam's direction and held up a soggy, half-eaten cracker.

"Share," Ike whispered.

Liam bent down and picked up the toddler, turning his face away from the proffered cracker.

"No, thanks, buddy," he said. "Maybe later."

Ike smiled, a tiny uplifting of the corners of his pink mouth. That was the closest thing to a smile Liam had seen from the kid, and he felt gratified. He'd wanted this so badly—to be a dad to someone—that holding Leanne's son was both painful and a relief at once.

Lucille led the way into the house and Bernie followed, her dress dragging along the carpet behind her. The screen door banged shut behind them. The suitcase, which Liam had retrieved from the trunk of the Rolls, was still in the back of the pickup truck, and he idly wondered when Bernie was going to want to change out of that soiled wedding dress.

"Did you have a nice day?" Liam asked Ike. What would nice even be like for a two-year-old who'd lost his mother and was now with a bunch of strangers? He remembered what that had felt like when he was a kid in the foster system, and it hadn't been warm and fuzzy.

Ike stared at him mutely, then leaned forward and rested his head against Liam's shoulder, and the little body deflated in a long sigh.

"That bad, huh?" Liam murmured. He patted the boy's back and followed Bernie into the kitchen where Lucille was pouring tall glasses of iced tea.

"So you're my aunt, then?" Bernie asked, accepting a glass.

"I am." Lucille held up a glass toward Liam, and he shook his head. She put it onto the table, paused, then turned to him. "I didn't lie... I just didn't mention my family. They cut me off. I have no access to their fortune or their influence. I had to start fresh. Alone."

Liam nodded slowly. Except that for the entire time he'd been nursing his heartbreak over Leanne's affair, she'd never once even hinted that the Senator Morgan who stole his wife was part of her family. She'd acted as cool as anyone else—a distanced stranger from that set of powerful politicos in New York.

"It wasn't a lie," she repeated.

"Okay." What else could he say? She'd certainly not told the whole truth, though.

"And what brings you to Runt River?" Lucille asked her niece. "I mean, besides the obvious run out on your wedding."

"You."

Bernie plucked at the veil affixed atop her head, and Lucille stepped closer and began pulling out pins and clips, dropping them onto the tabletop in a small pile.

"I had no idea you even knew I was here." Lucille dropped another couple of pins onto the table and pulled the last of the veil away from Bernadette's hair. Bernie ran a hand through her dark tresses as if in relief.

"You're the only Morgan not at the wedding." Bernie smiled wanly. "So really, you were my last hope…dressed like this, at least. I was just focused on getting out of there, and I didn't even want to stop and get changed. Someone would have spotted me. I could have hopped on a plane and gone somewhere sunny, I guess, but not without my passport. And I wanted—"

"Family," Lucille concluded.

"Yes."

"And little Ike there had nothing to do with this?" Lucille asked, her expression hardening.

"What?" Bernie shot a confused look between them. "The boy? Why would he? Whose is he?"

"Mine, for the time being," Liam said. How much did they want to tell this woman about his private business? Ike was looking at Bernie fixedly now, leaning toward her so that Liam had to tighten his grip to keep the kid from dropping out of his arms. He knew what Ike was seeing—a woman about his mother's age with the same dark hair and flawless complexion. The same things that made Liam wary were comforting to this little guy.

"Leanne Wilson," Lucille said. Bernie didn't even flinch.

"Who is that?"

"My late wife," Liam replied.

"Ah." Bernie frowned. "You two are acting like the name should mean something to me."

"Doesn't it?" Lucille pressed.

"No." She shook her head. "I came here because I thought you, of all people, might actually understand what I was going through. I just walked away from the political marriage of the decade. I thwarted my parents' plans that go a whole lot further than a simple wedding. There aren't a lot of people who would understand what that means, and since you've gone head-to-head with my dad, I thought you'd get it. Maybe I made a mistake." She licked her lips. "Liam, if you'd be so kind as to take me to a hotel or something, I'll sort myself out."

"No, no..." Lucille sighed. "You'll stay here with me, of course."

Ike squirmed, and Liam set him down on the ground. He toddled straight to Bernie and looked up at her. Bernie's face softened into a smile.

"Hi there, little guy. What's your name?"

"Share?" Ike held up the sodden cracker.

"Mmm." She pretended to take a bite. "Yummy."

That seemed to be the response that Ike was looking for, because he grinned and shoved his cracker toward her again.

"Share?"

Ike had smiled—not just a hint of a one, a real smile. Liam wasn't going to cut it, was he? This kid needed a mom who knew how to play his games, how to coax an honest smile out of him. He'd had Ike for a month already, and he still hadn't managed that.

"What's his name?" she repeated, looking up at Liam, her expression still softened by her game with Ike. She was beautiful, and he was irritated to be noticing that right now.

"This is Ike," Liam said. "I'm his legal guardian."

"Oh." She frowned, seeming to be adding it all up. "So, he's your late wife's son…"

"We were estranged," Liam said. "She moved out three years ago, so Ike is hers… and no, I'm not the dad."

"So it's complicated, then," she confirmed.

"Yeah, you could say that."

"Do you know who his father is?" she asked, running a hand through the boy's hair. Ike leaned his head into her hand.

"Yep," Liam said. He wasn't ready to get into that with Bernadette. The last thing they needed was a posse of lawyers from New York descending upon them. What Liam needed was some time and space to keep thinking. Lucille followed his lead and remained silent.

Color rose in Bernadette's face, and she shrugged. "Sorry, didn't mean to pry. He's a sweetie." She paused, then looked at Ike a little closer. "Did you say Leanne Wilson?"

Liam suppressed a sigh. This was what he'd been waiting for—for her to connect the dots.

"That's right," he said.

"I'd hate to suggest something untoward—" She winced. "There was a woman caught up in a scandal with my cousin Vince."

"That would be her," Liam said. Leanne had stayed out of the news, but the couple of times that Liam had talked to her, she'd mentioned how hard it was to have her silence purchased. The lawyers had swarmed her, and she'd been worried about all the papers she'd signed.

"So Ike—" Bernie looked down at the toddler more pointedly. "Ike is *Vince's* son?"

Liam didn't need to answer, because when she looked up and met his gaze, she heaved a sigh.

"Obviously, Vince didn't acknowledge him," she surmised. "And he wouldn't."

"Has he done this before?" Liam asked. "Get a woman pregnant and pay her to keep her mouth shut?"

Bernie shot him a tight smile. Liam had doubted that she'd admit to any of that. Senators had to keep big secrets if they wanted to stay in their jobs. They were all silent for a few beats.

"I think I'd count as an aunt, then, wouldn't I? Sort of..." She ruffled Ike's hair. "I'm technically a second cousin, but I think he could call me Auntie."

Liam exchanged a look with Lucille. This was quickly getting into dangerous territory. He didn't know what he wanted to do exactly, but he didn't *want* a Morgan bonding with Ike, getting attached.

"We'd appreciate it if you could be discreet," Liam said.

"What do you want?" Bernie asked. "Money? For Vince to acknowledge Ike as his?"

Money? That was what she thought of when she saw an orphaned child? But then, she came from a different world. He was worried about keeping the kid out of the foster system. She seemed more worried about lawsuits.

"I don't need anyone's money," Liam retorted. "Nor do I want it. I'm doing just fine. But I'd like a bit of time to think this through. I want what's best for the kid. I have no intention of making anyone acknowledge him if they don't want to."

In fact, he hadn't even considered that option. That would make little Ike nothing more than a pawn. The boy needed a family to raise him with love, not to treat him like a problem to be solved, a political liability. The kid needed a childhood—sprinklers in summer, sleds in winter, maybe even a dog— not to be known as a politician's illegitimate child.

"Sorry…" She sighed. "I get this is difficult."

"You have no idea," Liam muttered.

"Well, we all seem to want the same thing," she said. "A bit of quiet so that we can think." Ike tugged at Bernie's dress, and she picked him up and cuddled him close. "I just ran out on the wedding of the century, and my family is furious. You've got this little guy to consider. So maybe we can agree to discretion all round."

"Deal," Liam said.

Could he trust her? He didn't have a whole lot of choice, but of one thing he was certain: Ike needed to come first. If that meant he ended up with his relatives, or if he stayed with Liam, the priority had to be what was best for this little boy.

He's not yours, Liam reminded himself. But without Leanne, this boy needed someone tough enough to look out for his interests, and Liam would be that person. There was no way he was tossing this kid into the foster system or into a family of political jackals. Even if Bernie seemed sweet right now, he wasn't fooled. She came from a different world than he did, where the Morgans were near the top of the food chain, and ordinary Joes like him were nothing more than scenery.

Ike put the last of his cracker into his mouth, followed by his thumb. And for the first time since he'd arrived, the little guy looked comforted as he rested his head on Bernie's shoulder.

THAT EVENING, BERNIE sat on Lucille's couch in a borrowed bathrobe, since the clothes she'd packed were more fitting for a Caribbean honeymoon. At least she had a few outfits to wear, and she was mildly proud of herself for having had the forethought to dump Calvin's suitcase in the parking lot when she made her escape. It was strange, the things that felt like victories now, like saving her tears for when she was alone on the highway.

If she hadn't found Calvin halfway down Kimberly's throat, she'd be Mrs. McMann… Instead of sitting on her aunt's faded couch, she'd be strolling down a moonlit beach with a handsome husband. She hadn't been head over heels in love with him, but she had loved him. She wasn't some kind of heartless robot who married a man for nothing more than political ambitions. She'd been willing to build on the love they had, and hopefully as the years passed, their feelings for each other would have grown and deepened. Apparently, he hadn't been able to wait.

How long had he been cheating? She'd known that Calvin had been quite serious about Kimberly before they were introduced, but he'd assured Bernie that it was over—completely. She knew that his decision to marry her had been largely political. He wanted to be president, and a wife was a big part of the campaign. Kimberly wasn't First Lady material. She wasn't senator's wife material, either, in Bernie's humble opinion. But it was possible to make the wise choice in mate and still feel affection. Had he kept up with Kimberly all along, or had this been a final goodbye of some sort? What did Kimberly have that Bernie didn't that drew Calvin in like that?

It didn't matter—cheating was cheating. Bernadette had expected fidelity in their marriage, and Calvin had wholeheartedly agreed. The less to hide the better, he'd said. And if she wasn't sure how well she could trust his love for her, she could definitely trust his ambition. And they both knew that in order to get where they wanted to go, fidelity was imperative. She'd never be able to trust him again after what she'd witnessed. But she still wanted to *know*. Blast it, how could he be making out with Kimberly mere minutes before he was supposed to be saying his vows? What kind of man did that?

Bernie leaned her head back. Her life had been so carefully planned. She was going to marry Calvin, and they were going to make their bid for the White House. Bernadette would learn the family business for when she eventually took over from her father, and one day when Calvin's presidency was behind them, they'd run the Morgan dynasty together. And perhaps she'd been naïve, but she'd honestly believed that she was beautiful and intelligent enough to capture her husband's heart. The flames to their romance might have been fanned with money, but she'd expected monogamy. But now everything—absolutely everything—was going to be different. And that included her running the Morgan family business, because she'd just infuriated her father so badly that he might very well change his mind. She passed a hand over her face.

Liam had taken Ike back to his place across the street earlier in the evening. That mechanic had been kind to her. Heaven knew how crazy she'd looked when she'd driven up. After he and the toddler had left, she'd gone to the washroom and seen herself in the mirror for the first time; it wasn't a pretty sight. She had makeup streaked down her face from crying, her hair was in tangles, and the dress was dusty and torn.

She'd wrestled her way out of the dress—popping a few buttons and managing to tear the skirt even further—and then sat on the closed toilet lid and had a good cry.

Vince's wife, Tabby, was used to this. Vince had always had some girl on the side—that was just the way he was.

But Bernie wasn't as tough as Tabby was. She couldn't stand next to Calvin in a campaign, declaring him to be twice the man he really was. She wasn't that good a liar, and she didn't care to be.

"Hot chocolate?"

Bernie roused herself from her thoughts, and looked up to find her aunt standing in front of her, a cup of frothy cocoa in her hands.

"Thanks." Bernie took the mug with a grateful smile. "I haven't had unnecessary calories in five months in order to fit into that stupid dress."

"Then time to make up for it," Lucille replied with a low laugh, sinking onto the sofa beside her. "I've got pie in the kitchen, too."

Bernie took a sip. "I couldn't do what Tabby does."

"Vince's wife?" Lucille asked. "How do you think she'll react if she finds out about Ike?"

Bernie shook her head, then glanced out the living room window again toward Liam's house. "She probably already knows."

Tabby was the genius behind Vince's political campaigns. She acted meek, beaming up at her tall, meaty husband, but somehow she'd managed to disconnect her heart from the game. How did a woman do that? How did she support a man whom she *knew* was a cheater?

"You aren't like her," Lucille concluded.

"No," Bernie replied. "I'm not. I couldn't just stand there and pretend everything was perfectly fine when it wasn't. I actually thought Calvin would be faithful."

"I'm glad you came," Lucille said with a sympathetic smile. "And I'm glad you aren't that good an actress. It says something about you that you can't fake it."

"My parents wouldn't agree with that," she replied in a low voice.

"What did they tell you about me?" Lucille asked. There was tension in her voice, and she looked away.

"Oh, you don't want to know that." Bernie laughed uncomfortably. Her father had never had anything good to say about his sister.

"No, I do." Lucille looked back. "I always hoped your dad would come around one day and make contact. He never did. Then I hoped that you'd get curious about your aunt…"

"Why didn't *you* come around?" Bernie asked.

"I wasn't welcome. I was also a little scared. I didn't know what he'd told you."

Bernie grimaced. "He said you were a social and political liability."

That was the kind way of putting it. What her father had actually said was that Lucille was low-class, and even with money, she acted like a poor person with nothing to lose. He said she was grasping and selfish, and he suspected that she had some untreated mental illness.

"My father told me about your grandmother's engagement ring," Bernie said after a moment. "Is that really what started this whole feud—a ring?"

"It was more than a ring." Lucille's mouth turned downward, and she fell silent.

"What was it?" Bernie pressed.

Lucille heaved a sigh. "It was your father's domineering ways. He didn't ask me for the ring, he demanded it. He told me that unless I came with a sincere apology for my insulting behavior *and the ring*, then I was dead to him."

"And you couldn't do it."

"I had my pride," she replied. "I still do. He demanded that I genuflect like the household help, tug at my cap like a chauffeur. He'd inherited the whole shebang, and I was slotted in below him. He liked that role—ruling us all. And I didn't."

Bernadette could understand that, actually. Her father was a prideful man, and he took his position in society and in the family very seriously—perhaps more seriously than anyone else did. A lot of people would have complied with that demand, but they weren't his sister.

"I get it," Bernie said. "But you walked away from an awful lot of money."

"I still get my lifelong allowance from my father's inheritance," Lucille replied. "It's enough to live on now that Arnie's gone. I didn't walk away from that. I walked away from the duties, the social obligations. I walked away from the houses that would be paid for by my brother—and all the strings that came with them. I refused to be handled. And Milhouse wouldn't bend. So—" She spread her hands. "It is what it is."

She'd refused to be handled. Bernie had just done the same thing when she'd turned off her phone and driven west. Her parents had always "handled" her, and until today, she'd never minded. She'd done her duty, shown up at cocktail parties and dinners and made nice with various politicians. She was a general media favorite, and she liked the attention.

But now she wouldn't do what they wanted. She wouldn't smile for the press and say something sweet and submissive like, "Calvin and I are so sorry to disappoint everyone today, but we've done some soul-searching together, and we really feel…"

That would be a lie. They'd done zero soul-searching, least of all together, and she wasn't going to stand there, making the cad look like a decent man to protect his ambitions.

"I think I want some of that pie," Lucille said, rising to her feet. "I'll bring you a piece."

Looking around that living room, Bernadette saw the worn patches on the sofa, the slightly shabby furniture, her aunt's wide hips and grubby slippers. Lucille had walked away from the obligations and social demands that came with wealth and a privileged family, and she'd landed *here*, in a town called Runt River. Here, in the midst of ordinary. There were no maids or housekeepers. Everything looked faded and worn instead of chic and elegant. Personal indulgence came in the form of a mug of hot chocolate made from a pouch of powder, instead of European truffles or a crystal dish of chocolate mousse. Gone were the luxuries and comforts Bernadette had been accustomed to, because with a similar sense of outrage and commitment to utter truthfulness, Bernadette had done the same thing her aunt had done—defied Milhouse Morgan.

What have I done?

CHAPTER THREE

IT WAS THREE in the morning, and Liam stood in the middle of his living room in a pair of pajama bottoms and an undershirt, with Ike screaming in his arms. When Leanne died, he'd gone down to her apartment and gotten Ike's things—toys, clothes, diapers. Her parents had died years ago, and she had a cousin who had some addiction issues, but no one else. Liam hadn't put together a funeral. Leanne had been cremated, and he'd sprinkled her ashes in a field.

She hadn't owned her home or anything like that, so besides paying off her credit cards, there hadn't been too much to deal with. He'd left the last of her things in the apartment for the landlords to clear out. It might not have been their job, but he'd done as much as he could with the help of his foster brother, Tim. He couldn't face any more.

A few local moms had dropped off some

hand-me-down clothes for Ike over the past few weeks, but the boy was wearing pajamas with trains on them that Liam had brought from the apartment. They were a bit small, but he seemed to sense that they were part of his life with his mom, and he wouldn't wear anything else. Liam didn't push the matter. The poor boy had enough change to deal with.

Ike's face was wet with tears, and his crying hadn't slowed. They'd both been up for an hour already.

"Hey, buddy," he said, raising his voice above Ike's wails. "Let's talk about this."

Ike didn't seem so inclined, and Liam heaved a sigh, closing his eyes for a moment, looking for his own calm. He understood Ike's anger—his mom was gone, and he was with a bunch of strangers who couldn't possibly make up for her absence. But Liam was trying.

For the past month, Ike had responded to being held, liked some stories. Liam had let Ike stay awake in front of the TV until he dropped off in exhaustion and slept through until daybreak. But tonight was different— something had triggered a meltdown, and

Liam couldn't help but wonder if it had been Bernie's arrival. Ike had been raised without a father, and maybe right now he needed a woman's touch.

Ike's sobs weren't abating. His hands were bunched into rage-filled fists, and he stiffened like a board as he howled.

"Hey, buddy…" Liam looked across the street, and there was a light on in the kitchen at Lucille's place. That meant she was up, and he wouldn't be imposing. Not too much, at least. Lucille had been here for him for all the bumps this month, and while he always swore he wouldn't impose again, he always did. He picked up the cordless phone and dialed his neighbor's number. It rang twice before a female voice picked up.

"Hello?" She sounded cautious, and was barely audible above Ike's crying, but Liam could tell it wasn't Lucille.

"It's Liam, across the street," he said.

"Hi, it's Bernadette. Is the little guy okay?"

"Not really. I can't seem to calm him down. I was trying to reach Lucille to see if she'd give me a hand. Is she up?"

"No, just me. Don't worry. I'll be right over."

Liam blinked at the phone when he realized she'd hung up, not giving him a chance to decline. Not that he wanted to, exactly. He needed help; *Ike* needed help. He'd just preferred that help from the neighbor he knew.

"Come on, Ike," Liam pleaded. "I know you're upset…"

He really had nothing to offer, though. He couldn't bring Leanne back—and maybe Bernie had reminded him of her. But something suddenly occurred to him.

There was a knock on the front door, and Liam pulled it open to see Bernadette standing there in a white terry cloth housecoat. Her hair was back in a ponytail, and she looked like a different woman from the tattered bride of earlier. Ike blinked at the new arrival in surprise, his howls stopped for the moment.

"Hi, sweetheart," she said softly. "Hug?"

Ike reached for Bernie, and she took the toddler into her arms, snuggling him close. Seriously? How did she do that? He'd been hugging the kid all evening, and again ever since he'd woken up at two in the morning. How did she simply show up and make it all okay? He resented that. He was the one Ike had, and he was doing his best, but tonight it wasn't enough.

"If you could just hold him for a couple minutes, I have an idea," Liam said.

He didn't wait for an answer, he just walked away, his nerves completely frazzled. A crying kid was difficult in a way he'd never imagined before. Somehow, he hadn't thought parenthood would be like this.

Liam opened the door that led to the basement stairs and flicked on the light. He'd shoved all the pictures of Leanne into boxes after she'd left and dumped them down here. He'd added the few boxes of personal items he'd taken from Leanne's apartment after she'd died. He'd meant to go through it all eventually, but there hadn't been time. While pictures of his estranged wife didn't do much to comfort him, they might help Ike.

He had to rummage through a few boxes before he found what he was looking for—a framed photo of Leanne smiling into the camera. He'd taken it the summer before she left him. She'd probably already started her affair with the senator at that point.

He headed back up the stairs, and when he came into the living room, he found Bernie seated on the couch, Ike leaning his tear-stained face against her shoulder, his breaths coming in shuddering gasps.

"I brought something for you, Ike," Liam said. "It's a picture of Mommy. Do you want it?"

He held it up for the boy to see, and Ike stretched out one pudgy hand and pulled the picture against his chest. Maybe it would help. Maybe it wouldn't, but he had to try. Liam was most definitely out of his depth here.

"So that's her." Bernadette craned her neck to get a glimpse of the photo.

"Yup."

He couldn't explain the pain attached to that photo. He'd still thought he had a happy marriage at that point, totally oblivious to the fact that her new interest in politics had more to do with the senator himself than with his political platforms. And he'd held on to that photo because deep down, he'd always hoped that she'd come back. She'd *married* Liam. The senator hadn't left his wife. So maybe she'd come back eventually.

Some days he imagined her coming back to him and settling back in again, happy to have a decent, hardworking man instead of some philandering politician. Other days, he imagined getting the chance to tell her exactly what she'd lost, and he'd do the rejecting. The fantasies depended on his mood, but he still hoped she'd come back.

Obviously, she never had.

He leaned back, rubbing his hands across his face. How did Bernie manage to look so fresh in the middle of the night?

"Why are you up?" he asked.

"I couldn't sleep." She smoothed a hand over Ike's sweat-damp curls. "I can't stop thinking about yesterday."

Yeah, that also made sense. He felt a wave of sympathy. He'd been dealing with Leanne's betrayal for three years; she'd only started with Calvin's.

"Did you see it coming?" Liam asked. "The cheating, I mean."

She shook her head. "No. That's the thing. I didn't notice at all…until the last minute, that is."

"That was the same for me," he admitted. "I thought she was just really into politics. I didn't know there was a problem until she told me she was pregnant and she was leaving me."

"So there's a chance Ike is yours?" she asked.

He wished. If he'd been the father, maybe it would have changed things for Leanne. Maybe she'd have seen something worth staying for.

"No. I can't have kids." That was uncomfortable to talk about, but it was the truth. When Leanne had announced her pregnancy, it had been like a kick in the stomach. He knew what it meant, and she'd been holding a suitcase at the time. He'd begged her to stay. They could figure it out. But she didn't want to, and she'd walked out to the waiting cab.

"Do you still miss her?" Bernie asked quietly.

"Sure." He nodded. "I guess I miss what we had—what I thought we had. We'd both changed over the last three years, so I doubt we'd ever have been compatible again, even if she'd lived."

"Hmm."

Bernie looked like she wanted to cry, but she was holding it back. Her eyes got misty, and she pressed her lips together.

"You want to know how long this is going to hurt, don't you?" Liam asked.

She nodded. "Yeah."

She was just at the beginning, and he knew exactly what that felt like—like being gutted and left alive.

"It'll hurt for a while. But it'll get better and easier. Some days you'll forget. And guaranteed, the days you actually forget him are the ones he'll call you up and remind you of his existence."

"Did Leanne do that a lot?"

Leanne had never fully gotten over Liam, either, it seemed. She'd call about twice a year just to see how he was doing and tell him she missed him… That was hardest. It brought him right back to the starting line again for a day or so. For the first year, she seemed to believe that Vince would leave his wife since he was financially supporting Leanne, but then the senator must have tired of her, because he told her straight that he wasn't leaving his wife and kids. His career depended upon his honesty and his credibility. At that point, Liam and Leanne had discussed possibly reconciling, but that hadn't been possible. He couldn't do it. There was no going back to blissful ignorance.

"She'd call every once in a while," he admitted. "I sent her money a couple of times. It hurts a lot when they call—it reminds you of better days. But you get over it. And while it's hard to have that reminder, it also confirms how far you've come."

Ike's eyes had closed, and Bernie leaned her head back against the back of the couch. She was rubbing the toddler's back with her palm in slow circles. She didn't belong here—not in Liam's living room, and not in Runt River. She was too pretty for this place, too polished.

"You mind if I ask you something?" he asked.

She turned her head to meet his gaze. "Sure."

"Why aren't you going home to New York?"

"Because my parents will side with Calvin."

"I find that hard to believe," he said.

"You don't know my family." She sighed. "He's going to be running for president in the next few years. He has all the party backing. He's the Republican golden boy. My parents wouldn't try to make me marry him, but they would insist that I protect his reputation. My dad has already invested too much money in him, and backing a successful candidate is good for business. Calvin would owe my dad big-time once he was in the Oval. We don't back presidents out of patriotic fervor alone."

Liam raised an eyebrow. Wow. This wasn't just a wedding between two people who'd fallen in love; it was a political alliance. That was a world he was glad to avoid.

"What business is your dad in, exactly?"

"Real estate development, and he owns a line of hotels, and has some heavy investments in the oil industry. After the wedding, my dad was going to hand one of his hotel chains over to me to get some hands-on experience."

"That sounds…fun." It actually sounded stressful.

"Totally." She didn't seem to pick up on his tone. "But I'm not sure it'll happen now. Dad doesn't react well to being crossed." She looked down at Ike and smiled. "I think he's out."

As quickly as that, the window into her strange political world was shut. She glanced from Ike toward the hallway. "Should I put him to bed?"

"Yeah." Liam slowly stood. "Thanks. He really seems to like you."

Bernie attempted to get up, then chuckled. "I'm going to need a hand here."

Liam paused for a moment, then held a hand out to her. Her fingers felt cool and silky soft in his rough grasp, and he tugged her to her feet, Ike balanced in one arm. She came up to his chin, but when she looked at him, her lips parted in a gentle smile, he found himself thinking how easy it would be to bend down and kiss her... He cleared his throat and took a step back.

"I'll show you the way," Liam said.

He'd bought a twin-size mattress and put it on the floor in his bedroom. He thought Ike might be comforted by having someone close by...and Liam would sleep better knowing the toddler couldn't wander off in the night.

"Sure," she said. "Lead the way."

Bernie put Ike down on the mattress on the floor, but Liam knew he wouldn't stay there. It didn't matter. He was in the right room for the night, at least.

When Leanne had left, she'd taken with

her the soft scents, the tinkle of laughter and a reason to come back at a reasonable hour. This house, so full of memories, had become a purely male abode: Liam cooked with barbecue sauce; his soaps were deodorized, not scented; and he came and went as he pleased.

Having a woman walk down his hallway with a sleeping toddler in her arms, leaving a waft of sandalwood in her wake—it reminded him too keenly of what he'd been missing these past few years.

He'd told Bernie that it got better, and it did, but what he didn't say was that trusting again was next to impossible. When you missed something that big, you stopped believing that you saw what was really going on. And he was pretty sure he couldn't survive that again. Bernie would sort out her family issues and head back to her life in New York soon enough. He just had to hold out until then.

THE NEXT MORNING, Bernie woke up late, having finally fallen into an exhausted coma somewhere around four. When she did wake, it was to the sound of a lawn mower outside the open window, the smell of fresh-cut grass wafting in. She lay there for a couple of minutes staring at the popcorn ceiling. The light fixture was an old-fashioned square plate of glass. She'd never seen such a thing before, and she stared at it for a long while, wondering if this was how the rest of the country lived. Could they? It seemed impossible, but here she was in a bed with a hand-made quilt on top of her and a light fixture that looked like nothing more than a bent piece of frosted glass covering a light bulb. It felt poor, and at the same time, strangely liberating. There wouldn't be any cameras waiting for her outside, no pressure to appear happy and collected, to look perfect from every angle to avoid any tabloid speculation about why she looked tired or bloated.

Her cell phone vibrated on the plain white bedside table. She'd finally turned it on when she got back from Liam's place. She picked it up and looked at the caller—her dad.

She could answer and have this conversation now, or she could put it off. She let the phone buzz twice more in her hand before she heaved a sigh and accepted the call.

"Hi, Dad."

"Bunny! Thank God. We've been worried sick. Are you okay?"

He sounded like dear old dad, right now, gruff and stressed. If only she were a decade younger and her father could still fix most of her problems.

"I'm fine," she said. "I mean, I'm heart-broken, but fine."

"What happened, exactly?" her father pressed. "Because Calvin is a wreck, and he says he has no idea what you're talking about."

The liar. Anger started to seep into the sadness, and she pushed herself up onto her elbows.

"I don't really care what Calvin says," she retorted. "I know what I saw."

"I believe you." And by the tone of his voice, he did, which was comforting. "Still, we could have done this a little more grace-fully."

"No, I couldn't have."

Why did she owe any of them grace right now? She sat up and turned her gaze out the window where a middle-aged man pushed an old mower in straight lines across the grass.

"All right, all right…" Her father muttered.

"We can discuss that later. What matters right now is getting you home and deciding on the family position."

"How about Calvin McMann is a cheating louse?" she suggested.

"You aren't helping."

Of course not. The truth was seldom the option when it came to spinning a scandal.

"Where are you?" her father asked. "I'll send the security team to bring you home."

"I don't need to be fetched," Bernie retorted. "I need some space, time to think. I don't want to come back just yet."

"Are you in the Bahamas?" her father pressed. "You could stay for a week or so, but we need a consistent story we can all stand behind with reporters."

"No, I'm not in the Bahamas. Look, Dad, I need you to promise to leave me alone for a bit. I promise not to breathe a word of anything to reporters."

"Where are you, for crying out loud?" he demanded.

"I need your word." For all of her father's insistence on a public face, he'd honor a promise to his daughter. He always had.

There was a moment or two of silence, then he sighed. "Fine. Now where are you?"

"Runt River, Ohio."

There was silence again, this time complete as if he were holding his breath. Then he exploded. *"What?"*

"I drove out here after the wedding. I didn't really mean to—I just hit a highway and kept going. Then I remembered Aunt Lucille was out here, and I figured I could use a bit of family support."

"From Lucille? After all I've told you about her—"

"She's pretty harmless, Dad."

"She's not harmless. She has a vendetta against me, and you're my daughter. She is not the person to trust with something this volatile—"

"Too late," Bernie confessed. "I told her what happened. But I'll be careful. I'll keep a low profile—wear something unattractive. I'll blend right in with the locals."

"This isn't funny," her father snapped. "Your face has been on the covers of magazines and newspapers for the past four months because of this wedding. You are not going to blend in."

"I don't care!" Her anger was rising again. "Dad, if I get into a bind, you're my first call. That's a promise. But give me space, or I will find the nearest reporter and give him an exclusive about Calvin McMann's cheating ways."

"Don't you threaten me."

"I'm half joking." She sighed. "Dad. Space. Please."

"Fine. But don't believe anything your aunt tells you. She's a master manipulator."

Lucille hardly seemed like the manipulative shrew her father made her out to be, but Bernie hardly knew the woman, either. Maybe it would be wise to tread carefully with her aunt.

Except that Liam trusts her.

She hardly knew Liam, either, and the men in her life hadn't exactly been the most trustworthy lately. Calvin had cheated on her, and her father seemed more concerned with the family political future than he did with his only daughter's emotional state. At this point, she was wary of everyone.

"I'll be careful, Dad. I promise. But I'd better hang up. I'm hungry. Tell Mom—" She sighed. Her mother would be furious. Tell her mother what, exactly? "Tell her I'm okay."

After their goodbyes, she ended the call and got out of bed. She needed to get dressed and face the day. One step at a time.

There was a tap on her door.

"Yes?"

"Everything okay?" her aunt asked.

"Come in."

The door opened, and Lucille peered at her cautiously, a folded, faded towel in her hands. "Sorry about the thin walls. Was that your father?"

So her aunt had heard that conversation? Bernie was used to more privacy than this.

"Yes." She ran a hand through her hair. "Aunt Lucille, could you tell me something?"

"Sure." Lucille deposited the towel on the top of the dresser.

"Why not just give my father the ring?" she asked. "It's been, what, thirty-five years?"

"Forty," her aunt countered. "And for the record, he didn't want the ring to propose to your mother. This was before he met her. He wanted it to propose to one of the kitchen workers in our family's home. Everyone was against it—even the girl's family. It's rather ironic that he had such a problem with Arnie, and he was a lawyer! Just not blue enough blood."

Her father had wanted to marry the kitchen help? That didn't sound like the Milhouse Morgan who hardly knew the names of the squadron of people who kept his home immaculate.

"And you were against that engagement, too," Bernie surmised.

"They were all wrong for each other." Lucille shrugged. "And she was after the money."

"Oh." All this time, she'd imagined that ring belonged on her mother's finger, but the story was never quite what it seemed. "So why not give it to him now?"

Lucille was silent for a moment, then a small smile tickled the corners of her lips. "Because I don't want to."

Bernie stared at her aunt in surprise. That was it? She didn't want to? A country of politicians pandered for her father's support, and this one stubborn woman could thwart him with a whim? Laughter bubbled up inside her, and she shook her head.

"Okay, then," she said.

"The towel is for your shower." Her aunt

turned back toward the hallway again. "The hot and cold are switched, and it takes a few minutes for the water to warm up. Not what you're used to, I'm sure, but it does the trick."

None of this was what Bernie was accustomed to, but she couldn't help but feel mildly envious of the aunt who got to do what she wanted to and felt no obligation to the Morgan family.

But what did Bernadette want? She wanted to get to know this aunt who held odd family secrets, and she wanted to hide from all the fallout of her failed wedding. And now that she'd met Ike, she wanted to get to know this tiny Morgan who had lost his mother too early.

Family had to be about more than influence and politics, didn't it?

CHAPTER FOUR

IKE REFUSED ALL the breakfast options Liam
had offered him the next morning. Liam was
starting to get better at buying foods Ike
would eat. So far, the kid was a fan of macaroni and cheese, toast, yogurt and scrambled
eggs—but only if the eggs were room tem-
perature and the perfect fluffiness.

He'd also been known to eat a banana,
but only if it was just a smidge shy of being
ripe. Five minutes past Ike's liking, and he'd
calmly walk to the couch and dump the banana onto it—his version of the garbage,
it seemed. A lot of things ended up on the
couch—apple slices, toast that was cut di-
agonally, grapes that were too soft, grapes
that were too hard, the half of a cookie that
got soggy in his hand… He was a picky kid.

When Liam finally brought Ike across the
street to Lucille's, Ike looked up at the older
woman with big, unblinking eyes and whis-

pered "Hungry…" in a tone so plaintive any-one would think he was kept in a cage in the basement, which couldn't be further from the truth. The twin-size mattress on the floor in Liam's bedroom was supposed to be for Ike, but the tables had turned somehow, and now Ike slept in Liam's bed and Liam got the mat-tress on the floor.

Lucille shot Liam a curious look.

"I feed him!" Liam said defensively. "At least, I try to. I made him breakfast this morning. He just wouldn't eat it."

Most of it had ended up on the couch cush-ion. Liam rolled his eyes. They were being played by a two-year-old, but there didn't seem to be any way around it.

"What would you like to eat, sweetheart?" Lucille asked. "Auntie will make it."

They'd been calling her "auntie" from the start—a term of endearment for the woman taking care of him. Liam had never guessed how accurate that name really was. Appar-ently, Lucille had, though.

Liam glanced around the kitchen.

"Where's Bernie?" he asked. He'd been thinking about her more than he should, but she was also one of *them*, and he didn't trust that family.

"She's having a late start," Lucille said with a shrug. "She's been through a lot. I'm just waiting for the tears to start."

Liam nodded. He knew better than most what Bernie was going through.

"Well, be good for Auntie," Liam said to Ike. "I'll see you tonight, kiddo."

Ike looked back at him wordlessly, and Liam headed for the door. He had Bernie's car to evaluate, another couple of vehicles coming in for scheduled maintenance and while his part-time employee, Chip, would be coming in later in the afternoon to help him out, he wanted to get a good start on things before then.

Liam drove the eight minutes to the shop and parked in his usual spot. Life had gotten more interesting—more layered—since Ike's arrival. Now, as he unlocked the office door and flicked on the lights, his mind was on the boy. He was wondering what he could get the kid to eat in the mornings. But now that Bernie was on the scene, he had even more to distract him from his work, and that frustrated him. He wasn't supposed to be noticing her glossy dark hair or the way her eyes glittered when she was amused.

Liam let himself into the garage and ambled over to the Rolls-Royce. Pretty or not, Morgan or not, he had to fix her car. The white paint was dusty from the long drive from New York, but there was no muting the beauty of a well-maintained classic car. This was a Phantom V, and between 1959 and the late sixties, there had only been about five hundred made. He pulled open the front door and peered into the dim interior. Tan lambskin leather and burl wood veneer—true to the original design.

And Bernie had just hopped into this vehicle and driven off. He could only dream of taking a beauty like this for a spin, yet there were people for whom bombing around in a Rolls-Royce was nothing at all.

He opened the hood, and over the next few hours, he started evaluating the severity of the engine trouble. Troubleshooting engine problems was part "ear" and part mechanical knowledge. He started the car, listening to the grind in the motor, then turned it off and came back around to the engine. He could be lost in time while he tinkered, finding the problem. He liked engines—they were fixable. So many other things in life weren't. Marriages, for example. People weren't as easy to decipher.

Looking back on it now, he wished he'd been more flexible about their plans for children, but he had a feeling that their issues ran deeper than how to have a child—it was how they related to each other. The infertility had been taking a toll on Leanne. She'd been getting more withdrawn, and every time one of their friends or family members got pregnant, it seemed to stab her just a little bit deeper.

"Why not me?" she'd asked, tears glistening in her eyes. "Why won't you let me have this?"

And that had felt like a direct attack on his manhood, too. For her to get pregnant, it wouldn't be by him, and that bothered him a little. Maybe it wasn't entirely fair, since an adopted child wouldn't be his biologically, either, but it still rankled him that she needed that genetic link, no matter how he felt about it. For him, the priority had been to give a loving home to a child who might otherwise have been lost in the foster system. They'd never been able to find a solution that they were both happy with.

A man's virility was a large part of his identity, too, and he'd had to come to terms with the fact that he'd never be a biological dad, so watching her grieve her lack of a baby hurt him, too. Deep down he knew it was a little different for Leanne, and looking back on it, he wished he'd considered using some donor sperm, given her what she wanted.

There was a tap on the garage door window, and he looked around the hood to see Bernie's face in the glass. His heart sped up a little at the sight of her, and he glanced up at the clock. It was almost eleven. Had that much time really passed?

He went over to the side door and pushed it open. She stood in the yard, her hair pulled back in a loose ponytail that made her look younger, somehow. She wore a summer dress that was long and flowing with a busy pattern of pinks, reds and oranges. It was the perfect contrast to her big dark eyes. He had to swallow before he could say anything.

"Hi," he said. "Come on in."

She smiled and slipped past him into the

shop, her perfume lingering in the air. How did women do that—make walking through a door somehow more than that. She crossed the garage and stood looking at her car, hands folded.

"So you've started," she said.

"Yep. I've figured out what the problem is, but I'll need to order parts. We don't carry Rolls-Royce parts in Runt River."

"Hmm." She nodded. "How long will it take?"

"To get the parts—a week, maybe ten days," he said. "Then I'll have to work on it, which will take a few more days."

"Hmm."

She wasn't giving much away, and he waited to see if she'd say anything more. She didn't.

"I've drawn up an estimate for parts and labor as it stands now," he went on. "Then you can decide if you want me to continue or not."

He grabbed a paper from the workbench and handed it to her. She scanned it, then shrugged. "That looks fine to me. I honestly don't know much about cars, but if I get back to New York and find out you took advantage of me—"

"I'm not that kind of guy," he said. "I'll give you fair prices and honest work."

She met his eyes for a moment, then smiled wanly. "I believe you." She adjusted her purse on her shoulder. "Truth is, I'm kind of relieved to be stuck here for a little while. I'm not ready to go back."

"Yeah?" He eyed her cautiously. Would she still feel that way when they were waiting for late parts? These things happened in his business. The last thing he needed was a car in pieces and his client raging mad that she couldn't leave town fast enough once the novelty had worn off. He headed over to the sink and turned on the water to wash his hands. She was silent for a moment while he lathered up, scrubbing around his nails with a brush.

"There are two sides to every story," she said, turning toward him. "I heard one side for my entire life, and meeting my aunt is giving me a glimpse at the other side. This is an opportunity I never realized I wanted before."

He turned off the water and reached for a

towel. It was a strangely sensitive comment, and her expression made her look almost ordinary—if that was the right word for it. For a moment, she was no longer the wealthy heiress. She could have been any woman born and raised on these plains.

When he turned back, Bernadette was looking at his shop more closely, her gaze moving over the tools hanging on the walls, then across the floor and up the opposite wall.

"You said you're the only garage in Runt River, right?" she said.

"That's right."

She nodded slowly. "Did you ever consider moving to a larger area?"

"You sound like Leanne." He smiled wanly. "She wanted to move somewhere bigger. I didn't."

"Why not?" she asked, her gaze on him.

Liam shook his head. "She was really having a hard time with not being able to have a baby," he confessed. "And I think she wanted to move in order to get away from all her friends who were pregnant and growing their families. I was too practical for that. Like you said, it's a local monopoly. I couldn't have done better somewhere bigger."

"That seems logical." Her expression softened. "You seem to have a solid business sense."

He could hear the compliment in those words. He didn't know Bernie, obviously, but she struck him as a rather straightforward kind of person.

"Thanks," Liam said. "Call me old-fashioned, but in my books, a man provides. And I might not have been able to give her a baby the old-fashioned way, but I could provide a decent income. I was just sticking to my strengths."

He'd also been stubbornly holding out on the one thing that would have soothed his wife's grief.

Why was he talking so openly with this woman? It had started the night before when she'd helped him with Ike, and it seemed like that hadn't turned off. He'd probably regret this later.

She glanced at her watch. "I'm hungry."

He could use a bite, too.

"Want to go get some lunch?" Ordinarily he wouldn't have dreamed of asking her to a meal, but she was different inside this garage, somehow. More accessible.

"Sure," she said. "My treat."

Liam laughed softly. "Bernie, that's not how it works around here. I'm taking you to lunch. After what you've been through, I think you could use it."

She eyed him for a moment, then shrugged weakly. "Thanks."

She might be the heiress in New York, and she might bomb around in a Rolls-Royce without much thought, but here in Runt River she was a client, and he was a man. Men provided, and sometimes that was all a guy had left. Simple as that.

BERNADETTE STOLE A glance at Liam walking down the sidewalk next to her. He wore cowboy boots that clunked against the pavement, a pair of jeans and a T-shirt—the same casual dress he'd sported the day before, too. She estimated him to be late thirties, so about ten years older than she was, but there was something about him that felt oddly reassuring, and it wasn't just the fact that he'd been friendly when she needed it. Maybe it was the slow way he had of looking around himself, as if he had all the time in the world.

The road was webbed with cracks, and trees grew large and stretched leafy limbs between buildings. Her first impression of this town had been that it was so empty it was almost eerie, but now that she was walking down the road toward Main Street, the quiet was soothing. No traffic, honking or sirens. She hadn't been given the bird once by a passing cabbie since she'd arrived.

She'd been serious about wanting to stay in Runt River for the time being, and she certainly had a good excuse. If her car were fixed, she'd feel obliged to head out—it was something in her nature that didn't stand still very easily. She liked to be moving forward, achieving something. If it weren't for her vehicle being in the shop, she wouldn't feel comfortable staying here without some actual business. She was looking for privacy to lick her wounds and think through her next step, not somewhere she'd draw constant notice, and Runt River wasn't the anonymous bastion she'd hoped it would be—she stood out here.

A truck rumbled past them, and the driver

gave her a curious once-over. Liam waved absently. That wasn't the first time she'd been scrutinized since arriving. This town was small enough that a single newcomer could cause a whole lot of double takes. That was nothing like New York. She'd been able to drive a classic Rolls through the city in full bridal regalia and not draw a second look.

"Does anyone know you're here yet?" Liam asked.

"I told my dad where I was," she said. "And warned him to give me space."

"They'd probably be worried sick, otherwise," he conceded.

"It's damage control." She pulled her dark hair out of her eyes. "They need a family story to stand behind for the media, and they're afraid I'll leak the secret."

"Which is?" he asked with a small smile.

"That Calvin is a cheating louse." She shot him a smile. "That makes him less electable, you see. And they have plans for him."

"Even after he cheated on you?"

"It isn't personal," she quipped, quoting a line she'd heard a hundred times from her father. "It's politics."

"Hmm." He put a hand on the small of her back and nudged her. "Let's cross here."

His touch was firm and warm, and she found the gesture oddly comforting. Calvin hadn't been the demonstrative type in private. When they went out into public, he'd hold her hand, brush her hair out of her eyes, smile down into her eyes—and the photographers got some great shots. But once they were alone, he was distant and wanted his space. "I'm used up," he'd say. "I just need to unwind." So Liam's casual gesture felt more intimate to her than he'd probably intended, especially since no one was watching.

They crossed the road just as they came to Main Street and stepped up onto the first sidewalk she'd seen in this town.

"You say it isn't personal, it's just politics. Well, it can be very personal for the people who get tilled under," Liam said once they were on the other side.

"You know, this is the first time I can identify with that," she admitted. "But my family expects me to have 'broader vision,' as my dad puts it." She used air quotes. "I might be humiliated, heartbroken, angry, unfairly treated, but I'm supposed to think about what's best for the family."

"Namely, your father," he clarified.

Yes, he was the patriarch, and he called the shots. He held the majority of the family assets. Even her cousin Vince had to make nice to Uncle Milhouse to keep any kind of financial backing. Vince was a placeholder for the family's political ambition, but Calvin was the future, and his image could not, under any circumstances, be tarnished.

"So what do *you* want?" Liam asked.

She smiled warily. "Does it matter?"

"Maybe not to your father, but it does to me. If you could have anything you wanted, what would it be?"

She hadn't actually thought about that. She was a practical woman, and she'd followed her father's lead. She had a degree in economics and marketing from Harvard, and her father was grooming her to take over their massive fortune. That meant learning the family business—how to keep all the balls in the air—and maintaining a respectable image. Nothing too flashy or undignified. If journalists probed into her past during an election year, which they would if her husband was running for president, they'd need to come up empty. Bernadette was far from free.

And yet, the silver lining to this whole ugly mess was the discovery of a little boy she'd never known existed—Ike. Funny to be bonding with her cousin's illegitimate son, but she was glad that she'd had the chance to meet him. Now that she knew him, she'd make sure that he didn't want for anything. He'd need family support, and she felt some responsibility in that respect. Now that she knew about this tiny Morgan's existence, she couldn't just turn her back on him.

They approached a small restaurant. The faded sign read Uncle Henry's Restaurant, and Liam angled his head toward it, then led the way to the front door. He held it open for her, and the smell of sausage and eggs wafted out to greet her. She was hungrier than she'd thought, because her stomach gurgled in response.

The restaurant had a few patrons—mostly men past fifty wearing baseball caps. One waitress was taking an order, her pad of paper perched above a pregnant belly. Liam led the way to a table by the window, and he pulled out her chair for her before sitting in the other.

"You never did answer my question," he said as they got settled. "What do you want out of this mess?"

Bernie leaned her elbows onto the table and considered for a moment. How much could she say without sounding unbearably rich? "My aunt Ellen Morgan runs a charity just outside the city for single moms in crisis. They provide medical care, groceries, baby supplies… They even have a residence where the girls can stay if they get kicked out of their homes. It's called Mercy House, and she's been passionate about it for years. If I could step away from the spotlight and do anything, I'd like to do something like that— an organization that makes a difference."

Liam looked mildly surprised, and she shot him a rueful smile. Truth was, she didn't just admire Mercy House—she was a sponsor. But being more personally involved had always appealed to her.

"Didn't expect that?" she asked.

"Not really," he admitted. "So why not do it?"

"I've never had the time. I have a lot to

learn before I take the reins from my dad. But, you're right. I could juggle some priorities. After I get back and face the music, that is."

The waitress came over with two glasses of water, then she pulled out her notebook and perched it on top of her belly.

"What can I get you two?" she asked, shooting Liam a friendly smile. "Your usual?"

"My usual," Liam confirmed. He glanced at Bernie. "The waffles here are great."

"Waffles, then," she said. "With a side of bacon, not too crispy, but definitely well done. I'd also like a slice of lemon and a slice of orange in my water, and I don't want the syrup in a cup on my plate—it just gets sticky. I want the syrup in a separate container on a different plate."

The waitress eyed her for a moment, then reached over to the table behind them that hadn't been cleared yet, and put a bottle of store-brand syrup in front of Bernie with a clunk.

"On the side," she said with an icy smile, then turned and walked away.

Bernadette stared in surprise. That was downright rude—and no way to treat patrons of any establishment. She'd never been treated this way in her life.

"It's like she's never taken an order before," Bernie muttered. "She should be grateful she doesn't work in a coffee shop."

"She's nine months pregnant," Liam said. "Her boyfriend left her a few months ago. Said he was going for a job and then just disappeared. She's living with her aunt at the moment. So she's having a tough time. Cut her some slack."

Bernie sobered. And she was the one who was supposed to be sympathetic to the plight of single moms... She swallowed, feeling immediately awful for her attitude. She watched the waitress as she peeled the paper off her pad and stabbed it onto a spinning wheel of spikes on the counter of the kitchen window and turned it to face inward.

"Obviously, I didn't know that." Heat rose in her cheeks. Apparently, this place wasn't as sophisticated as she was used to, but she didn't want to look like the heartless heiress in front of Liam, either. Considering the beating her image was about to get in the press, his opinion mattered to her.

"If you want to help her out," Liam said,

taking a sip of his water, "eat here again and leave a big tip. That's what the rest of us do."

"She needs more than tips," Bernie countered. "I know that Mercy House is quite a way from here, but there must be something similar in Ohio. There are doctors who would see her at no cost, and there are programs to pay for the cost of a hospital delivery—"

"Tips." Liam's tone deepened, and he fixed her with a steady look. "And a bit of respect."

Bernie gave him a tight smile and stopped talking. Obviously, he already had an opinion about her, which stung. Even if he disapproved of the way she ordered a meal, what was his problem with charities? Mercy House made a difference in the lives of these girls, and their cheery waitress over there wasn't exactly too good for some charitable help.

A few minutes later, the waitress came back with their food. Apparently, Liam's regular order was eggs, toast and sausage. Bernie's waffle was topped with fresh strawberries and a ruffle of whipped cream, and really did look delicious.

The young woman put the plates in front of them, then cleared her throat. "Sorry, I forgot the lemon and orange wedges." She swallowed. "I hope it's not too rude, but I overheard what you were saying about that place that does things for single moms."

"Mercy House," Bernie confirmed.

"If you had the phone number or something... I'd be grateful."

Bernie rummaged around in her purse and pulled out a business card. "This is their card. Just tell them—"

She stopped. Tell them what, exactly? She couldn't announce her name here without bringing all sorts of attention that she was trying to avoid.

"Just tell them you need help," Bernie concluded. "They have a lot of resources. They might even be able to tell you about something closer."

The young woman smiled and tucked the card into the pocket of her apron slung underneath her belly. "Thanks. Enjoy your meal."

She moved on to another table, leaving Liam and Bernie in relative privacy again. If Mercy House could make this young woman's life a little bit easier, Bernie would be glad to have helped. But she was embarrassed by her knee-jerk reaction to be judgmental and mildly catty. This wasn't a brunch with girlfriends in an upscale bistro. This was… more real, somehow, and she felt like she'd already managed to make a fool of herself. She didn't want to be that kind of woman. Her appetite had vanished, and while the food looked amazing still, she wished she could cut this meal short and leave.

But Bernie had nowhere to go, and her car was in the shop. For the next little while, she'd just have to learn how to blend in—there wasn't any other option.

CHAPTER FIVE

AFTER THEY'D EATEN and Liam had paid, he and Bernie left the restaurant. The rest of the meal had been less relaxed. Bernie had closed herself off, her expression became more polished and she left a quarter of the food on the plate. Something had changed after their discussion about the waitress, and he knew he'd been a little hard on her. But this wasn't just any waitress—he'd known Melanie since she was a little girl, and she was twenty now. He fixed her aunt's aging Toyota. He'd even employed her deadbeat boyfriend for a few months. In a place like Runt River, everyone had a story, and it was invariably intertwined with everyone else's.

It looked like Melanie wanted the information about the charity, and that was fine. He wasn't trying to keep her from resources; he just didn't think it was right to embarrass her at her place of work. And she wasn't exactly without help. Her aunt was a loving woman, the local church had thrown a baby shower and pitched in for a new crib and stroller. Melanie's ex-boyfriend's family were doing their best to make up for their son's poor choices, too. Runt River didn't just abandon their own. They took a fierce pride in that.

As they stepped outside into the sunlight, Liam cleared his throat.

"Look, I hope I didn't offend you in there—"

"No, I'm fine." Her expression was still controlled and distant, however, and she looked away from him down the street.

"Things are different in a place this size," he tried to explain. "People have their pride. Even if someone needs help, you can't always walk up and just offer it… So—" He sighed. "It's just different here."

"Understood." For a moment, that polished shell cracked, and he thought he saw some real emotion underneath—sadness, mostly. She was trying to pretend everything was okay when it wasn't.

"I can understand the pressure you're under," she went on. "I know you think I'm naive to how hard things can be for people, but I'm not. At Mercy House, I learned how much children cost to raise, and that can't be easy for you."

"I do okay," he replied.

"Vince hasn't done the right thing with Ike," she added. "I know it might be a lot to think about right now, but what if I stepped in for him?"

"In what way?" he asked cautiously.

"I could take care of Ike a lot more easily. I have the financial—" Color rose in her cheeks. "Again, I don't mean to offend. But my family has the means to provide everything Ike could ever want."

Liam's stomach clenched. Was she seriously offering to take Ike off his hands?

"No," he said curtly.

She blinked. "I wasn't meaning to be crass—"

"I'm his legal guardian," Liam said. "And I'm doing just fine. I don't need you to take over."

She nodded, color flooding her cheeks. "Okay. Loud and clear. But if you need anything, tell me. I'm happy to help."

That offer had been Liam's fear—that the Morgans would find out about Ike and sweep him off...to where? And would he be loved and understood? The problem was, Liam was already attached.

"Is that Lucille?" Bernie was looking down the sidewalk, and her aunt had just come out of the ice cream shop, Ike in tow behind her. Ike carried a kiddie cone, and his face was covered in blue ice cream.

"That's her," he said.

"I'll catch up with her." She looked back at Liam and gave him an apologetic smile. "Thank you for lunch. It was kind of you."

He nodded, and she headed off down the sidewalk toward her aunt. Ike brightened at the sight of her and toddled in her direction. It took a moment for Lucille to realize that he wasn't following her, and she looked panicked before she caught sight of Bernie. The kid was in good hands. Except, Bernie seemed to be getting attached, too, if she was making that kind of offer. The law was on his side—for now.

Liam turned in the opposite direction toward Anderson Avenue, but he wasn't quite ready to head back to work. He had two hours before a scheduled oil change arrived at the shop, and he had another fifteen minutes on his lunch break. He decided to take a few more minutes and continued down Main.

His mind kept going back to Bernie, though. She wanted to help, but was there more to it? Did she honestly want to raise Ike herself? Because if she did, he had no doubt she'd make it happen. And yet mingled with his own distrust of her was an image of her with her big, brown eyes. She was sweet, vulnerable even… She didn't *seem* like the political shark, unless the teeth only came out when she was cornered. But wouldn't her current situation count as that?

He passed the hardware store, then a yarn shop—which was busier than the hardware store, funnily enough—and continued up Main Street. There were a few signs stapled to poles, all with the same bold lettering: Stop The Railway! Make Morgan Listen! Too many capitalized letters, but it showed how strongly people felt about this blasted railway. Morgan had promised them jobs, but a noisy train clattering past their town at all hours of the day and night hadn't exactly been their idea of improving things.

At the next corner there was an empty storefront that used to be a travel agency that had gone out of business about fifteen years ago, and now was leased for various seasonal purposes. Right now, it had a makeshift banner tied over the old travel agency sign—Make Morgan Listen. Coincidentally, this was the exact office that had been used for Vince Morgan's local campaign office when he was running for senator, and right across the street from the Runt River Christian Church.

That was the church the Eagers, his foster family, had brought him to every Sunday, and that was the church where he'd married Leanne. The memories came back like bile. Leanne had always loved politics—never missed a debate on TV, and last election, she'd had a candidate she'd truly had faith in.

Looking at the signs going up, the flutter of paper pamphlets stapled to telephone poles, it was like being transported back in time to when he'd honestly believed she was just excited about their candidate. And maybe she had been… Heck, even Liam had been, through her. He and Leanne never discussed who they were voting for. It was just safer that way. One less thing to fight about. Besides, they both took their votes very seriously. But that year, he would have voted Morgan, given the chance.

Vince Morgan—Ohio's Choice. That had been his tagline. He'd been Leanne's choice at the very least, and maybe Liam should have taken it a little more seriously when she came home gushing about the man. He should have noticed something more happening behind the scenes—maybe been a little less trusting.

Runt River was demanding their senator's attention, and Liam couldn't help but wonder if old Vince would show his face in this town again, because while Leanne had signed nondisclosure agreements, he hadn't—and he never would.

Liam turned and walked resolutely away from the campaign office. Vince Morgan had torn his life apart, and now Liam was having lunch with the man's cousin. Was that largeness of character or just plain old stupidity?

The Morgans were a powerful political family, capable of a whole lot of damage when they wanted something. Liam couldn't let himself forget that Bernie was one of them. Sweet, pretty, ill-treated even… but still a Morgan, and a polished smile was their nastiest weapon.

As Bernadette caught up with Aunt Lucille, Ike looked up at her with shining eyes. His curls were damp from sweat around his face, and his shirt had a smear of blue ice cream down the front. He was sweet, and just looking down into his babyish face made her smile.

"Share?" He held up his kiddie cone toward her.

"Oh, that looks so yummy, Ike." She bent down and took a pretend nibble. "I'll eat it *all.*"

Ike squealed and pulled his cone back, obviously not willing to lose the entire thing in his fit of generosity, and Bernie ruffled his hair. Lucille laughed, then glanced over Bernie's shoulder.

"How's Liam?" Lucille asked.

"Fine." Bernie glanced back, too, and saw Liam sauntering away from them. Jeans and a T-shirt worked for him, accentuating the strength and confidence in his gait. He didn't look back. She'd irritated him back there, but he'd also irritated her. She wasn't the bad guy here, but he seemed to be trying to protect the waitress from her. That stung.

"Liam likes you," Lucille said.

Lucille obviously hadn't witnessed that tense lunch.

"He puts up with me." She was a customer, with a weird connection to his late wife, that was all. She shot her aunt a wry smile. "So what are you two up to?"

"We're getting out of the house." Lucille looked down at Ike. "Right, Ike?"

Ike nodded and took another slurp of ice cream.

"The town is all riled up over that railway line, and they're demanding that their senator come and face them," Lucille said, bending to wipe some ice cream from Ike's cheek with a napkin. "That'll be hard for Liam. I don't think he's seen the senator since Leanne left."

Bernie glanced over her shoulder again— Liam had disappeared. She hadn't realized what Liam was probably dealing with right now. And his wife left him for *Vince*? She knew her cousin well…and Vince had never been her idea of a heartthrob. The woman obviously had questionable taste, but then quite a few women seemed to share it. Liam was strong, quiet, ruggedly handsome. Vince was posed, fake, slightly pudgy. Unless Leanne was attracted to power, there was no comparison. If only Leanne had known what was waiting for her. Vince might be a sweet talker when he wanted something—like votes or a fling—but his wife wasn't going anywhere. Not only did Vince rely on Tabby for his public image, but she was tougher than she looked. Leanne would have been torn to shreds. Perhaps she had been—the affair hadn't lasted long, from what Bernie understood.

"You probably never knew Vince," Bernie said. Aunt Lucille had been out of the picture before she and Vince were born, from what she'd been told. "He sleeps around a lot, but I've never figured out why he can get so many women."

"Money," Lucille said bluntly.

"Probably. And honeyed words. I remember overhearing him talking to some financial backer, and that man can schmooze. Still… When she had a man like Liam—"

"So you like him, too." Lucille chuckled, and heat rose in Bernie's cheeks.

"Oh, stop." Bernie laughed and shook her head. She didn't want to talk about Liam or her latent attraction to him. "Maybe it's because Vince is my cousin and I know his dirty secrets. He comes off as so honorable and determined, and I can see how that would be appealing. But I know the truth."

"Which is?" Lucille asked with a sidelong glance.

"That his wife runs the show. Tabby's the brains behind his campaigns, and if he ever thwarted her, she could undo him."

Lucille arched one eyebrow. "But she's okay with the womanizing?"

"She seems to put up with it, in exchange for influence. He might be senator, but the job is done by the two of them."

Vince was still smarting from Milhouse's refusal to back him as the Republican nominee in the next election. Vince thought he was owed it, by merit of DNA. Milhouse wanted a candidate who could win.

"From what I understand, Leanne fell in love with Vince," Lucille said. "She idolized him—truly believed that he was what Ohio needed. It was a mixture of political fervor and attraction, I suppose. There is no accounting for chemistry sometimes, because Liam couldn't talk her into staying. She was determined to stick close to Vince.

She must have thought the baby would make a difference."

Idiot. That was all that Bernie could think of a woman who would make that choice.

"What were they like—Liam and Leanne, I mean?" she asked.

"Oh, they were an ordinary couple. He was a good husband, from what I could see. He'd get her flowers every so often, always came home to her. She wanted a baby so badly, and they couldn't have one. That kind of pressure on a marriage takes a toll."

Bernie looked down. "He mentioned that."

"Did he? Well, everyone knew about it. There was a lot of arguing toward the end, but just before she left him, it actually looked like they were doing better. I thought they were patching things up a bit. But I could overhear those arguments from across the street. She was desperate to move to the city, and he wanted to stay here with the garage. She didn't think he could make enough money here—if she couldn't have a baby, she at least wanted more material comfort."

Maybe he thought Bernie was looking down on his home the same way. And if she had to be brutally honest with herself, perhaps she had been.

"That might explain a few things," Bernie said, almost to herself.

"Grumpy, is he?" Lucille asked with a small smile.

"It was more than that." They started walking down the sidewalk. "There is a waitress in that restaurant who's pregnant."

"Melanie," Lucille confirmed. She held out a hand to Ike who caught up and grabbed her little finger.

"Well, I was mentioning Aunt Ellen's work with Mercy House," Bernie said, and then she stopped when she saw Lucille's face. The older woman fixed her with an intense glare—almost angry. "What?" she asked.

"No, no," Lucille looked away again. "Go on...what about Mercy House?"

"I was just talking about all the resources available there for young women in her situation. Ellen has doctors who volunteer their time for checkups, there are all sorts of parenting classes, baby supplies, all available for free to the girls who meet the criteria. I'm not sure I told him this part, but they also have a maternity wing at a small local hospital that will give free care to these girls when they deliver. There's a wealthy sponsor who kicks in a rather large donation to the hospital every year to help fund this, but still—"

Bernie didn't think it would be polite to point out that she was the sponsor right now...

"And..." Lucille prompted. "He didn't like this idea?"

"Not really," she said. "I suggested that our waitress might find some valuable resources there, and he flipped out. He said it would insult her to even suggest it."

"Well, Runt River has its ways," Lucille said, visibly relaxing. "You'd do well to listen to Liam on that sort of thing. He knows what he's talking about. She's not exactly destitute."

"Except she overheard us," Bernie said. "And she asked for the information. So I gave her one of Aunt Ellen's cards."

Lucille froze, then slowly turned that glittering gaze back onto Bernie. "You did what?"

"I gave her a business card." Bernadette frowned. "She asked for it. And you can rest easy that she wasn't insulted."

Lucille closed her eyes for a moment, then

slowly shook her head. "I'm going to say this as nicely as I possibly can, Bernadette." Her tone chilled. "Runt River doesn't need Morgan charity. That girl doesn't *need* Mercy House." Her lips curled in distaste. "We take care of our own, and we are doing just fine without your well-meaning intrusions. Don't give that card out to anyone else here. And I mean that. No mention of that blasted charity. Runt River doesn't need it."

Bernadette stared at her aunt in shock. Did Lucille hate the Morgans so much that she couldn't allow a pregnant woman to get proper medical care because the funding came from the family? She'd known that the divide was a bitter one, but this was nuts.

"All because you and my dad can't stand each other?" Bernie demanded.

Lucille shook her head, then smiled bitterly. "I'm looking out for a vulnerable young woman right now."

"Heaven forbid she have access to some resources!" Bernadette was angry now.

"Bunny…"

"Bernadette to you," she snapped.

"Bernadette." Lucille lowered her voice

and took a moment to calm herself. "Stop trying to help. Okay?"

Bernie felt a touch on her leg, and she looked down to see a sticky hand planted on her skirt. Ike looked up, eyes wide and welling with tears. They'd been doing this in front of Ike, and somehow she hadn't even thought of how much the little guy would understand, but kids certainly picked up on tone.

Bernadette bent and scooped him up in her arms.

"It's okay, Ike," she said quietly. "Auntie and I were just talking. It's all okay now."

Lucille pinched her lips together in disapproval, but she didn't say anything more on the subject.

"Let's get home," the older woman said instead. "Ike needs a nap."

Perhaps Lucille wasn't the kindly, hard-done-by relative that Bernie had believed her to be. Maybe her father's bile had held a tinge of the truth, too. Because Lucille seemed to have a vehement dislike for all things related to this family, and while Bernie chafed at the demands, she was still a Morgan, and she loved her parents. This wasn't supposed to be about choosing sides; it was supposed to be about building a bridge.

But there was obviously more to this feud than she'd realized...and in her eagerness to get away, she may have gone from the frying pan straight into the fire.

CHAPTER SIX

A COUPLE OF days later, Liam stood over a pot of macaroni and cheese, stirring the orange powder into the noodles with a lump of butter. Ike stood at his side, looking up at the pot like a puppy.

"Smells good, doesn't it?" Liam asked, looking down at the little guy.

"Hungry."

"Me, too, buddy. Almost done."

He finished stirring, then grabbed a plate from the cupboard and dumped a slosh of pasta onto the plate. He should probably provide a side of veggies for Ike to turn his nose up at, but he wouldn't. Not today. He'd battle the veggies another day. Today, he just wanted to feed the kid. That would feel like victory enough at the moment.

"Go sit down. Time to eat," Liam said, and Ike scampered off to the table and climbed up onto his seat. There was a booster chair on the seat cushion, a much appreciated hand-me-down from a neighbor. Liam put the plate in front of Ike and handed him a spoon.

"Yummy, yummy, yummy..." Ike sang to himself as he ran his spoon around the plate, gathering up a bite. Liam couldn't help but smile. What was it about feeding a child that felt so satisfying? It hit him in the same pleasure center as fixing a car—a personal victory of man over complex problem. And two-year-olds counted as "complex problems" most of the time. Cute, but complex.

There was a triple knock on the door, a pause, two more. Liam knew who that was, and he sauntered over to open the door.

"Hey, Tim." His foster brother stood on the step, and as Liam stood back, the other man stepped inside.

Tim Eager was about six months older than Liam, and he'd been the biological son in the foster home he was raised in from the age of ten. The Eagers were a kind enough family who took in a few different foster kids over the years. They just liked kids, and they wanted to make a difference, but they tended to be a little too idealistic, in Liam's humble opinion. They figured church every Sunday and someone to talk to would be enough to heal the wounds that a lifetime of neglect and rejection had inflicted. And really, what more did Liam expect of them? At least they'd tried. Tim, being the same age as Liam, had seemed to understand better, and the boys had bonded, despite the wariness from Mr. and Mrs. Eager. Somehow Tim had known that what Liam had needed was a friend, someone who would just hang out with him without trying to fix him.

"How're you doing?" Tim asked now.

"Good." Liam raised the pot of mac and cheese. "Want some?"

"No, no… I ate already. Go ahead."

Liam put the pot back on the stove. "So what brings you by?" he asked.

"I have a problem with my truck—it's grinding when I change gears. Wondered if you'd take a look?"

Tim wasn't a rich guy. He worked as a supervisor at a nearby tire factory, and Liam had been helping him to keep his old Ford roadworthy for the past few years.

"Yeah, sure," Liam said. Work was steady enough that he could help without jeopardizing his livelihood. "So how's the family?"

Tim talked a little bit about his pregnant wife and their two little girls. Liam's foster parents still had two foster kids in their home, which kept them busy, despite their advancing age. But Liam was included in the invitations to family dinners on the holidays, and they still felt like "home," more than anywhere else did.

Ike finished his plate of noodles.

"Do you want more?" Liam asked.

"Uh-uh. TV!"

"Okay, go ahead."

In the month he'd been here Ike had mastered the TV remote, and he could find the kids' channel lickety-split. As Ike trotted out into the living room, Tim's expression turned sober. They were getting to the real reason for his visit.

"What?" Liam asked, grabbing a fork and taking a bite from the pot.

"Look, man, is this good for you?" Tim asked.

"It won't kill me," Liam joked, looking into the pot of orange noodles.

"Har, har," Tim said. "You know what I mean. Taking care of this kid. Is this really healthy?"

"What would you have me do?" Liam sobered. "I'm not sending him to a foster home. No offense, but that's not the life for a kid."

"What about Leanne's family?"

"Her cousin is still partying it up, and there isn't anyone else. I'm the most stable home for Ike right now."

"This is the child Leanne had when she cheated on you." Tim shook his head. "This can't be easy."

"It isn't easy," Liam admitted. "It's downright hard, but he's a sweet kid, and he deserves better."

"What about Ike's father?"

That hit a little too close to the heart of the matter, and anger rose up to cover a tender spot. He hadn't resolved any of his anger toward Vince Morgan. The man was a snake—lying, slithering, dangerous. By the time Leanne signed her nondisclosure agreement, all of Runt River was aware of who had fathered her child. News like that spread faster than the flu.

"If the senator was going to acknowledge Ike, don't you think he'd have done it by now? I'm sure he knows of Leanne's death—it happened in his city, after all. And he hasn't made contact. I doubt he would. Ike is his little mistake, and he has a reputation to maintain."

Tim nodded and leaned back against the counter. "What about the rest of the Morgan family? Bernadette, for example?"

Liam had told his foster brother about Bernadette's identity, knowing that Tim could be trusted, but Bernie hadn't exactly earned his confidence yet.

"She's one of them," Liam replied. "Her priorities aren't going to be the same. When a family's power comes before a toddler's happiness—"

"Are you sure about that?" Tim asked pointedly. "You have a personal bias against them. Are you positive that you're better for this boy than his relatives?"

Liam stopped and shook his head. He didn't trust any of them, and that wasn't just because he hated Vince. He might be biased, but he wasn't stupid.

"And if Bernadette asks to take Ike?" Tim asked. "I don't even know if she would, but it's a possibility, and you need to be ready for it."

She'd already hinted at it—taking over her

cousin's responsibilities for the boy. And that had stung. He didn't need her to take anything over. He could provide for Ike without any help from them.

"I'm Ike's legal custodian," Liam said with a sigh. "He stays with me until the courts say otherwise."

There were a couple of beats of silence, and Liam knew he sounded hardheaded. But deep down he felt certain that the Morgans weren't good for the little guy, and that included Bernie.

"I'm worried about you, man," Tim said.

"I'm fine." Liam raked a hand through his hair, then shook his head. "Am I grieving? Sure. But I'm doing okay."

"You're hanging in there," Tim admitted. "But you're not fine. You're taking care of the very child that ended your marriage. You're soldiering on like you always have, but you are *not* fine."

"What would you have me do?" Liam demanded. "Do you want me to break down?"

"We're all worried about you," Tim said. "Mom and Dad are, too. You've got to put yourself first for once, Liam. You need to take care of yourself."

"You're a dad," Liam said with a bitter smile. "When's the last time you got to put yourself first?"

"Except you *aren't* Ike's dad. You don't have to do this."

Tim's words stung, and Liam looked into the living room where Ike sat in front of a cartoon. No, he wasn't Ike's dad. He'd never be anyone's biological father, and that had been the biggest obstacle in his marriage. He'd already failed on the most fundamental level of manhood.

"I'll never have kids of my own," Liam said. "You know that. So any kid in my life is going to be someone else's, biologically speaking."

"But this kid..." Tim sighed. "If it were me, it would be too much. If Tiffany cheated on me, left me and had a child with someone else, I wouldn't be able to do what you're doing. No one expects this of you, Liam. You don't owe Leanne anything."

That was the thing—Tim was used to "normal." He had two parents who'd stayed together, extended family. He had friends, he had a wife, he had kids of his own. Tim was the poster child for normal. Liam wasn't, and never would be. Might as well embrace that now.

Ike was glued to the TV, enthralled with a show that seemed to be about hand-washing. There were worse things to hammer into a kid's head. But those curls, those big brown eyes, the tiny body and big head…the kid was cute, but it was more than that. The kid was vulnerable. He needed someone to protect him from all the garbage out there, all the people who might take advantage of that innocence.

"I know I don't owe her anything," Liam said after a moment.

"So why are you doing this?" Tim asked.

"Because someone has to, and they dropped him off on *my* doorstep. If they'd brought him to someone else, I wouldn't have stepped in, but—" He sighed. "Someone has to take care of him, and they brought him to me. The only other option is the system, and I can't do that to him."

Tim stepped up next to Liam, and they silently watched Ike for a few moments.

"You're a dad, Tim," Liam said quietly. "Could *you* just give him away because it was easier?"

Tim swallowed hard, then shook his head. "No, I guess not."

It felt good to have Tim see the situation through his eyes for a moment. This whole thing was complicated and messy, but at the heart of it all was a little boy who needed love. And Liam could identify with that.

"Look, if you need a hand," Tim said, "we're here. Tiffany says she'll babysit if you need a break, and you could bring him by to hang out at our place sometime. We're family, man. We're here for you." He paused and heaved a sigh. "Just be careful."

Liam understood that wariness. He was hip deep in this, and there would be no getting out easily. Whatever he did from this point on would hurt. If he gave Ike to his biological family, he'd have to say goodbye. He'd gotten attached to the boy, almost in spite of himself. And if he kept Ike and raised him, then he'd be raising Leanne's love child, the baby she had with another man—the child that showed her that life with Liam wasn't enough. That would be painful, too. There was nothing easy about this situation, just different ways to hurt.

And Tim cared.

"Thanks," Liam said. "Why don't I come by tomorrow evening and take a look at your truck?"

They were family—as close to it as Liam could get. And he was a man who took care of his own.

BERNADETTE STOOD IN Runt River Revival, a women's clothing shop that consisted mainly of blue jeans and tops. She needed to blend in, and the dresses she'd packed for her honeymoon were pretty, but they stood out here.

She'd chosen a few pairs of jeans, tried them on, and set them aside. Now she just needed a few tops. She angled toward the T-shirts.

"I love your dress," the young sales associate said.

"Thanks." Bernie cast her a smile. "I'm looking for a more casual look, though."

She grabbed a couple of white T-shirts, a black one, a pink one. She had some cash on her, thankfully, so she wouldn't be forced to pull out her platinum credit card and announce her real name unnecessarily.

She mentally tallied up the total. She had enough to cover it, but she couldn't go overboard. She put back a chunky necklace. When was the last time she put something back because she wouldn't have enough money?

"Aren't you, like, famous or something?" the girl asked.

Bernie froze for a second, then forced herself to relax. It was like nosy questions from the press—she had to just let it roll off her.

"I'm Lucille Neiman's niece," she said with a shrug.

"Oh." The girl looked mildly disappointed. "Maybe it's that you look like someone famous. I heard that you've been in the papers."

Bernie didn't like to lie. Honesty was the best policy, and when honesty wasn't possible, hiding was the second-best policy. But never lying.

"Did you get your jeans here?" Bernie asked instead. "They look good on you."

"No, I got these in Cleveland," the girl replied. "Are you taking those tops, too?"

"I am." She dropped them on the counter and waited while the salesgirl tallied it all up. She seemed to have forgotten her earlier curiosity, and Bernie made a mental promise to herself to dial it down from now on.

She'd even go without makeup if that helped her fly under the radar around here.

Bernie paid and accepted the plastic bag with a smile. "Thanks. Have a nice evening."

Her phone rang from inside her purse, and she pulled it out as she exited the shop. She recognized the number immediately. Calvin had been calling constantly since she'd turned her phone back on, but she hadn't been willing to talk to him yet. She stopped on the sidewalk, her heart hammering. Was she ready to face him now? She swallowed hard, then picked up the call.

"Hello, Calvin." She sounded more sure of herself than she felt at the moment.

"Bunny! My God. I've been worried sick. What happened?"

"You know what happened," she retorted. "Kimberly happened."

"You could have talked to me about it, Bun. You didn't give me a chance to explain."

"Explain what?" she asked, starting to walk again. "Why you were groping at your ex-girlfriend minutes before you were supposed to marry me?"

"It wasn't like that." His voice hardened.

"Stop being so emotional. It was a goodbye, nothing more."

"Goodbyes don't require tongue."

"Funny. Look, Bunny. I thought you were more mature than this. We knew what we were doing when we got engaged. We were becoming one of America's power couples. And that can be complicated. I chose you, but that doesn't mean I don't still have feelings for her. I can't just turn that off like a switch. I chose you. That should count for something."

Bernie pulled the phone away from her ear and looked down at it incredulously. He honestly thought he was being the mature, logical one right now. Or perhaps he was just being utterly honest with her. For once. But there was something underneath it all that made her anger simmer.

"It doesn't count for enough," she retorted. "I was expecting monogamy. We *agreed on* monogamy. It was what was best for your political career, remember? Nothing to hide?"

He was silent, and she looked at the phone again to see if the call had been dropped. It hadn't.

"A lot of successful couples have certain…

understandings," he said. "I can promise to stay married to you for the rest of our lives. I can promise to put you and our children first in everything. I can promise to be discreet, and to protect your image—"

"Not enough, Calvin!" She clamped her mouth shut and lowered her voice. "It's over. If this is your way of trying to make up, you're failing miserably. I'm done."

"Okay, okay…" He heaved a sigh. "Then we need to talk damage control."

"Discuss it with my father," she snapped.

"I have. But you're the obvious liability here. We need a story that we both stick to."

"I liked the truth," she said.

"Yeah?" His tone turned ugly. "Are you going to like it when your name is dragged through the papers? Because not everyone is going to side with you, you know. There will be people who say that you're cold and unfeeling and they don't blame a man for seeking some warmth elsewhere."

She'd known that Calvin could be dangerously practical when necessary, and she'd found that exciting when it was focused on his competition. But pointed at her, it made her blood run cold. This was a threat. If she lashed out at him publicly, he'd make it as ugly for her as possible. Public opinion was fickle, and a beautiful heiress didn't get a ton of sympathy.

"Is that what you think?"

"Bunny, I'm just trying to paint a realistic picture for you." His voice softened again. "We need a story we can both live with. Something like, you realized that you didn't love me enough to commit to me for the rest of your life. You needed some freedom to explore who you are, and you feel terrible for running out like you did—"

"So, the official story would be that it's my fault?" she demanded.

"Considering I was the one left in front of cameras, reporters and a church full of people, yes."

How had he managed to turn this around already? "Forget it!"

"Bunny, I have a reputation to protect. You know my career plans, and if you don't want to be a part of it, I can respect that. But at the very least, I'm asking you not to sabotage what we're all working toward."

"Your cheating on me doesn't count as a little self-sabotage?" she quipped. "I like how you manage to make it my fault. Because I didn't grit my teeth and accept a lifetime with a philandering louse and simply march down that aisle and marry you?"

"You're being too emotional about this."

"And how *should* I be?" A lump rose in her throat, and she blinked back tears. "I just want to know one thing—how long was this going on with Kimberly?"

Silence again for a few beats. "Fine. I'd never exactly...stopped."

And she hadn't noticed. Bernie shut her eyes for a moment and sucked in a deep breath. It was even worse than she'd imagined.

"So that wasn't a goodbye."

"It was. Bunny, I was *marrying* you. She knew what that meant. She'd never be my wife—you had that role. She'd never come first—my wife and kids would. She knew what that meant. It was most certainly a goodbye—a goodbye to any possibility of more."

"More than being a mistress," she clarified.

"Bunny..."

Kimberly had been in the picture all along, and she would have stayed there. Bernie had dodged a bullet in running out on that wedding, she realized as she stopped at a street corner and stared up at the pale blue sky, the bubbling cumulus clouds that sailed across it. A truck rumbled past, country music blaring out an open window, and she looked down at the bag of "blending in" clothes in her hand. It didn't matter what she said; Calvin would turn it around on her. And if he could do this in a private conversation, he'd be able to do it with the press. She couldn't win against this man—not alone—and he had her father's backing.

"Calvin, I'm going to have to give this some thought," she said.

"That's fair. Look, Bunny, I'm sorry."

He wasn't. She knew that. He was sorry she wouldn't go along with the arrangement, but he wasn't sorry for his actions.

"Goodbye." She disconnected without waiting for a response, and she dropped her phone back into her purse.

She was free here in Runt River—freer than she'd been in her life. And she wasn't about to agree to anything prematurely. Very likely, they'd start spreading a story without her consent sooner or later, and she'd have to deal with that when the time came. She'd seen politicians mow down people who got in their way, and up until this point, she'd always thought her father's position made her immune. But she wasn't.

Jeans. T-shirts. No makeup. She'd give this a try. She wasn't "Bunny" anymore. She was Bernadette Morgan, and she had yet to discover what exactly that would mean. But of one thing she was certain: she'd never accept the blame.

CHAPTER SEVEN

THE NEXT EVENING, Liam took Ike down to Tim's place. They had dinner there—burgers on the barbecue—and Tim's seven- and nine-year-old daughters were over the moon with "a baby" to take care of. Ike didn't mind the babying in the least, and allowed them to wash his hands, feed him cookies and generally parade him about like a prince. When he offered them soggy pieces of cookie, they rapturously praised his generosity. Ike was in his element.

In the meantime, Liam got Tim's truck up and running again. It wasn't too complicated a fix, and his foster brother was grateful. Tim and Tiffany didn't have a lot of extra money, so every little bit helped.

As Liam drove back to his place, the radio playing a jaunty tune, Ike chattered in the backseat in a mixture of baby talk and real words. He seemed to be talking about playing with the girls from what Liam could decipher.

"You liked playing with the girls, did you?" he asked, glancing over his shoulder.

"Yep!" Ike declared.

"That's how it starts, buddy." Liam smiled wryly. It didn't take little boys too long to discover that they liked the doting attention.

He pulled into his driveway, and when he got out of the truck, he glanced across the street. Habit, he told himself, but it was more than that. He found himself looking toward Lucille's house more and more often now since Bernie had arrived in town. And he had to do a double take when he saw a young woman sitting on the steps. She wore a pair of jeans and a fitted white tee. Her hair was pulled back into a ponytail, and if she hadn't lifted one hand in a half wave, he wouldn't have immediately recognized her. It was Bernie—without the makeup and the city clothes. He let out a soft whistle of surprise, and waved back.

Liam opened the back door of the pickup and reached in to unbuckle Ike. Ike squirmed against the harness which only made it harder to get the kid out, but once out of his car seat and back on the ground, Ike wandered off and found himself a stick to play with.

Bernie didn't move from her position on the step, and Liam paused, wondering if it would be pushy to cross the street and say hi. Except the last time he'd seen her they'd been at odds, and he wasn't sure if she'd want his company right now. Just because she wanted some cool evening air didn't mean she wanted him.

Liam turned toward his front door.

"Come on, Ike," he called. "It's time for a bath."

Ike looked over at Liam, then back at the flower bed he was poking with the stick. The dirt was going to win this one, he could tell.

"Come on, buddy," Liam chuckled. "It's already late. Do you want bubbles in your bath?"

Ike loved bubble baths, and Liam was hoping to do this the easy way. Ever since Bernie's arrival, Ike had opened up and started smiling and laughing. Liam wasn't sure what she'd done exactly, but Ike was a happier kid now. Maybe it was her resemblance to Leanne—the one thing he couldn't provide.

Ike dropped his stick and looked across the

street. "Bunny," he said, pointing with one pudgy finger. He was trying to say "Bernie," but he couldn't say his *r*'s yet.

"You'll see her tomorrow. Time for a bath."

"Bunny!"

Liam turned around to unlock the door, hoping that Ike would follow him inside, but when he glanced back, he saw that instead of losing interest, he was heading toward the road at a trot.

"Shoot!" Liam dropped his keys and dashed across the yard toward him. Ike saw Liam coming and let out a squeal and started to run, too. Just like Ike to think it was a game.

"Ike, no!" Liam called, and in the periphery of his vision, he could see Bernie jump to her feet and run toward the street, too. As the toddler's shoe hit the pavement, Ike tripped and fell hard into the asphalt.

There was silence for a moment as Liam closed the distance, and by the time he got to Ike, his mouth was wide and the first wail pierced the quiet evening. Ike had scraped both his knees pretty badly—they were bleeding—and there was a scrape on his forehead and nose. The poor kid. That had to hurt. Liam scooped him up and held him close. Bernie arrived a second after him.

"Is he okay?" she asked breathlessly. She looked Ike over and winced. "We need bandages. Do you have any?"

"Yeah, upstairs." Liam nodded toward his house. "Care to help me out with this?"

"Sure."

Ike was wailing, and he held out his arms for Bernie. She gathered him into a hug, and Liam noticed some blood from the tyke's knee smear against her white shirt. She didn't seem to notice.

"Oh, poor Ike," she crooned. "That really hurt, huh?"

Bernie followed Liam inside and up the stairs to the bathroom. He was relieved that she'd come along. It wasn't that he couldn't deal with this alone, but having another adult here to help him calm down Ike would make it all a whole lot easier. And he was new to this kid stuff.

Bernie sat down on the edge of the tub with Ike on her lap, and Liam grabbed a cloth, ran it under some cold water and started cleaning up the blood. Ike cried even louder, and Bernie held out her hand for the cloth.

"Let me," she said.

Liam passed it over, and Bernie cuddled Ike close and murmured into his hair as she dabbed at the blood. Ike calmed down, and his cries subsided into sniffles as she worked.

"It's not going to hurt, Ike," she said softly. "See? Look, that didn't hurt a bit. And we'll get you bandages and maybe even a cookie if Daddy has some…"

Daddy. She'd said it so easily, but Liam had never called himself that. He wasn't the kid's dad; he was just a stand-in.

"Daddy?" Ike looked up at Liam and wiped his runny nose with the back of his hand. He looked so small and sad with the scrape down his forehead and his face wet with tears.

"I—uh—" Liam cleared his throat. "He just calls me Liam."

"Oh." Color rose in Bernie's cheeks. "Of course. Sorry. Liam might have cookies, right, Ike?"

"Daddy," Ike whispered, and Liam's heart constricted. If only it were that easy. How many times had he seen men with their kids, heard those little voices asking their daddies for something special. He'd thought that if he had a kid who called him Daddy, he'd never be able to say no to that plaintive little voice. Yet here he was, and he couldn't just make it all okay again. All he had was a box of bandages.

"Let's get you patched up first," Liam said, forcing a smile.

Bernie turned her attention from Ike's knees to his forehead, and she dabbed at the road burn on his face.

"I got an owie," Ike announced. The horror of his ordeal seemed to be over, and he was enjoying the attention now. Liam tore open the wrappers and started applying bandages to the worst of the scrapes. When he got to Ike's forehead, he wasn't sure what to do about it.

"Kisses," Ike said, lifting his face up toward Liam. "I gotta owie. Kisses!"

A lump rose in Liam's throat, and he bent down, and he planted a kiss on the soft little forehead. Ike smelled like baby shampoo from his last bath and cookie crumbs from his evening at Tim's place.

"Better?" Liam asked.

"Again." Ike lifted his face, and Liam kissed him once more.

It felt strangely comforting to him, too, as if by simply pressing his lips against that fragile head, he could take all the pain of the world away.

"Okay," Ike said, sliding down from Bernie's lap and bending to inspect his bandages. That kiss had been enough, apparently, and Liam stood there for a moment, his throat tight with emotion. When he looked at Bernie, he saw tears misting her eyes.

She looked younger without the makeup, and he noticed for the first time that she had faint freckles spattered across her nose. In that moment, under the fluorescent bathroom light, he found himself wishing that he could close the distance between them, too. It would be the most natural thing in the world to slide an arm around her waist and kiss the top of her head. She'd feel warm against him, and maybe she'd lean against his shoulder. He pulled his thoughts away from the precipice.

Bernie was a part of a cutthroat world he was trying to protect Ike from. One word from her would bring her family's legal team onto him, and Ike could very quickly be swept away. Attraction shouldn't factor into this, and entertaining these feelings would only blur his perspective. She'd already offered to contribute to Ike's raising, and he needed to be careful. Having the Morgan family's undivided attention could be a dangerous thing.

Except that he *was* feeling something for this woman—something he hadn't felt in a good many years. Was it just that he was lonely, or was it the combined effort in sorting out Ike's scrapes? Whatever it was, he needed to keep it in check.

"Yeah, well…" he said gruffly. "You've promised the kid cookies, so I guess we'd better make good on that."

Bernie nodded and stood. "A promise is a promise."

As THEY HEADED down the stairs toward the kitchen, Bernadette smiled at Ike who was peeking at her over Liam's shoulder as he carried the toddler. Ike blinked at her, small hands wrapped around Liam's neck. He was a Morgan, and that melted something inside her. There was something about a family tie that was special—and she could feel it with Ike.

One of us.

She'd been thinking about her conversation with Calvin, and she realized that the part that hurt the most wasn't Calvin's infidelity, but the way her family had sided with him. She knew that they had plans for him, and by extension for themselves, but they were family, and she should be able to count on their support. They probably thought the same thing about her.

"Family first" meant something different for the Morgans—it meant the group came before the individual. Bernie couldn't really count on the family, but the family should be able to count on Bernie, and they'd all prosper together. It was messed up—she recognized that, but it was what it was. She was one of them, therefore she owed them. Liam hadn't been open to her offer of help, but it was the one thing she could offer. Morgans stuck together.

They came into the kitchen, and Liam put Ike down and rummaged in a cupboard. He pulled out a box of chocolate cookies and handed one to Ike.

"I like the new look." A smile flickered at the corners of his lips. She could see his approval, and for some reason she liked that.

"Thanks." She looked down at her shirt and saw a smear of blood from Ike's knee. She grimaced. Whatever—it was only a shirt.

"So what brought this on?" he asked.

"If I want to lie low, I'd better blend in a little more," she replied.

"Makes sense."

She eyed Liam for a moment, wondering how much to share. "While I was picking up my new casual look, I got a call from Calvin."

He shook a few cookies onto a plate and nudged them down the counter toward her. "Begging for a second chance or something?"

She wished that were the case—it would have been easier to take. She gave him a brief summary of the conversation.

Liam smiled wryly. "And you told him where to shove that, I imagine."

Bernie was irritated with herself for her cautious response to her ex-fiancé. She should have let him have it—but things were more complicated. Calvin had the power, and her family's support. She'd never felt more vulnerable in her life.

"I can't win," she admitted. "I'm in the way of a grand machine that's already in motion. My father thinks Calvin has a real chance at the White House, and my ego isn't important enough to derail that."

"That's insulting."

"It is."

"So what are you going to do?" Liam met her gaze and held it. That was the question, wasn't it? What was her next move? She had no idea…there was no going back to the way things used to be.

She sighed. "I don't know."

Bernie took a cookie and bit into it. As she chewed, she watched Ike poke at his bandaged knees.

"Ike is lucky to have you," she said.

"You offered to take him," he countered, and she heard the challenge in his voice. He wasn't looking for compliments; he was looking for facts.

"I didn't say take him."

"You said you'd take over Vince's responsibilities."

She had said that. "That wasn't a reflection on what you're doing with him here," she replied with a shake of her head. "I'd discovered an orphaned relative. What was I supposed to do? He's a part of my family, and

I have an obligation toward him. But looking at how you're taking care of him... You put him first." She licked her lips. "In the long run, that's worth a lot. It's more than I've got."

What she wouldn't give right now for her father to side with her—to tell her not to worry because any man who would break his daughter's heart wasn't good enough for him, either. Somehow all of this would be easier if her father's loyalties to politics were a little weaker and his loyalties to his only daughter were a little stronger. Milhouse Morgan wasn't the kind of man to let sentimentality get in the way of his goals, but what woman didn't want to come before money in her father's heart?

"I actually used to dream of a family like yours," Liam said.

"Like mine how?" she asked. Did he have any idea how cutthroat her family really was?

"Genetically related." He smiled wryly. "Someone who was connected to me in some undeniable way. I was a foster kid. My mom gave me up at birth, and I ended up in the system. I bounced around for a bit, until I landed in a foster home here in Runt River when I was ten. I stayed there until I was eighteen and aged out."

"And the foster family?" she asked. "Are you still in contact?"

"They're all the family I've got," he replied. "I spend Christmas and Thanksgiving with them, but there's a difference between their kids and the foster kids. I have to admit that blood counts."

"That would have been tough," she admitted.

"It could have been a whole lot worse," he replied. "My foster brother Tim and I are pretty close. I've made the best of it, and I have a life here. The thing is, when you don't have a family of your own, you tend to take what you do have more seriously. You don't take it for granted, and you don't trade it away."

Like Ike—Liam wasn't willing to just hand the boy over, and she admired that. But were there other relatives somewhere? How much support did Ike actually have?

"Did your wife have family here?" Bernie asked.

"Leanne's parents died when she was young. Her cousin is in Akron, but she's got some addiction issues, so she isn't an ideal guardian for Ike."

"Hmm." Her expression clouded, then she nodded. "It isn't a bad thing for Ike to have more family, you know. I'm just offering to be that family."

"I appreciate the sentiment," he said, his voice low. "But I've got this."

She nodded. He didn't trust her—that much was obvious.

"You really don't trust me, do you?" she asked.

"Your family has ground me down in the past," he said. "I'm not eager to have it happen again."

"Well, they're grinding me down, too," she conceded. "I can't say I blame you."

He met her gaze, and they exchanged a wry smile. Funny to be bonding over her dysfunctional family.

"Thing is," Liam said quietly, "when you marry someone, it's supposed to be for better or for worse, in good times and bad. When Leanne and I got married, we didn't talk about the possibility of bad times. When we weren't able to conceive, we got the fertility tests and figured out I was the problem. That was a real blow to my male pride. I promised her the world, and I couldn't deliver. But I'm trying to make up for that now by sticking by this kid. I'm not giving up on Ike."

She noted the hard-won wisdom in those words. People didn't get married thinking about the possibility of tough times.

"Calvin and I were no better," she confessed. "I loved him, but I wasn't in love with him. We were getting married because we had joint goals, and together could have achieved them. I naively thought that we might grow closer over the years. But you're right—what if he didn't make it to the White House? What if my father disinherited me? I don't think either of us would have wanted that for the rest of our lives. We had no business getting married."

"You should have been enough for Calvin," Liam said.

She should have been. But she wasn't—even that shiny future wasn't enough. He needed another woman in the arrangement, too. That was painful on several levels. Running the free world with Bernie wouldn't have been enough…

"And you should have been enough for Leanne," she said. He caught her eye, and they smiled—this time with more warmth.

She took a cookie off the plate and offered it to Ike. The toddler took it and trotted into the living room.

"He's dumping it on the couch," Liam said.

Bernie watched to see what Ike would do with the cookie, and sure enough, he tossed it onto the couch cushion.

"Ike!" she called. "If you don't want it, bring it back."

Ike ignored her and picked up a toy truck from the floor.

"It's his thing," Liam said with a low laugh. "He's a funny kid."

Liam knew Ike rather well. He'd be a good dad to Ike, she realized—better than Vince would ever be, even if he acknowledged the boy. Vince was too much like Calvin—a ferocious dedication to the legitimate family without the actual faithfulness to make that mean something.

Liam passed her another cookie. "We'll both be okay, you know."

"You think?" she asked. She wasn't sure what okay even looked like anymore. Everything was on its head.

"Getting over your ex gets easier," he said. "I know I keep saying this, but it doesn't hurt as much after a while. When you have some time to think it all through, it starts to make some sense. That probably helps the most— when it stops seeming like some random thunderbolt. Besides, we have family," he said. "Mine is a little less conventional than yours, but I still belong somewhere."

Family. That's what it always came down to, except hers expected her to put her dignity aside, and make Calvin McMann electable by smiling for cameras and taking the blame for their canceled wedding. It was the last thing she wanted to do, but maybe it was the smartest. After this humiliation and betrayal, perhaps she could get her payback when he was in office. He'd owe her, as well he should after what he'd done. She was a Morgan, after all, and if she had nothing else, she had her family.

CHAPTER EIGHT

LIAM ADJUSTED THE light above the Rolls-Royce engine. It had been a few days since he'd seen Bernie. The first part he'd ordered had arrived, and he could install the new carburetor now, and do the rest of the work when the other shipments arrived. The timing was perfect. He had the morning to work on the Rolls before he had another vehicle coming in for a tune-up and a flush of the brake fluid.

Ordinarily, this kind of coordination soothed him. It was that nitpicky part of his brain that got flooded with endorphins every time his schedule settled into place. He had the bottom line to consider, and days that stayed consistently busy made up for the slow ones where he sat in the office, wondering if it was bad karma to wish someone's car would break down. Today, though, his mind wasn't on his work; it kept flitting back to the night before.

He hadn't expected to feel that kind of alarm when Ike fell down. He'd seen Tim's kids fall and get scraped up—it was part of childhood—and he'd never felt that kind of heart-lurching panic. Still, Bernie could soothe the boy better than he could, and while he could appreciate that a two-year-old would long for a woman's gentle touch, he'd been the one caring for Ike for over a month now, and the toddler still hadn't reached for him.

That shouldn't sting, should it? Bernie was all beauty and gentleness—heck, if he scraped his knee, he'd prefer her, too. Besides, he hadn't even made up his mind about what to do about the boy, besides protect him from Morgan manipulation.

But it did sting, and for more reasons than wounded pride. Bernadette was a Morgan, and the fact that the Morgans could provide more for Ike than he could wasn't lost on him. And Ike had managed to wriggle into a part of his heart that had never been touched before. Was this what it felt like to be a dad?

Bernie might think his devotion to Ike was worth more than money, but Ike might have other ideas on that as he got older. When he was sixteen or seventeen, would he feel the same way, or would he feel cheated?

Liam hadn't appreciated a whole lot when he was a teen. He'd hated his foster family because he wasn't really theirs... He'd resented their kindness and generosity because it reminded him that he was charity. It was only when he reached his twenties that he started to see that having a foster family was better than having no family at all, and that was when he'd finally gone over for Christmas after five years of keeping to himself. And the Eagers had pulled him in close and showed him what family was all about.

But adulthood didn't give everyone the same dose of wisdom. Ike might very well feel the same way his mom did—and if Liam had stood between Ike and his biological family, would Ike appreciate all he'd sacrificed to raise him, or would he resent his meddling? Good intentions didn't guarantee appreciation. And he had a beautiful, gentle, very appealing relative right here in town who had offered to do what Vince wouldn't. It was between the lines—she could take him in.

Was Liam holding back for Ike's sake,

or for his own? Was it that Bernie was really such a bad choice for Ike, or was Liam just biased against the family? He wished he knew, but his gut still held him back. Not only would he have to let go of the little guy, but there was no guarantee that Bernie would be his caregiver. Once Liam let go, anything could happen, and he couldn't let these strange, growing feelings for Bernadette sway that decision.

The side door opened, and he glanced up to see Bernie in the doorway. Her figure was silhouetted against the backlight of morning sunshine, and she hesitated. His heart gave a leap.

"Hi," he said—a little too quickly. "Come on in."

When the door clanged shut behind her, Liam noticed that she was wearing jeans again, this time with a pink blouse. Her hair was loose around her shoulders, and if she'd thought that no makeup and a more casual style was going to make her blend in, then she'd better try a bit harder, because she was gorgeous in a way that didn't require extra effort.

"The first part for your car came in." He

gestured to the box. "I'll install it this morning, but then I have to wait on the others."

As if that was all they'd been sharing lately…

"Okay." She gave a nod, then met his gaze with a tentative smile.

"You okay?" he asked.

Color rose in her cheeks, and she shrugged. "I got a little lonely."

He'd been missing her, too, actually. He shouldn't be doing this—getting emotionally entangled—but pulling back wasn't so easy.

"And before you suggest that I call my friends, I don't dare." She smiled wryly. "They'll ask questions."

"And you aren't ready to answer."

She shook her head. "I need to have a clear goal before I do that."

A goal. Not a clear head. Not settled emotions. A goal.

"Don't you do anything based on your heart?" he asked, leaning against the car and crossing his arms over his chest.

Bernie laughed and looked away. "I came here, didn't I?"

Was she referring to Runt River and her quest to find her aunt, or this garage this morning? He paused, and he remembered the way she'd looked in the bathroom, Ike on her lap and her eyes shining… She hadn't mentioned offering to raise Ike as further proof of following her heart. But then, he wasn't one to act emotionally either, because if he had been, he would have pulled her into his arms yesterday.

"You're a grown woman," he said. "You can do what you want."

He grabbed a rag and proceeded to wipe his hands, and when he looked up, Bernadette was next to the car, looking into the interior.

"Do you like classic cars, Liam?"

That took him by surprise.

"Uh—" He shrugged. "Yeah, of course. Do you?"

She ran a hand along the door. "I learned to. I'm an only child, and that was a way to get my dad's attention—hang out with him in the garage. He never did his own work on them, of course, but once they were polished and prettied up, he'd walk around the garage appreciating them."

"Sounds like a special time."

She nodded. "It was. I think my dad would

have preferred a son, but he made do. I was all of their eggs in one basket, so to speak."

Liam smiled. "And you chose the Rolls for your wedding?"

"My mother did. It was about aesthetics." She was silent for a moment. "It felt so good to drive this car across state lines, though... I can't even describe it. When I was a little girl, I used to imagine being a princess in this car. I'd sit in the backseat, and I'd pretend my chauffeur was driving me to the ball. Well, I got to do the driving this time, and it felt amazing." A smile flickered at her lips, and she raised one eyebrow. "I did that based on heart."

And she was here in Runt River for a while, but that didn't mean that she wouldn't go back to it all in a week or two, after having had an emotional vacation. There was more to her than being some potential political wife, or even the eventual heir to her father's fortune. He'd seen that as they'd bandaged up Ike together, and it hadn't only been Ike who'd softened around her.

"But are you going to follow through, or go home?" he countered.

She met his gaze easily enough, and before he could think better of it, he tossed the rag aside and stepped closer. She tipped her chin back to keep the eye contact. She smelled good—was that perfume? He wasn't supposed to be getting sidetracked. He was supposed to keep a level head.

"You mean, was this a minor rebellion, or a real bid for freedom?" she clarified.

"Yeah, that's what I'm asking." His voice was low. A tendril of dark hair slipped in front of her eyes, and he reached forward without thinking and tucked it behind her ear, but in that movement, he'd moved closer still, and she hadn't retreated. Not one inch. If she'd flinched, if she'd blushed, if she'd dropped her gaze... But she hadn't, and that directness drew him in.

"I'm still sorting it out," she whispered.

That's what he'd thought—because if she went against her family, she might find herself as ordinary as the rest of them. But those pink lips, slightly parted...there was nothing ordinary about them, and he was holding himself back from closing those last few inches and—

The door opened behind them, and Liam dropped his hand. He shut his eyes and pressed his lips together, trying to calm the beating of his heart.

"Morning, boss," Chip sang out as he came inside. "Oh, sorry. Didn't realize you had a customer."

A customer—that's what she was supposed to be. And he'd forgotten about Chip coming in today. He felt like a fool. What was he doing?

"This is my employee, Chip," Liam said, clearing his throat and stepping back. "I should probably—"

"Yes, of course." Bernie nodded and quickly dropped her gaze. There it was—if only she'd done that earlier. She made a beeline for the door, a little more rushed than was graceful, he realized ruefully. He'd unsettled her, and while he knew he'd regret all of this later, something deep inside liked that he'd had an effect. The scent of her perfume mingled with the smell of grease and dust from the shop. She smelled better to him than cars, and there weren't many scents he could say that about.

He exhaled a pent-up breath as the door shut behind her.

"Was I interrupting something there?"

Chip hooked a thumb toward the door. "Sorry, I thought—"

"Of course not," Liam snapped and turned back toward the Rolls.

This was getting out of hand, and he knew it. Bernadette Morgan wasn't a woman to be trifled with, and she wasn't a woman who could offer him anything personal. If he hadn't been enough for Leanne, there was no way he could offer Bernie anything but a momentary distraction. And he wasn't offering that.

"Give me a hand with this carburetor, would you?"

Cars made sense, and it was high time he looked to the pleasures that were actually an option in his life, because Bernie was fire, and he knew it.

WHAT AM I DOING?

Bernie let the door slam behind her as she headed out of the garage. That hadn't been the plan when she'd arrived…but there was something about Liam Wilson and those gentle eyes and strong hands that made her think things she really shouldn't be thinking. She was in no way ready to be tangling with another man, but if he'd kissed her, she wouldn't have stopped him.

She headed down the road toward the highway. She wasn't ready to go back to Aunt Lucille's place—her heart was still pitter-pattering.

Had he been going to kiss her? She wasn't even certain now. She'd wanted him to. She'd have regretted it, of course. Was it just her emotional turmoil that made her want more, or was it that basic male quality about Liam that appealed to her on a primal level—the car grease, the strong shoulders, the broad hands...

She couldn't afford to just start up with some man she hardly knew. Flings weren't an option, no matter how good-looking he was, or how tender he seemed under the surface of that tough shell. Her parents had fully vetted Calvin before anyone had even introduced them. They knew everything from his elementary school records to his food allergies. Shellfish—if anyone cared to know. As if that even mattered, but they knew everything about him and his family before she even got the chance to see if she liked him. That was how Morgans did romance. Unless you counted the men, in which case, they slept around and paid off their conquests with a chunk of cash and a nondisclosure agreement.

But what did Bernadette know about Liam? He was the guardian of her second cousin, her aunt seemed to think very highly of him and he'd tangled with the Morgans in the past. None of that was enough to make him trustworthy—not to her family, at least. The funny thing was, she was starting to trust him in spite of it all...without any defendable reason.

Bernadette sucked in a steadying breath and slowed her pace. She'd reached the service station beside the highway, and she stopped, putting her hands on her hips. A few cars passed, and another turned into the service station.

Where exactly was she going? She was marching off...where? Liam had been right—she was all bravado and no plan. She needed a goal. She needed to know what she was working toward, and Liam's appealing belief in following her heart wouldn't work. There was too much at stake to do something so foolhardy.

Her phone rang from inside her bag, and she rummaged around and pulled it out.

"Hi, Dad," she said, picking up the call.

"Hi, Bunny. I'm at the golf course and I'm alone. Ninth hole."

"How's your game?"

"Three under par," he replied. "I didn't call to talk golf."

No, of course not. But he'd waited until he was away from her mother, and that was a small gesture that she appreciated. Kitty wouldn't be happy until Bernadette netted them a future president.

"What can I do for you, then?" she asked with a sigh.

"I called to tell you that we have a story that you need to get behind."

"Is it the one that Calvin suggested?" she asked bitterly. "The one where I'm a selfish child who doesn't know what she wants?"

"We aren't phrasing it quite like that," her father retorted. "And if you'd been willing to discuss this earlier, you could have been part of the solution. As it is, we've gone too long without an official response, and this one covers all our bases. So this is the official stance—you realized that marriage was a solemn institution, and you weren't ready to make that kind of commitment yet. Calvin is heartbroken, but he's soldiering on. He's asking the press to leave you alone during this fragile time—"

"Fragile!" Heat rose in her cheeks, but maybe she was…

"And in time," her father went on smoothly, "you will tell people that you loved him, you have parted as friends and that you will personally be voting for him in the next election because a man of his character would be a leader you could believe in."

She was to be the woman who still looked to Calvin McMann for leadership, even if a personal relationship weren't possible. The papers would gobble it up. She had known this was a possibility, but it still stabbed. At least her father was telling her himself instead of letting her find out the hard way. It wasn't exactly being thrown under the bus— it could technically be worse.

"What makes you think that Calvin can even behave himself over the next few years?" she demanded. "He's already proven himself to be a womanizer, and I highly doubt he'll stay your chaste angel long enough. Voters like a family man, and they definitely don't like a president who can't be faithful to his wife."

"These things can be covered up," her father replied.

"Like Vince?" she snapped. "It doesn't work."

"It *has* worked with Vince," her father shot back. "None of his dalliances have made it into the paper, and if he were just a tad better-looking, he might have actually gotten the Republican ticket. Besides, it's a he-said-she-said situation unless there's DNA involved. And what do you mean it didn't work? Unless you know about another woman that I don't—"

"You should ask Tabby about that," Bernie said drily. Tabby kept an eye on her husband's escapades, and she was probably the one who knew more about the senator than even his mistresses did.

"That Wilson woman died recently. It's very sad, but convenient."

Did her father really think that this would all just go away?

"She came from Runt River, Dad."

Her father was silent for a moment, then

he cleared his throat. "Really. And your aunt knew her, I'm assuming?"

"Her neighbor."

Her father let out a soft whistle. "Was Lucille involved in introducing them?"

Bernie knew where her father was going with this—had Vince been set up? But Lucille, for any of her faults, wasn't the kind of woman who set up affairs for politicians. Of that, Bernadette was positive.

"I really don't think Lucille had anything to do with it," she replied.

"Then we're probably in the clear," her father said. "Vince knows enough not to father any extramarital children. Calvin could take a note from him."

Irritation sparked into full-blown anger, and Bernadette closed her eyes for a moment, but before she could think twice, the words came out of her mouth. "If Calvin took a note from Vince, he'd go nowhere," she snapped. "Vince does have an *extramarital child*, as you put it. And do you really think Kimberly is going to carry Calvin to the White House? Not a chance."

There was silence on the other end, and Bernadette paused, waiting for an explosion that didn't come. Misgiving wormed its way up into her stomach. She'd said too much... far too much. Shoot...she should have just shut her mouth. This was why she couldn't just blow up—caution was imperative at all times.

"Dad?"

"I'm assuming this child is in Runt River, or you wouldn't know about it. And it must be the child of that Wilson woman. Boy or girl? And how old?"

Her father had summed it up quickly, and she knew that tone—he was moving straight past reasonable and going into cleanup mode.

"I shouldn't have said anything," she said. "I was just—"

"Of course you should have," her father interrupted. "Vince might not make president, but vice president isn't out of the running yet, if we can keep his reputation clean."

"Dad!" Misgiving was replaced by panic. "No one is threatening anything. The person who is legal guardian to this child just wants a quiet life. That's it. Consider the child here—"

"I am. We have another Morgan."

The words were chilling. *Another Mor-*

gan... She'd considered taking Ike in herself, but that only worked as long as the rest of the family saw him as a charity case and not a threat. However, her father's reaction was not one of charity. Ike was so close to being in their grasp, and she felt a wave of nausea at the thought. Those big brown eyes, the pudgy fingers holding up a cookie to share...

"An illegitimate Morgan," she countered. That had to make a difference, didn't it? Couldn't they back down for the bastard child of an oily politician?

"That only means a harder fighter, sweetheart," her father said with a bitter laugh. "The sooner we get this straightened out the better."

"Meaning?"

"Meaning I'll take care of it," he replied. "I'm actually glad you're out there. You can do some damage control."

Ironically, that was what she'd been doing already...keeping it quiet, keeping it calm. But that wasn't what she wanted to be doing. She wasn't here as a Morgan representative until the cavalry arrived. But if she refused, her father's lawyers would arrive that much sooner.

"It's under control, Dad." And she hated that sound in her voice: icy, hard, calculating. This wasn't the woman she wanted to be.

"That's what I wanted to hear," he replied. "Thank you, Bunny. Now I'd better play this hole."

Bernadette hung up her phone and let out a wavering breath. She was already dreading what she'd put into motion. Being right—saving her own pride—wasn't worth sacrificing the calm and quiet that Ike enjoyed out here in Runt River.

What had she just done?

CHAPTER NINE

BERNADETTE WALKED FOR more than an hour down the streets of Runt River the next day. She needed a plan. If her parents had taught her anything it was that following her heart only led to heartache, and a goal was paramount.

After her honeymoon, she was supposed to go back to attend some board meetings with her father in preparation of taking over the hotel chain. But her life goals had always revolved around the family money. She was the only child—the obvious heir—and the study of economics had interested her because of her personal link to a veritable fortune.

What would she do if she didn't have that money to fall back on? What would her future look like if Milhouse changed his will and left his estate to a cousin? He'd told her repeatedly how much he appreciated her loyalty and her ability to "see the bigger picture" when it came to the family's goals. Except this time, she'd thwarted those family goals. This could very well change everything, unless she proved herself loyal once again.

Runt River had a stretch of businesses that looked like they dated back at least fifty or sixty years. There was a corner store with a faded sign, a dry-cleaning place next to a Laundromat… She watched her reflection in the windows as she walked past. What did she have to offer without her family's money? A degree and a pretty face… It was rather depressing. She could stay in the wealthy circles if she married well, but she'd grown accustomed to the idea that she'd be more than an influential man's wife—she'd run her father's empire herself. And all of those plans could slip through her fingers if she didn't watch herself.

As she came to Main Street, her feet had started to hurt. Sandals for this long of a walk weren't a great idea, and she paused in the shade of the building on the corner. An eye-level sign caught her eye—Make Morgan Listen!

Vince. She'd known that her cousin was the senator of Ohio, but it felt strange to see local people reacting to him this way. He'd moved to Ohio when he started his political career, and only visited New York. She'd assumed he was well-liked, but that was politics. She came around the front of the building and peered into the window. There were some folding tables set up with flyers and pamphlets. Two middle-aged women sat at another table with telephones in front of them, but they didn't look terribly busy. They were sharing a box of donuts between them. Behind them was a banner that declared the same slogan.

She should just walk on by—Bernie knew that—but she was curious. She pulled open the door and stepped inside.

"Hi," she said.

"Hi there." The first woman put down her donut and licked her fingers. "Are you new around here?"

"I'm just visiting my aunt for a couple of weeks," Bernie said with what she hoped was a disarming smile. "So I'm not local."

"Well, you could still sign our petition," she replied. "Big business is all fine and good when it brings our constituents jobs, but the jobs aren't coming for us—they're sailing right past us! A new rail line is projected to go straight by our town without so much as a pit stop. We'll get all the noise and risks without any of the benefits! And we say no to that. There is even talk of moving the tire factory out to a town where the train will stop…so we'll end up with even fewer jobs than before!"

"That's awful." Bernie scanned the map that showed the proposed railway, then picked up a brochure.

"So we're demanding that the senator come down here and face us. We voted him in, and we want answers. Either that train needs to stop in Runt River so the tire factory can stay, or they need to put that railway far enough away that we won't have to deal with all that noise pollution."

"Do you think Senator Morgan will come?" Bernie asked.

"We've already been on the local news, and we're not done. We'll host demonstrations, and we'll take ourselves right to his office door if we need to. We might be a small group, but we're not scared."

The second woman nudged the petition toward her. Signing her real name wasn't an option right now. She was trying to keep a low profile, and she could only imagine what these women would do with a Morgan's signature on their petition.

"Thank you." Bernadette raised the pamphlet in salute. "I'll give this a read."

She headed back out to the street, and she glanced at the paper in her hand. They wanted their senator's attention, but she doubted that they'd get it. Runt River was tiny, and there were very likely countless other towns with similar outrage over the new railway. It would have to pass somewhere, and their righteous indignation wouldn't amount to much. It was sad, but true. And right now, as heartless as it might make her seem, she hoped that her cousin stayed away and let her continue in some relative privacy.

Bernadette's stomach rumbled, and she looked down the street. Uncle Henry's was just a couple of blocks away. She'd eat, get her head on straight and figure out her next move. If Vince could make things work his way, even with questionable moral integrity, then she could do it, too. She just needed to get her emotions under control.

LIAM CLOSED THE hood of the Rolls-Royce with a bang. The old cars were built to last—metal and leather, no plastic in those old vehicles. There was a time when people bought cars with cash and expected them to last twenty years. But nothing seemed to last anymore, and holding on to the good old days didn't change that. He headed to the sink to wash his hands.

"I'm taking lunch," Liam said. "You coming?"

Chip wheeled himself out from under another vehicle. "Not done yet, boss," he said. "I'll finish up first, if that's okay with you."

"Sure. Take your time."

It was just as well. Liam wanted a few minutes to himself, and it was possible that Chip sensed that. He was tired, but he was also irritated with himself. If Chip hadn't arrived when he did the other day, he'd have kissed Bernie. There was no question about that— and it would have been stupid. While he'd worked on the Rolls this morning, he'd had a lot of time to think it over, and while he wanted to blame it on a healthy male reaction to a beautiful woman, he knew better. It wasn't like Liam hadn't been around any women since his wife walked out. Bernie had a strange combination of steel and vulnerability that dropped his defences, and that was dangerous. She was a Morgan, and while she might feel terrible about tilling him under, it wouldn't necessarily stop her. He had Ike to worry about, and that was enough.

Liam walked down the street toward Uncle Henry's, his usual lunch destination. The sun baked his shoulders as he walked, cowboy boots clunking against the sidewalk. Since Leanne had left, he'd been leaning on his routines—the odd lunch at Uncle Henry's, working at the shop, church a couple of times a month. But with Bernie here, even those weren't enough to keep his mind focused.

He'd have to explain himself...eventually. Normally, he wasn't put in the position of having to tell a woman why he wasn't welcoming her advances—it wasn't her, it was him. He took pride in having self-control, doing the right thing even when it was hard. He didn't play with women's emotions, and he was always up-front about where he stood. So why had he lost his grip on that when it came to the least appropriate woman in town?

Uncle Henry's was always busy at lunchtime, and as he came inside the diner, he glanced around for an empty table. Routines—they helped, and he'd still have them once Bernie had driven out of town again.

His gaze landed on Bernadette at about the same time that she spotted him, because her eyes were wide, and she froze mid-chew.

Great. She was probably trying to avoid him, too, but they'd seen each other now. The only other option was to turn around and walk out, and that would be downright rude. He couldn't punish her for his own lapse in judgment. It looked like he'd have to deal with things now.

Liam angled around another table, and headed in her direction. Color tinged her cheeks, but by the time he'd arrived, she'd regained her composure.

"Hi," he said. "I think I owe you an apology. But I'd rather do it seated…"

She nodded and gestured to the other chair. He pulled it out and sat down. She was eating a plate of fries and a toasted BLT. It looked good, actually. He might order the same.

"It's okay," she said quickly. "No harm done."

"No, it's not okay," he said, keeping his voice low. "I know you probably won't believe me, but I'm not that kind of guy. You've been through a lot, and you're probably pretty vulnerable right now—"

"Why does everyone keep saying that?" She grabbed a napkin and wiped her fingers.

"Because you just walked out on your wedding," he said. "And that's not pity you're getting from me, it's empathy. I've been there—cheated on, not the wedding part— but I can understand how infuriating and heartbreaking and—" He cast around, looking for a word, and came up empty. "So taking advantage like that was wrong. You can feel safe to come by the shop any time you want, and you don't have to worry about me crossing any lines. That's a promise."

She licked her lips and looked down at her plate for a moment. Was that anger? Had he hurt her feelings, or something? He glanced up as Melanie brought him a menu.

"I'll just have the same," he said. "With a Coke."

She jotted his order on her pad of paper and gave him a thumbs-up before leaving them in relative privacy again.

"Nothing happened, Liam. I'm fine."

"Okay. Well, good." That took care of that…right? Was this over?

"You can stop beating yourself up about it." She shot him a small smile. "I'm not exactly a drowned kitten. We're both adults, so I think we can admit that there is some attraction here. There's nothing to be ashamed of."

"No, of course not." He nodded, trying to tamp down the elation. "So you're feeling it, too."

She inclined her head in acceptance. "Admittedly, you aren't my usual type."

He chuckled. "Admittedly. So what is your usual type?"

Bernie plucked a fry from her plate. "Ivy league. Polished. Good family." She dropped the fry.

"How has that worked for you?" he asked, and when her cheeks colored, he felt a certain satisfaction at having upset that calm of hers.

"Not as well as you'd think," she admitted with a low laugh. "So far, they've mostly been self-absorbed. What about you? What's your type?"

He'd only had one type—Leanne. There had never been anyone else, and moving on from that had been harder than he'd ever imagined. It was a big change to wrap his brain around.

"I only really dated my wife," he admitted. "I haven't had a chance to develop a type, so far. But if I were to try…" He paused, trying to imagine a woman who could entice him. "I'd say she'd be willing to get her hands dirty, and she'd choose the back of a pickup and a starry night over a nice restaurant in the city."

Bernie met his gaze quizzically. "Back of a pickup? Is that even legal?"

"Not to drive!" Liam couldn't help but laugh. "You spread out a quilt and you lie down in the truck bed away from town where the night is so dark you can see every star…" He arched an eyebrow at her. "You ever tried it?"

"Not me. It does sound nice, though…"

Had he tempted her? He wasn't supposed to be flirting, but she was missing out on more than she realized.

"I did go to a country fair once, though," she offered.

"Yeah?" That struck him as surprising.

"You'd probably come within spitting distance of a pickup, then."

She laughed at that. "I went on a rickety old Ferris wheel and thought it would spin free and I'd die that night. I ended up throwing up in a ditch. Very ladylike." She rolled her eyes. "I would have preferred the pickup truck. Our driver had to buy me a ginger ale at a gas station, and I sipped on it all the way back to the city." Bernie relaxed as she told the story, her dark eyes glittering with humor. "I ruined my favorite shoes, too."

He liked this side of her—the laughter, the smile. This must be what she was like when she was in her comfort zone, and she was even prettier, if that were possible.

"Your driver?" he asked. "Didn't you ever just drive yourself somewhere?"

"Yes, I do drive myself places, but if I was going out of the city, I erred on the side of safety." Her smile faded. "That's where I stop being relatable, isn't it?"

Her world was completely different from his, but he felt bad for pointing that out. In his books, making someone feel like an outsider was rude. And it wasn't his intention.

"You told the truth," he said. "Can't fault you for that."

"Thank you. That's something." She was silent for a moment as her expression clouded. Then she met his gaze again. "And if I'm going to continue telling the truth, I'd better get something out into the open."

"What's that?" A new kind of worry worked through his gut.

"Well, I was a bit flustered after I left the shop, and you're right, I was all mixed up, thinking about Calvin and you, and attraction, and—"

Bernie reached out and moved the ketchup bottle to line up with the vinegar.

"My dad called," she went on. "He pushed my buttons, and I accidentally told him about Ike."

Her words landed like a brick against his chest, and Liam stared at her, mute. She'd told Milhouse Morgan about Ike? What about their deal to keep everything quiet?

"How exactly did that happen?" he breathed.

"He compared Calvin to Vince, and suggested that Vince was some prime example for Calvin to follow, and… I was angry. It just came out. I didn't give him any information. He just knows there's a child. That's it."

Liam's mind spun. "So what does this mean, exactly? What will he do?"

"I don't know," she admitted. "And I'm so sorry, Liam. It wasn't intentional. I'm normally much more in control. I'm a planner. I think things through. I shut my mouth when in doubt. I'm not the kind of person who normally just blabs like that—"

He'd just been defending himself using the same logic. He wasn't normally the kind of guy who lost control like that.

"What did your father *say*?" he asked.

She shrugged faintly. "He's interested."

The Morgans would want Ike back—he could feel it. They were a powerful family, and if Milhouse Morgan's interest had been piqued, then Liam's time with the kid was likely going to be short, and that realization sparked a fierce protectiveness.

Melanie slid a plate in front of him, along with a tall glass of cola. He gave her a nod and what he hoped was a smile of thanks, but he suspected he'd just bared his teeth. As he looked down at his now unappetizing meal, his gaze fell on a pamphlet lying next to the sugar packets.

Make Morgan Listen.

Was that even possible from ordinary people like the residents of Runt River? That family wasn't just powerful, they were influential, and they had more money than he could fathom. He could bankrupt himself with legal bills and still not win this. Ike was a Morgan, but if Vince had cared one bit about the boy, he'd had years to do something about it. If the Morgans were interested now, it wasn't out of familial love, and that realization curdled his blood.

"Ike is just a little kid." He couldn't help the tremble in his voice. "He's already lost his mother, and he's just barely adjusted to being here with me..."

"Liam, I'm on your side." She picked up the pamphlet and tore it in half. "I didn't mean to do this, but I'm not exactly powerless, either. I'm one of them, and I have some clout. My family has big hopes for Calvin, and I'm sure with some well-timed publicity stunts, I could make him highly unappealing to the female vote."

"Would that be enough?" he asked.

Bernie pressed her lips together and glanced away for a moment. "I have a goal, Liam, and that's the first step. Now I just need to figure out my plan. So far, we have our fears and that's it. But the first rule of politics is to never react to a rumor. Deal in facts. Respond to people. Period."

"Is this your way of telling me not to worry?" he asked incredulously.

"No." She sighed. "I'm telling you not to freak out."

They both looked at their food. There was no way that Liam was going to be able to eat anything now. As if on cue, Melanie slipped the bill onto their table on the way by. Liam reached for his wallet.

"This one is on me," she said, reaching to stop his arm.

"That's not how things work out here," he said, but her expression remained granite.

"Liam," she said softly. "Let me do this much."

He shrugged, and she pulled out a couple of bills and tossed them into the center of the table. It would be a significant tip.

He could pretend that she was no different from any other woman, but it wouldn't be true. She might like to be called Bernie, but she was Bunny Morgan, and as she'd pointed out, she was far from powerless.

CHAPTER TEN

BERNADETTE SAT AT her aunt's kitchen table, a cup of tea and a photo album in front of her. Lucille had offered to show Bernie some pictures from before she was born, and she'd been flipping through photos from the seventies—her parents in polyester, drinks in their hands… Lucille and her husband looked happy together, but when Lucille and Milhouse were in the same frame there were crossed arms, tight smiles, sidelong looks. Apparently, there wasn't much love lost there. Her aunt and her father did share a strong resemblance, though. The Morgan nose, the chin.

Lucille stood by the counter, her arms crossed over her chest and worry creasing her brow—oddly reminiscent of those old photos.

"I just need a plan," Bernie said. "I'm thinking I might be able to sway my dad by threatening to tarnish his golden boy's reputation, but…"

Would that even be enough? In all likelihood, they'd just make her appear emotionally unstable—something that the general population would believe in a heartbeat considering her dash from her own wedding. She might have a few friends who would stay on her side, but her father could very easily disown her and name Vince his heir instead. She'd have lost her family, her support network, her inheritance and she'd have gained nothing. The family would still get their way.

"Are you willing to take them on?" her aunt asked.

Bernie sucked in a breath, then sighed. "I have to fix this."

That wasn't really an answer. She had let the secret out, and she was responsible. Whether or not she wanted to take this on didn't really matter.

"Sometimes you get involved in something without meaning to," Lucille said. "I knew that bonding with Leanne's son was a bad idea from the start, but I also knew he was my relative, and I couldn't say no. I truly believed that Ike had a chance at a normal life here in Runt River. I shudder to think what your father would want with him now."

Bernie didn't need the guilt trip. She was perfectly aware of what she'd done. She took a sip of tea and looked out the back window at the golden evening sunlight that splashed over the neat rows in the garden.

"My dad isn't a complete monster, Lucille." She felt an obligation to stand up for her parents. They might be stubborn, strong-willed and self-interested, but they were still her parents.

"Maybe not to you. Ordinary people don't have the same kind of armor that you do," Lucille countered. "They don't have access to lawyers—not without giving up their basic necessities. They don't have the thick skin, or the lavish vacation to give them an escape from stress."

"I know," Bernie said quietly.

"Do you?" Lucille rubbed her hands over her face. "Because I've been living an ordinary life—or as close to it as possible—for the last thirty-five years. I know what your father is capable of when he decides he wants something, and it won't be about what's best for that little boy."

"I know!" Bernie shot her aunt an irritated look. "My father is concerned about the optics. He thinks that Vince might still have a shot at vice president."

"Vice president." Lucille barked out a bitter laugh. "I remember when that boy was six months old. He was a fat little baby who loved having his piggies counted, and even back in those idealistic days, I didn't think he'd be vice president."

Lucille came over to the table, then flipped ahead in the album and tapped on a photo. Bernie looked closer. Aunt Ellen looked so young and trim, and she held a pudgy Vince in her arms. Vince was a big baby, and he looked even larger compared to his petite mother.

"But your father did," Lucille said with a sigh. "Even then, the Morgans had plans for him. Vince was groomed from the start. He didn't have a chance."

Bernadette scanned the photos and found her mother in several of them. She'd looked sad back then—weaker, somehow. Perhaps her bravado had developed with age. Her father looked the same, though. Younger, slimmer, more hair…but that regal expression hadn't changed a bit.

"And you think they'd groom Ike, too," Bernie concluded.

"No, I think they'd hide him. He'd be a second-class Morgan his entire life, jumping when told to and never in the picture."

Bernadette agreed with that, and the thought of that sensitive boy being shunted into a cold world of nannies and boarding schools was heartbreaking. But she'd noticed something in the photos—something that went against all the stories she'd been told.

"Wait—" Bernie looked up at her aunt. "I thought you and my dad had a falling out over your grandmother's engagement ring. But my parents were married here, and you and Uncle Arnie are still in the photos."

Lucille froze for a second, then swallowed. "Well, the tensions built up over time, I suppose."

"So what happened to make that final cut with the family?" she pressed.

Lucille was silent for a few breaths, then she shrugged weakly.

"There are things you probably don't want to know, Bunny…" Her aunt's voice was distant, and the old nickname sounded oddly tender.

"I might not want to know, but I think I *need* to."

Lucille looked out the window, the lowering sun illuminating her face in a splash of gold. "Have you ever wondered why you look nothing like your mother?"

Bernie had the dark hair, but other than that, she didn't really resemble either parent. She assumed that she'd taken after a more distant branch of the family tree. These things happened.

"The genetic gamble. I look more like Dad's side."

"You look *nothing* like your father's side," Lucille said sharply, and Bernadette felt like she'd been slapped. "Have you ever seen pictures of your mother pregnant? Or from when you were born?"

"Mom thought she looked fat and wouldn't let any cameras into the hospital," Bernie said. She knew this story well. "She always said that childbirth was dirty and private, and she hated those photos of women in hospital gowns with IVs still in their arms."

"Those photos are normal," Lucille said

with a roll of her eyes. "People take those pictures because they want to remember the moment their child came into the world."

"So Mom is a little icy." It hardly seemed kind to rub it in. Her mother loved her—there was no question of that.

"Bernadette, listen to me." Lucille sucked in a breath. "The first picture of you is when you were two weeks old." She flipped the album forward again, her movements brisk. She stopped at a picture that Bernie recognized. She was propped up for a formal photo shoot. "And there is a very good reason for that."

"Which is?" Bernie asked cautiously.

"Your mother wasn't there when you were born."

Lucille's words landed like a cannonball on her lap, and Bernie stared at her aunt in perplexed silence.

"My mom—"

"Your real mother was a teenager staying at Mercy House. She gave birth to you at the age of fifteen."

"So my father—"

"You are not the biological child of either

of your parents," Lucille said gently. "You're adopted."

"Adopted?" Bernie shook her head. "If that were true, there is no reason they'd keep it a secret." Her father had warned her about Aunt Lucille—not to believe anything she said. Maybe this was why. Was Lucille vindictive, or did she honestly believe this garbage?

"Your father told you that our fallout was over a ring," Lucille said. "And it started that way, but the ring wasn't the nail in the coffin. *You* were."

"I don't get it!" Bernie shoved the photo album away. "This doesn't even sound true!"

"Your aunt Ellen, Vince's mother, was running Mercy House," Lucille said. "And your mother—Kitty—was having fertility issues. They'd been trying to conceive for years, and it wasn't happening. Your father's eye was wandering, and your mother decided to take things into her own hands. There was a pregnant girl at Mercy House who had the right look—long dark hair, big brown eyes. Her baby would look enough like a Morgan to pass scrutiny. She was only about five months along, so your mother hatched a plan."

"My mother couldn't have faked a pregnancy—" That was just over the top.

"She didn't fake it," Lucille countered. "She simply refused to be seen in public for several months. Ellen gave the girl the best of care, as she did for all the girls who came there...but then there was a hitch. Your birth mother didn't want to give you up once you were born. She wanted to keep you."

Bernadette swallowed hard, tears rising in her eyes. Could this be true? Was it even possible? It explained a lot about the family picture record and all of that, but—

"They couldn't have forced her," Bernie countered.

"She was fifteen..." Lucille shook her head. "She was scared. Her parents had kicked her out for getting pregnant. She was still a child herself, and the Morgans knew what they wanted. Do you really think she stood a chance against them?"

Bernie could see the scared girl in her mind's eye. Fifteen was very young—certainly not old enough to stand up to an influential family.

"What did they do?"

"Your parents pressured her. Hard. They told her horror stories of the life she could expect if she kept you—poverty, loneliness. And then they offered her money—enough to support her for a few years while she got back on her feet."

"And she sold me—" Bernie's voice caught.

"No, she refused." Lucille shook her head. "In the end, they threatened her with something—I don't know what. Everyone kept their mouth shut about that, but they scared her so badly that she agreed to sign you over. They brought me in as a witness to her signature, and I saw the look on her face when she handed you to Kitty. It was a mixture of fear and loathing. If looks could kill…"

"My mother stole me from a teenager?" Bernie stared at her aunt in shock.

"I'm afraid so," Lucille said softly. "And that was the reason we fell out. I told Kitty that she'd been wrong. That poor girl was your mother, not her. Kitty was furious with me, and your father demanded that I back up the family story."

The family story. It was always about

a narrative they could all get behind. The truth? That could be flexible.

"And when I told him that what they'd done was downright evil, your father told me to get out and stay out. I was cut off."

"What about my biological mother?" Bernie asked. "What happened to her?"

"I don't know." Lucille shook her head. "I tried to trace where she'd gone, but she'd disappeared. I thought perhaps it was for the best. What was I going to do, go remind her of her heartbreak? Your parents had provided her with a decent sum of money, so she certainly wouldn't be destitute. I let it go."

It sounded agonizingly possible, but her father had warned her about Lucille... This could all be a lie. There was nothing to back this up but a lack of photo evidence. That was shaky.

"What would my parents say to this?" Bernie asked.

"They'd call me a liar," Lucille said quietly. "They'd say I was unstable. They'd shake their heads and make up stories about my struggle with mental health. What would they do if you told the world the real reason you walked away from your wedding?"

Something quite similar. Bernadette heard the truth in her aunt's words. Her parents had always had "the lawyers" arrange for her ID. Her personal papers were in the safe with her father's. She'd never thought to look for her own birth certificate. She'd never looked like either of her parents, and they'd told her horrible stories about Aunt Lucille for as long as she could remember…

Bernadette stared down at the photo album, a lump forming in her throat. Family—she'd been raised to count on family for everything, but she'd never once suspected that she wasn't really a Morgan. If they'd stolen her, then she had a biological mother out there—a mother who had desperately wanted to keep her. And despite this knowledge, she didn't love her parents—Milhouse and Kitty—any less. They were still her parents…the father who'd walked through the garage of classic cars with her and let her play princess in the car she'd one day use for her own wedding… the mother who combed her hair every night and listened as Bernie talked about her day at school. They were her *parents*.

"Why did you tell me this?" Tears welled in Bernie's eyes.

"Because you need to keep Ike out of their clutches," Lucille said, pulling out a kitchen chair and sinking down into it next to Bernie. "If you need some leverage to use against your parents, this is it."

"You want me to threaten them with *this*?" She could feel her mouth turning down in distaste. "You want me to blackmail them—"

"I'm not telling you what to do." Her aunt sighed. "I'm simply giving you some information to use as you see fit. I'm giving you some wiggle room."

But using this information as leverage would do more than keep her family away from Ike; it would sever her own relationship with her parents. She'd be walking away from her inheritance, a life of comfort and privilege…and she'd be walking away from the only family she'd ever known.

"They're my parents," Bernadette said, her voice shaking.

Lucille didn't answer.

THE NEXT MORNING, Liam stood in the kitchen with Ike. It had been a rough night, and neither of them had gotten much sleep.

Ike had cried his little heart out most of

the night. Liam had held him, rocked him, sang snippets of lullabies that he could remember from TV shows…but he didn't call across the street for help. Ike might technically be a Morgan, but Leanne had been the one to raise him. Liam figured that Ike belonged to Leanne even more firmly than he belonged to the Morgans. He'd eventually pulled out that framed photo of Leanne that had comforted Ike in the past, and the boy had finally settled down and consented to lie down in Liam's bed, the photo clutched against his chest until he'd fallen into an exhausted sleep.

And Liam had crashed in his new spot— on the mattress on the floor.

This morning, Ike wouldn't relinquish the frame. It had a little dribble of toothpaste down the back now, because Ike wouldn't let go of it to brush his teeth, or to eat his breakfast. Okay, he hadn't eaten much breakfast, but he'd stared at a plate of scrambled eggs until it got cold. Now, Ike stood in the middle of the kitchen, the picture clutched against his chest in a white-knuckled grip, his big eyes filled with unshed tears.

Liam had gone to some therapy sessions as

a kid, and he'd learned a few lessons for the future, like not pretending you didn't hurt. And he figured Ike needed someone to understand exactly why his heart was breaking, not pretend everything was fine with a kids' TV show and cheerful faces. Ike wasn't fine, and he wasn't stupid, either.

"Hey, buddy..." Liam crouched next to him. "Are you missing Mommy?"

Ike looked down at the photo in his hands, his lips quivering. "Mommy."

"I know." Liam pulled Ike in his arms and held him close. "Mommy's in heaven now, Ike, and that means that you and I have to take care of each other. I'm pretty good at taking care of people. We'll be okay."

Ike leaned his head against Liam's shoulder and let out a shuddering sigh. Tears misted Liam's eyes. A mother's love was the closest bond a child could have...one he'd never experienced himself, but he'd imagined his mother over the years. He'd hoped that wherever she was, she was happy. He always imagined her happily single, though. There was a part of his boyish heart that just couldn't share her, and that image of her hadn't changed in his adult heart, either. He didn't want to share her, and since she was a figment of his own imagination, he didn't think he should have to.

But Ike had been forced to say goodbye to the mother he'd actually known. How was Liam supposed to comfort the kid? All he could offer was a hug in the middle of the kitchen floor, and that wasn't nearly enough. He couldn't tell Ike that he'd be here forever, that he'd take care of him for the rest of his life, because Ike had a biological family out there who now knew about his existence. Liam's claim to the kid by marriage counted for a whole lot less than blood. If Vince wanted to bring it to court, that was.

"I wanna cookie," Ike whispered.

Liam laughed softly. "That I can do, buddy."

Liam stood up, bringing Ike with him in his arms and headed for the cupboard. He'd never been one to have a lot of junk food in the house, but since Ike arrived, he found himself stocking up on the treats. He pulled down a bag of chocolate chip cookies and handed one to Ike.

Ike looked at the cookie for a moment, then up at Liam.

"Share?" Ike said, holding the cookie to Liam's mouth.

Liam took a small, careful bite. "Thanks, bud," he said around the crumbles.

Ike smiled, then shoved half the cookie into his own mouth. That would have to count for breakfast.

"Let's take you over to Aunt Lucille's place," Liam said. "I've got to get to work, kiddo."

Liam switched Ike to the other arm and grabbed his keys off the counter. Funny, but he didn't want to put Ike down. He wanted to be some support for the child, a boulder between him and a lonely world. Who knew how long Liam would have Ike, but while the boy was here, Liam was going to protect him.

He'd deal with goodbyes later, if he had to, but right now he had to deal with reality— a brokenhearted little boy who needed love.

CHAPTER ELEVEN

BERNIE SPENT THE morning with Lucille and Ike. Ike was restless and clingy. He didn't want to watch TV or play, and he wouldn't relinquish the photo of his mother. Bernie spent a good deal of time looking at that photo—Leanne's smiling face looking so peaceful and relaxed. She had been pretty, Bernie thought. She could see why Vince had zeroed in on her, but all that beauty and potential was wasted on her cousin. Vince knew how to get what he wanted, whether that was a woman's body or her silence.

"I don't understand why Leanne would have risked everything for Vince," Bernie said. Ike was sitting beside a window, the photo tucked under his arm.

"She and Liam married young," Lucille said. "And when hard times hit, they didn't pull together. That's the thing with relationships—you either pull together or end up fighting each other."

Her parents didn't seem to have that problem. They knew what they wanted, and they worked toward it as a team. Bernie could remember many times when her parents would stand together in their kitchen, mugs of coffee in hand, as they came up with a plan to get their way. It might have been a deal they wanted on a classic car, or rezoning a piece of land. Whatever they'd put their minds to, they got. And as a girl watching her parents plot, she'd thought that was what a successful relationship looked like: two people on the same team no matter what.

But the team wasn't just Milhouse and Kitty—it was the whole Morgan clan. And her parents hadn't stopped with real estate deals or political dreams. They'd wanted a baby, and they found a way to get one…and Aunt Ellen had made it happen.

"Makes you wonder what's worse," Bernie said quietly, "the couple that splits up over wanting a baby, or the couple that stops at nothing to get one."

Lucille picked up Ike and put a hand over his forehead. "I am sorry, Bernadette… I know what the truth has cost you, and I didn't want to tell you earlier because I didn't want to ruin what you had. None of this is your fault, dear. None of it."

"Except now that I've told my father about Ike, I'm part of the machine. One day, Ike will learn the truth about his parentage, and I don't want to be the relative that helped my parents get their way at all costs."

The Aunt Ellen. The willing helper. The one who used money and position to soothe her conscience. Her parents' laser focus was now cast in a sinister light. If they'd steal a baby from a teenage mother in order to make their dreams come true, what more would they do to protect those dreams? She used to feel safe in her parents' protective circle, but now she felt stifled.

"We won't let that happen," Lucille said. She felt Ike's forehead again. "You aren't alone in this, Bernadette. You have me."

Bernie watched as Ike rubbed a chubby hand over his eyes. "Is he okay?"

"He feels a bit warm to me." Lucille smoothed Ike's hair away from his face. "He'll be fine."

Ike made everything a little more complicated, though. Lucille's rebellion against the family had been more of a silent revolt—keeping a ring in spite of her brother's wishes. And she'd held information that her brother wanted to bury, so they'd let her hide in Runt River, safely out of the way. What would they do if Lucille decided to bite back? And were Bernadette and Lucille strong enough to keep an entire family at bay?

Through it all, nagging at the back of her mind was the image of a teenage girl with dark hair, a pregnant belly and frightened eyes. *Her mom.*

Yet, despite her new knowledge, Bernie couldn't just wipe Kitty out of the picture, either. Kitty had raised her, loved her, devoted time and energy to her. Bernie hadn't been one of those kids who was handed over to a nanny while her mother shopped and did yoga classes. Kitty was a hands-on mother, and while she was overbearing at times, Bernadette had never doubted her love. Didn't that count for something? Or did one horrendous act undo the rest?

Bernie hadn't spoken to her mother since the wedding. They had a strange balance in their relationship, and Bernie had needed her own space to think. She knew her mother's stance on marriage, and it was far from romantic. Her mother wanted her with Calvin. Being First Lady was worth some sacrifices in her mother's eyes.

For the first time, Bernadette wondered how much her mother had sacrificed to be Milhouse's partner. Her mother had told her that marriage wasn't about flowers or chocolates. She'd said that warm feelings faded over time, so it was better to have a solid foundation of mutual goals and a stock portfolio. A wife was a business partner, and the more successful the business, the more successful the marriage.

Had Kitty *ever* fallen in love? Did she know what she'd given up? Or had she plastered over that part of her heart for the sake of the family's financial success?

"I'm going to go out for a bit, Auntie," Bernie said. She needed some space to breathe and to think.

"Sure," Lucille said with a tired smile. "I'll get Ike down for a nap. Maybe he'll feel better after a rest."

All her life, Bernadette had been taught to put family first, but who was her family now? Where did her loyalties lie? And what did the Morgan name mean when she hadn't actually been born to it?

LIAM TIGHTENED THE last lug nut and slid out from under the pickup truck he'd been working on. He loved this garage. This was more than a job to him, and more than a simple small business. When Earl Henner had retired and sold the garage to Liam, Runt River Auto had saved him. Aging out of the foster system had left him adrift, but this garage gave him a place to belong and a goal to work toward. Sometimes that was all a man needed to get him going again.

"Say, boss—" Chip was sweeping up with a push broom. "I was wondering if you might need me full-time."

Liam looked at Chip in surprise. He'd been here part-time for the last couple of years. They hadn't discussed full-time. "That's something I'd have to think about." And look through his finances to see if he could even afford a full-time employee.

"Thing is, I want to ask Jessica to marry me, and I can't do that unless I can support her." Chip put his faded ball cap back on his head.

Yeah, Liam remembered that feeling. He'd had to psych himself up for weeks before he proposed to Leanne. She'd been sweet and pretty, smart and just a bit sassy. She wanted marriage, a house, the whole nine yards, and he wanted to be the one to give it to her. He wanted that stability, too—a family of his own where he wouldn't "age out." He'd asked her at a local restaurant, his shirt too tight and his hands all sweaty. And she'd said yes. Back then, the future was bright.

Here was hoping Chip had better luck than Liam had in marriage, though.

"I'll look at the books and see what I can do. We're a lot busier lately, and if I'm not mistaken, you're already working about thirty hours a week. Ten extra hours should be doable. Let me look into it and get back to you. And…congratulations."

Chip grinned. "Thanks. But I haven't even asked her yet."

Liam's cell phone rang, and he pulled it out of his back pocket and glanced at the number. It was Lucille—she didn't normally call during the day.

"I'd better take this," Liam said, then

picked up the call. "Hi, Lucille. Everything okay?"

"Not really." There was worry in her voice, and Ike's cry wavered in the background. "Ike has a fever—it's high. He's been listless all morning, and I thought if he had a nap he'd feel better, but he woke up just soaked in sweat."

"Like the flu...or—"

"High fevers can be dangerous for kids." Ike's cry got closer. Lucille must have picked him up. "I've given him some medicine, but it isn't helping right now."

Liam had become a bit of an expert on Ike's cries lately. He knew the difference between an angry cry and a bored cry, or a finger-pinched-in-the-cupboard cry, and this one was different altogether.

"I'll be there in ten minutes."

"All right. See you soon."

Liam hung up the phone, his heart racing.

"Speaking of extra hours, Chip, can you take over for the rest of the day?" Liam asked. "Ike is sick. I've got to run."

"Yeah, sure thing." Chip nodded. "We have that transmission fluid drain scheduled this afternoon. You okay with me doing that one alone?"

Liam paused. "Can you handle it?"

"Yeah." Chip nodded, licked his lips. "I can do this one, boss."

There had been a time when Earl had turned his back and trusted Liam's skill, too. Looked like Chip was about to graduate into a full-time mechanic.

"Okay, then," Liam said. "If you can do this one on your own—handle the whole job—then you've got yourself forty hours a week. Show me what you can do."

Chip nodded, then grinned. "Thanks. You won't be disappointed."

"And, Chip?" Liam pulled his keys out of his pocket and headed for the door. "Buy the ring already."

Someone around here deserved happiness in love. Might as well be Chip.

CHAPTER TWELVE

BERNADETTE WALKED FOR more than an hour, and as she ambled down the quiet streets of Runt River, a dull ache formed inside her chest. Bernie missed her mom—the one who had raised her. Kitty had taught her everything she knew—from how to eat at a formal dinner setting to how to write elegant thank-you notes. She'd taught her to appreciate jazz, how to sit with her knees together and her ankles crossed. Kitty taught her how to read the stock index, how to interview household help and how to choose a quality wine to sip alone in a quiet evening. For all that her biological mother had lost thirty years ago, Bernie still missed the mother she'd actually known.

Was that cold of her—not to miss the mother who had given birth to her right now? It wasn't that she'd never miss her, but her birth mother was more of an idea right now than an actual person. She'd have to adjust to this new information—absorb it, figure out exactly what she felt.

Bernadette had held back from calling Kitty—not wanting the lecture that she knew was coming, but maybe connecting with her mom would be worth a little discomfort. Bernie pulled out her phone and started to type a text:

Hi, Mom. I know you're mad, but I wanted to let you know that I'm okay. I'm just thinking things through. You know what Calvin did, and I couldn't live like that. At least Dad is faithful to you. You'll have to forgive me sometime. Bunny

There were so many more questions Bernie wanted to ask Kitty about the past, about her adoption, but she didn't dare. Still, reaching out felt good, and she cheered up a little in spite of it all. Was it possible to just forget the truth and move forward? Was it really so terrible to be part of a wealthy, influential family who wanted nothing but excellence for her future? How many women would have given their left leg for the privileges she took for granted? It was tempting to try to forget it, if that were possible.

She was back to Main Street, and she paused at the corner across from a coffee shop. She could use a little liquid comfort right now. So she jogged across the street in front of a rusted pickup truck that slowed down for her. She gave a wave of thanks to the gray-haired cowboy behind the wheel, and headed for the door of the coffee shop.

Inside, a few patrons sat at tables, sipping coffee and munching on muffins. She recognized the two women from the Morgan campaign office. Bernie headed to the counter and ordered her drink.

"A large mocha latte, please."

She'd learned not to complicate her order—people didn't seem to do that around here.

"Anything else?" the woman behind the counter asked.

"No, thanks."

Her phone blipped and Bernie looked down to see that Kitty had messaged her back: Come home to discuss this. Texting more than a coffee order is crude.

Her mother always did have a weird sixth sense when it came to Bernie. She sighed. Of course. She hadn't really expected anything less from her mom. Her mother was unbending. Kitty had signed on for Morgan success, not failure, and Bernie was thwarting some well-laid plains. Still, just getting a response had been a relief, and she smiled to herself.

"Love you, too, Mom," she murmured to herself. She wasn't going home—not yet. If texting was too crude a form of communication, Kitty would just have to wait.

As the milk steamer hissed, the conversation from the table of railroad protesters filtered over to her, and Bernadette idly tuned in.

"I can't believe he's actually coming!" the first woman said. "I wasn't sure he would."

Bernie glanced over to where the women sat hunched over their mugs, eyes shining with excitement.

"That TV news story must have done it," the other agreed. "If he won't come over here and explain himself, we'll bring it right to his door!"

"He made promises," the first woman agreed. "And he's going to be held accountable. We obviously got our message across, because his email said that he cared about our concerns and he'd come to make a personal appearance."

The women chattered on, but Bernadette stopped listening. Her mouth went dry. Vince was coming to Runt River, and she sincerely doubted that he was coming because he cared about one small town's concerns. Runt River wouldn't rank high enough on Vince's priorities to warrant a personal visit. If Vince Morgan was coming, it was to do some damage control of his own. This was about Ike.

LIAM ARRIVED AT Lucille's front door, and he could hear Ike's crying from the step. He didn't bother knocking, just went straight in. Lucille sat on the couch with Ike in her lap. She held a sippy cup of water in front of Ike, but the toddler kept turning away. His cheeks were flushed and his eyes looked glassy. And in that moment, Liam had a sickening realization—Ike wasn't on his health insurance yet, and a doctor's visit would cost a fortune.

"Hey, buddy," Liam said, kicking the door shut behind him.

Ike's cries paused, and he held out his arms toward Liam. That was a first. Liam crossed the room and scooped him up, putting a hand on his damp forehead. The kid was burning up.

"I'll get some cold cloths," Lucille said, already turning away. "And if you could persuade him to drink some water—"

Ike leaned his head against Liam's shoulder and started to cry again.

"You need to drink some water," Liam said, holding the cup up to Ike's lips. The boy took a couple of sips, then let out a shuddering sigh. Liam had never seen a kid with a fever before, and he wasn't sure how bad this was. But he did know that if Ike needed a doctor, he'd get one, even if he had to pay for it out of his savings.

"Have I ever told you about carburetors, Ike?" Liam asked softly, leaning back into the sofa. "Carburetors are a very important part of an internal combustion engine. That's where air gets mixed with a fine mist of fuel..."

He didn't really think that Ike cared at all about carburetors, but it gave him something to talk about, and his voice seemed to comfort the boy. Sometimes it wasn't what was said so much as being together. Ike leaned his flushed face against Liam's chest, and

Liam held up the sippy cup to the boy's mouth again.

"One more sip," he said. Ike complied.

"So when a carburetor stops working properly, that's when you've got to get in there and fix it…"

"Gotta fix it," Ike said softly.

Liam smiled down at the tyke. Who knew—carburetors comforted the kid. Maybe they had more in common than he thought.

CHAPTER THIRTEEN

As Bernie let herself in the front door, she saw Liam sitting in the rocking chair, Ike on his lap with a cloth over his forehead. Liam was a big man, and he barely fit in the chair, but he rocked as gently as a grandmother.

"Hi," she said, frowning. "Is everything okay?"

"He's got a fever," Liam said. "We're just trying to cool him off."

"It says here to give a dose once every four to six hours," Lucille said coming into the living room from the kitchen. "Oh, Bernie, you're back. Good—I'm going to run down to the drugstore and see what the pharmacist recommends. You can stay here and get cool cloths."

Bernadette took a bottle of children's acetaminophen and a wet cloth from her aunt's hands and turned toward Liam tentatively.

"I'll be back!" Lucille called over her shoulder, and a moment later the side door opened and then banged shut, leaving Bernie, Liam and Ike alone.

"Do you need a fresh one?" Bernie asked, and Liam handed her the cloth from Ike's forehead and replaced it. The cloth felt sickly hot in her hand, and she bent down next to the toddler.

"How're you doing, sweetie?" she asked quietly.

Ike just blinked at her, and she ran a finger down his cheek, feeling the heat radiating from him. She straightened. "I'll go put this one in the freezer to cool it off."

"Good idea."

She was back a moment later, and she sank into the chair next to Liam, regarding him thoughtfully. He looked like a regular dad with his child in his lap.

"You're good at this," she said.

"When he was crying earlier, you wouldn't have thought so."

She smiled ruefully. "Well, he's settled now."

Ike's eyes had drifted shut, and his breath was coming slow and steady. Bernie took the cloth off his forehead and blew against his damp skin. Then she mopped his face with the other side of it.

"I overheard something in the coffee shop today," Bernie said. "The women organizing the railway protest were talking about Vince coming to town soon."

Liam stopped rocking, and Ike squirmed in his sleep, so he started again but kept his glittering gaze locked on Bernie.

"What does that mean, exactly?"

"I can't say for sure, but given the timing of his visit—" She shrugged weakly. "I'd say he's coming to sort things out."

"Yeah…" Liam nodded. "That makes sense."

"I just wanted to give you a heads-up," she said. "I'm sorry, Liam."

"I'll talk to him," Liam said. "Man to man. I'll sign confidentiality papers. I'll play ball his way. Maybe it will make a difference."

And it was worth a try—but Liam was approaching this like an honorable man, and Vince was far from honorable. *Guys do this sometimes, Bunny.* Guys got their mistresses pregnant and figured out ways to protect their own reputations so they could continue in politics.

"It's worth a try." She hoped she sounded more convincing than she felt. If the Morgans were about to run someone over, sometimes it was just kinder not to see it coming. "So how was your day? Until now, I mean."

"Chip is proposing to his girlfriend," Liam said with a small smile.

"That's sweet." She smiled, too. "How long have they been together?"

"A couple of years..." Liam looked down at Ike, and his rocking slowed. "I'm going to give him full-time hours. He's earned it. When I first started at the garage, I'd just aged out of the foster system, and I needed to pay for my own keep."

"Your foster family just booted you out?" She frowned. That seemed harsh.

"We all knew it was coming," he replied. "And, no, they didn't boot me out, exactly, but they lost the state funding for me, so I needed to start supporting myself. So I got that job at the garage and rented a bachelor pad in town, and the rest is history."

"When did you get married?" she asked.

Liam's expression turned sad. "I met Leanne in the grocery store parking lot. Her car battery had died, and she needed a boost.

We dated for about two years, too, and she wanted marriage and kids and the white picket fence, and I wanted to be the one to give it to her."

Bernie felt a pang of envy at the tenderness in his voice. He'd loved Leanne, and love like that didn't come as easily as some people thought. She had money, family, position and had been ready to marry the most eligible bachelor in the state of New York, and she still hadn't experienced that kind of love.

"I was too stubborn to do things Leanne's way. I was so set on adopting, and I was still really struggling with the news that I was the infertile one."

Problems weren't smaller here in Runt River, they were just different. Or maybe not even so different, considering that her parents had struggled with the same thing. But there were fewer options here, fewer solutions.

"You can be thankful for one thing," she said. "Through all of this, no one followed you around with a camera and reported on your hardest times."

"Yeah," he nodded. "There is that."

"Small mercies, right?" She leaned forward and turned the cloth over on Ike's forehead. His cheeks were still red, and the medicine didn't seem to be helping too much.

"Will the photographers find you eventually?" Liam asked.

"Eventually." It was coming. She knew that. "Makes life here—I mean a real life here—seem a lot sweeter. When I first arrived it seemed almost creepy. No people. No cars. Everything is so—" She stopped. No word could be flattering.

"Poor?" he asked.

"Different," she qualified, but he was right. It had seemed poor. "But you have privacy here. Life might still knock you down, but you don't have the whole country watching it happen."

"Just friends and family," Liam said with a bitter smile.

"Family…" She shook her head, her mind going back to her own family. "They aren't always on your side, are they?"

"Not always," he agreed.

"When Vince got married, I was about sixteen. The wedding was set, and he and Tabby were finalizing all the details. They seemed very happy. Back then, we'd all go to my grandfather's place on Sundays for this mandatory dinner. Well, one Sunday, we all went down there, and I saw Vince's car on the street, and it was cold out and the car was running, so I thought I'd go over and say hi." She grimaced at the memory. "I tapped on the window, and inside I saw my engaged and very adult cousin making out with my best friend from school. She was sixteen, too, by the way."

"Seriously?" Liam's mouth turned down in distaste. "What did you do?"

"Well, Vince took me aside and said that I shouldn't be upset. It didn't mean anything. He was still getting married, and it was lucky that it was my friend in that car, because maybe I could help him in diverting her toward other guys her own age again." The memory still put a bad taste in her mouth. That was when she'd realized that family solidarity would often mean putting her own conscience on the back burner.

"So he's always been a creep," Liam said drily.

"It would seem," she agreed. But that concession to the family goals—that time of Vince's wedding—had left her feeling a little soiled, too. She'd never told Tabby what she'd seen, and she'd smiled brightly in all the wedding photos. She'd lost her best friend out of it, too.

"That's really awful, Bernie," Liam said quietly. "You weren't much more than a kid. Neither was your friend."

She had to agree. "I shouldn't be telling you this, though."

"I'm a nobody," he said with a quirky smile. "I'm no threat."

And in a way, maybe he was right. He was just a mechanic in a little town trying to keep a business afloat while he cared for an orphaned boy. He had no money or notoriety. But he certainly wasn't a "nobody." He was twice the man her cousin was.

IKE'S FEVER BROKE that evening. The day had been an exhausting one as Liam and Bernie took turns holding Ike and mopping his head, because every time they put him down he cried for more hugs. They gave him two cool sponge baths, and the fever rose and fell as the hours crept by. There was Jell-O, pudding, a bit of chicken soup, which Ike wasn't crazy about, but he did slurp up some noodles from the broth. He liked triangles of toast, and they turned the TV to the kids' channel and watched episode after episode of silly animated shows.

When his fever finally broke, they felt exuberant—almost victorious. Liam felt a rush of relief that he hadn't expected. Why was it that a little guy could wrap Liam around his fingers so effectively?

Ike was asleep—a different kind of sleep now that the fever was gone. Illnesses and fevers happened—he knew that—but somehow it had felt a whole lot more earth-shattering with this little guy suffering from it.

And he isn't mine. It was stupid that he even had to remind himself of this. Of course Ike wasn't his. Ike was Leanne's love child with another man—Liam had never forgotten that. Ike, on the other hand, had no idea; nor did he know that Liam might not be there forever.

"You want a hand opening doors and all that?" Bernie asked.

"Sure." He was grateful for the offer—not just because his arms would be full of a sleeping two-year-old, but because it helped to have another person in this. He'd started thinking about what being a single parent would look like, and he had to admit that it was scary. Did he really want this—the whole package? Bedtimes, bath times, childhood illnesses, first days of school, homework, preteen attitude…all of it alone. Dinner dishes washed alone, lectures given, lines drawn, discipline decided upon without any other input—no one else who would love this kid like he did. If he could talk to the senator man to man, and if Vince could be convinced to leave Ike where he was…

But still, it was a big responsibility—one that wouldn't end when Ike turned eighteen. Parenting was for life, and while he wanted to be a dad, did he want to be a dad on his own? That was something he needed to consider seriously.

Bernie walked with him across the street in the last rays of the evening sun and reached the front door a few steps before he did. He fished in his pocket for the key and handed it over. She let them in and turned on a lamp in the living room as he headed up the stairs to his bedroom. As he lay Ike down in the center of his bed, he tucked the boy's teddy bear in next to him. He glanced at the mattress on the floor with his own bedtime reading piled up next to it. There was a rustle in the doorway behind him.

"Liam?" He turned and found Bernadette smiling ruefully.

"Yeah?"

"You've been sleeping on the floor, haven't you?"

"I—" He paused, feeling sheepish. "For the last few nights."

"How many nights?" she prodded.

"Fine, all of them." He met her at the door, keeping his voice low. "It's just that he likes my bed so much better. It doesn't matter if he starts on his mattress, because he asks to be lifted up to the bed…and it's kind of hard to refuse. I don't really feel comfortable sleeping in the same bed as him, so I just took the mattress." He glanced back at Ike, snoring softly on the bed. "And he seemed fine with that."

She still looked mildly amused. "You're a softie."

"I'm practical," he countered, and they moved together toward the stairs. "I'm not losing sleep over a principle."

"Your bed wasn't worth fighting for?" she asked.

"Apparently not."

Who was he kidding? Ike already ran this place—Liam slept on the floor and bought completely different food than he used to eat because Ike didn't like it.

They headed down the stairs. She was so unlike any other woman around here, but she still had a comforting quality about her. People in Runt River didn't understand his predicament—they didn't sympathize too much, either. Leanne had left him, and in this town's opinion, she didn't deserve much pity. People wanted him to move on, and while his friends and neighbors didn't know who had fathered Leanne's child, they certainly knew that Ike was the result of that affair. Tim wasn't the only one to have pulled him aside about that. But Bernie could see the gray areas, and it was a strange relief to have at least one person understand, or at the very least, not judge him.

"Thanks for the hand," Liam said as they crossed the living room together. "All of it today. I appreciate it. I'm not sure I could have dealt with that alone."

"No problem. Glad I could help."

Bernadette stepped outside, and instead

of just shutting the door after her, he found himself joining her on the porch. Why had he done that? But he didn't want to retreat.

The sun was setting—golden streaks of light slanting across the grass as the sky blushed pink. Bernadette looked softer in the glow, gentler, or maybe it was the way she was looking at him. She pushed her hair away from her face, and she met his gaze with a tentative smile.

"Can I tell you something?" he asked, his voice low.

"Of course."

"I need to pull away from him," Liam said slowly. "That sounds really awful, but I'm too attached. I'm treating him like he's my kid, and he's not. Everyone knows that."

"What do you mean, pull away?" she asked.

"Take a bit of emotional distance," he said. "I'm not his father, and while his real-life dad leaves a lot to be desired, at least they share DNA."

Something flickered across her face, an emotion too fleeting for him to nail down. But he wasn't looking for permission here; he just needed to put it into words.

"Anyway," he went on. "I've been hoping I could hold on to Ike, take care of him myself, but that's probably not realistic. Maybe even selfish."

"I don't think it's selfish," she countered. "Being a single parent is anything but selfish."

"Okay, well..." He cleared his throat. "If Senator Morgan comes for his son, I can talk to him, but even if I have some legal leverage, I don't have the clout that Vince has. Or the money for a court battle. There is no reasonable hope that I'll be able to raise a kid that I have no biological link to. Vince would bury me."

"So you want to back off emotionally."

"You're making me feel cruel. I'm not leaving a puppy on the side of the road. I'm acknowledging facts."

"Facts—like DNA."

"It matters!" Why was she arguing this? Wasn't she the big "family first" person here? "It's hard, Bernie. I'm attached to that kid, and the more time I play at being his dad, the harder it's getting to think about giving him up. I know he's Leanne's, and Leanne and I had our problems, but that isn't Ike's fault.

He's just a little boy who lost his whole world when his mom died, and he needs someone to look out for him. When I stop and realize that I might have to let him go…" It hurt—in a place deep in his heart that had never been touched before. He needed to protect himself, too. "I like to think that I'm better for him than Vince, but am I? I'm just another flawed guy."

"You're a better man." Her voice was firm, but her eyes misted.

Was she serious? Did she really think that some mechanic in Runt River was a better option than a senator who could provide Ike with all the privileges money could offer?

"You think?"

"I'm sure of it."

"The law doesn't care about subjective things like that," he said with a sad smile.

"I do, though." She moved closer to him and put her hands on his chest. The slight pressure of her fingers made him want to wrap his arms around her, but he didn't dare. Instead he put a hand over hers, her silken skin warm under his palm.

"Ever think about sticking around Runt River?" he asked, meaning to tease, but not sure that he came across that way. "We could just keep doing this... You could help me out with Ike, and I wouldn't be on my own."

She smiled sadly. "Freezing time doesn't work. But I can see why Aunt Lucille chose Runt River. It grows on you."

Her eyes sparkled, and she looked up at him, her pink lips parting slightly, and before he could think better of it, he did the one thing his rational mind was screaming at him not to do. He bent his head and caught her lips with his. Her lips were as soft as he'd imagined they would be, and for a moment she froze. Should he stop? He was about to pull back—he hadn't wanted to take advantage—when she almost imperceptibly moved toward him. He slid his arms around her waist for the first time and she leaned into his body, her hands moving up to his sides and resting there as light as butterflies.

She smelled good, and she felt just right there in his arms, but then she pulled back, and her fingers fluttered up to her lips.

"Sorry," he whispered.

"Don't be." She smiled, then looked across the road toward Lucille's house. Good point.

Had her aunt just seen that? "I'd better get going."

"Okay."

He'd promised her to keep his lips to himself the other day, and he hadn't kept that promise. He could regret it later, but right now, the memory of her lips against his was too strong.

She was Vince Morgan's cousin, and she belonged to the family that had already destroyed his marriage. Leanne had discovered just how impenetrable they were, too. Lawyers and gag orders were common occurrences for them. Ike was now at the center of the Morgan family's interest, and Liam was kissing Bernie… He was stupid—there was no getting around that. She might have landed in this town, but this wasn't her life. This was some sort of vacation from the life that was awaiting her in Manhattan, and this temporary haze of attraction and longing would burn off eventually. And then the Morgans would have their way—they always did.

He'd said he needed to reel his emotions in, and that was probably the smart thing to do. He'd work on it. Tomorrow.

CHAPTER FOURTEEN

THAT KISS STAYED with Bernadette all that night—the memory of Liam's obsidian eyes meeting hers. When she'd looked up at him, she hadn't expected more than a shared smile. She'd been grateful for his understanding, for just being there. She didn't feel quite so alone with that rugged mechanic at her side, and she was glad that Ike had him.

She'd been serious when she said that Liam was a better man than her cousin—he was. He was kinder, more moral, more resolute. But he also wasn't backed by one of the wealthiest families in America. He might be twice the man, but he had no hope of winning. This wasn't a contest of man against man; it was man against financial empire. It wasn't a fair fight.

When Liam's lips had come down onto hers, she'd been surprised, and then everything had evaporated around her. He'd been in control of that kiss, his mouth moving over hers in a way that made her breath catch to even remember it. It was nothing like the kisses she'd shared with Calvin, and the difference wasn't because of his skill. It was from the tenderness in the moment.

Liam cared—that was as much as he'd probably admit to, but she'd felt the gentleness in that kiss, the protectiveness, and all that she'd wanted to do was move farther into those muscular arms.

This morning as she sat on the edge of the guest bed in her aunt's house, she felt foolish for letting herself melt into that kiss. Liam didn't know what her parents had done to get her, and while she loved the parents who raised her, this morning she felt more confident that she wanted to know about her birth mother. And she couldn't do that if she alienated the Morgan side of her family. If she tried to find her mother as a regular person, without the clout, money and privilege that opened doors for her, would she even be successful in her search? She doubted it. Even if what her parents had done disgusted her, she needed their influence.

Bernie's mother had been fifteen when

she'd given birth. She remembered herself at fifteen, and while she'd been a very sheltered, protected teenager, she knew the emotional maturity of a girl that age. That the Morgans had frightened her into giving up her baby was appalling, and Bernie wondered if her birth mother had ever fully recovered. Did she lie in her bed at night even now, silently cursing the monsters who stole her baby? Because monstrous behavior was in the eye of the beholder.

Guys do that kind of thing, Bunny. That was what Vince had told her when she'd caught him with her best friend in that car. None of the Morgans thought the word "monstrous" applied to them.

Bernie looked down at the Mercy House business card in her hand. Her mother had seen the faces of the people who took her baby. Had she ever seen them in the magazines in the years since then? Did she know who they were? Had she pieced together that the much-loved only daughter of Milhouse and Kitty Morgan was really her baby? Bernie at least knew of her mother's existence now, and there was no going back to blissful ignorance. While this would only complicate her life further, she needed to know more about that frightened teen.

What kind of woman had she grown into?

And does she miss me?

Bernadette picked up her cell phone and dialed the phone number for Mercy House. She got a receptionist who transferred her call to the records department.

"Hello, this is Verna in Records. What can I do for you?"

She'd already decided not to reveal her identity, knowing it would set off all sorts of alarm bells for the family if Verna told Aunt Ellen about the strange call from her niece.

"Hi, Verna," Bernadette said. "I was hoping you could give me some information about a girl who stayed at Mercy House thirty years ago."

"Our records are confidential," Verna said. "Unless the woman in question has passed away, in which case I'd need—"

"Look." Bernie sighed. "She's my birth mother. I know she was at your charity when she gave birth to me, and she gave me up for adoption."

"That happens a lot here, miss."

"Yes, I understand that. But I'd like to find her, if I could."

"I can sympathize." Verna's voice softened. "But there are privacy issues. The girls who come for our help don't necessarily want that information to be public. This is a delicate time in their lives."

"Don't they want to meet their children?" Bernie asked. "It's been thirty years. If I gave you my birthday, for example, would you be able to tell me about the girl who gave birth on that day?"

"I'm sorry, miss—"

Right now, Bernie was nothing more than a regular person trying to find some crumbs of information. As Bunny Morgan, she could have simply called the legal team and asked them to bring her results. They never failed. But the legal team wasn't at her beck and call right now—not if she wanted to keep this investigation a secret.

"All right, all right," she conceded. "You can't give me any personal information. But could you tell me some general things?"

"Like what, exactly?" Caution entered Verna's tone.

"If a girl wanted to find her child again,

and she contacted Mercy House, would she be given information about where her baby was placed?"

"The adoptions done at Mercy House are all closed adoptions."

"The girls have no other choice? They can't put on record that they'd like their children to be able to find them later on?"

Not that her mother would have been given that option, but it would be nice to know if any of the others got better treatment.

"The girls understand when they come here that if they decide to give up their babies—and that is by no means a requirement—the adoptions will be closed. They can always use other adoption agencies if they so desire."

"But we're talking about thirty years ago here, Verna." Bernie tried to control her irritation. "Was it always like this?"

"We do have a record of non-identifying information," Verna said.

"Such as?"

"The birth mother's medical history, her physical appearance, race, level of education, that sort of thing."

She knew most of that—Lucille had seen

her mother. A medical history might be useful later on, but that wouldn't ease the ache that had started in her chest.

"And to access this information?" Bernie asked.

"We'd need your birth certificate, two pieces of ID, and your physical presence here at Mercy House. We take privacy very seriously, miss."

Yes, of course they did. And Bernie didn't have access to her own birth certificate, nor did she believe she'd get very far if she showed up at Mercy House. Blast it! Was this what "ordinary" was like? How did people get anything done?

There was a murmur in the background, a rustle as Verna seemed to put her hand over the receiver. Then Verna's voice came back. "I have the site coordinator with me right now. She's asking for your name."

Bernie hung up. She'd been reckless to even try without a team of lawyers, and she shouldn't have even called if she wasn't willing to give her name. She knew that… The site coordinator would be relaying this information to Ellen Morgan in a heartbeat if she confided her identity. Frustration welled up inside her.

Whatever choices Mercy House had given other girls, Bernie's mother hadn't had one. She'd had the full weight of the Morgan legal team leaning on her, and she'd never had a chance. In exchange for the charity's help, she'd been forced to hand over her child, and they'd have buried the trail in the name of privacy protection.

Bernie might believe that her mother wanted her baby to grow up without ever knowing her, except Lucille had told her how desperately her mother had wanted to keep her. And she'd *tried*. That effort, that attempt to defy the Morgans and keep her baby, was what brought a lump to Bernie's throat. Isn't this what every child longed for—to be wanted? But once a woman had her baby stolen from her arms, she wouldn't forget and she wouldn't forgive. If she'd tried to keep her baby back then, she might try to find her again.

But without a name, Bernie couldn't even begin a search of her own. She wouldn't be able to weasel it out of the records department at Mercy House. If she was going to get this information, she'd need to get it from the source—her parents. And Milhouse and Kitty were on the same team here. There would be no dividing and conquering. They'd wanted a baby, they'd acquired a baby and their iron will wouldn't bend, even for Bernie's sake.

Bernadette heaved a sigh. Lucille had chosen an "ordinary life," but had she known how frustratingly inept the rest of the population really was? Bernadette might have been born to someone else, but she'd been raised a Morgan, and she had certain expectations about how things should work. Women in records didn't say no to her.

Liam had asked her if she'd considered staying in Runt River, and when she thought about a life free from the press and photographers, a life where she could make her own choices without being pressured on all sides…it was tempting. It was even more so when she considered kisses from a muscular mechanic and being able to be a part of Ike's life as he grew up. Tempting, yes, but not realistic. She needed to preserve the life she'd been raised with—because a life here left her just as powerless as everyone else. If she didn't have a birth mother out there—if it was simply a choice of privilege versus ordinary freedom—then she might think differently. But she did have a birth mother out there somewhere who had *wanted* her. As a Morgan, she could make things happen. Lucille had faced the same choice and had sacrificed privilege, but Bernadette intended to wield that privilege to find the mother the Morgans had tried to hide.

THE NEXT DAY, Ike had a lazy day of eating pudding cups and watching TV with Lucille, and the day after that he was at full speed again. Liam was amazed with the kid's recuperative powers. If that had been him, he'd have been down and out for a week at least.

Liam hadn't seen Bernie since their kiss. Maybe she was avoiding him—not that he'd blame her. He'd had some time to reconsider it, too, and she was in a vulnerable state since running away from her wedding, and with no future possible for them, what was he doing? He'd only make it harder. It wasn't right to play with people's emotions, and he had a heart to protect, too.

That morning, there weren't any scheduled

appointments, so Liam had Chip take charge of the shop.

"Come on, Ike," Liam said, holding the front door open. "Let's go to the park, buddy."

Ike clutched an oven mitt—he'd been playing with it since breakfast.

"Maybe we could leave that at home," Liam suggested.

"No." Ike's lip stuck out.

"It'll get dirty, though," Liam said. "You can play with it again when we get home."

"I wanna bring it." Ike marched obstinately out of the front door, then stopped and pointed. "Bunny!"

Liam's heart lurched—he'd known he'd see her again, but he wasn't exactly ready. He looked across the street to see Bernie standing on the sidewalk in front of her aunt's house. She wore a white sundress, her hair loose about her shoulders. Beautiful—that was the only word to describe her. This was obviously an effort at "dressing down," because she was without makeup again, but it did nothing to dull her glow. Her eyes widened in surprise, and she dropped her gaze.

Shoot. She didn't want to see him, either.

Ike dropped the oven mitt and bolted down

the steps and straight for the road. She'd be able to catch Ike before he could, he realized.

"Bernie, could you—" he called, and in response, Bernie jogged across the road and scooped up Ike in her arms, giving Liam the chance to toss the oven mitt back inside and lock his front door. He met her on the sidewalk.

"Hi." He met her gaze, but only for a moment. Was he really bashful after kissing her? He kind of was.

"Bunny come, too?" Ike asked, patting Bernie's cheek with a pudgy hand.

"I'd thought you'd be at the garage," she said.

"Can't do too much until the parts come in. Chip will give me a call if they do."

"Where are you going?" she asked Ike.

"Park." But his *r*'s were still lazy, and he managed to spray as he said the word.

"So fun." She kissed his cheek and put him down.

"You could—uh—come with us, if you wanted." Liam was hoping she'd say yes. He knew he needed to keep his emotional distance, but avoiding her wasn't an option.

"Sure. I can't do too much until my car is fixed, either."

He shot her a rueful smile. She'd actually agreed to come along—somehow he hadn't expected that, and he found himself glad of it. They turned in the direction of the park just down the road, and Bernie fell into step next to him. Ike trotted out front, already very familiar with the park. She walked comfortably enough next to him, but she'd also avoided him the last couple of days, so…

"Did I—" Liam swallowed. "I mean, the other day—the other evening, I should say—"

How was he supposed to say this?

"Liam, I'm fine."

"I made things weird between us, though."

"I'll give you that." She shot him a smile, but he saw forgiveness in her dark eyes.

He felt heat rising in his face, and he looked away.

"Do you know anything about your birth mother?" she asked, and he looked back, surprised at the change of topic.

"No… Well, I know that she had addiction issues, which was why I wasn't snapped up for adoption. I was a drug baby—not in demand."

"Sorry." She winced. "But did they give you her name or anything like that?"

"No." Why the sudden interest in his birth mother? "Look, we know who Ike's mother is. There isn't any question about that—"

"I know, I—" She paused, glanced toward him warily, then looked away again.

"Is something wrong?" he asked.

"I actually just found out that I was adopted."

He blinked. "Seriously? That's pretty big."

"Yeah. Apparently, it was the big family secret. Aunt Lucille told me, but it does make a lot of sense, looking back. So now I can't stop thinking about my birth mother."

"That's normal, I'd say," he replied.

She pulled her hair away from her face, glossy strands falling back over her shoulder. She sighed. "Didn't you ever want to know about yours?" She was looking at him earnestly now, dark eyes pinning him.

"I know that she was about twenty-five," Liam said. "She was a drug addict, and she couldn't take care of me. I went right into the system. And of course I've wondered about her, but there wasn't much information to go on, and while having a mother would be amazing…" He was afraid of being disappointed. He knew what addiction looked like, and if his mother was an addict, coming to him for money for her drugs, it would be worse.

"She never tried to find you?" Bernie asked.

"Not that I know of. I don't exactly have a difficult trail to sniff out, either, considering that I was raised in the foster system. I used to dream that she'd come back for me one day and I'd have a mother again. But life doesn't work out like that."

The park was located on a corner—a swing set, a play structure, a tube slide. A couple of benches were set around the perimeter, and as they approached the park, Ike ran ahead of them, going straight for the sandbox. There were a few trees, and Liam chose a bench in the shade. Bernie sat next to him.

"So it looks like I don't have the family you thought I did," she said quietly.

"Adoption counts, Bernie."

She didn't say anything else, and he wondered what she was thinking about.

"If the Eagers had adopted me, I'd have felt a lot differently," he went on. "Adoption means you belong to them, you're their kid. Foster kids don't get that final feeling. I'm not an Eager. I'm a Wilson. It's different. You had loving parents who apparently didn't even want you to know that you weren't biologically theirs. Maybe that was a bad call on their part, but there's no question that you're a Morgan."

She'd inherit her father's fortune, and she'd live with the privilege that wealth and political influence brought. She had parents who had paid for her wedding, who were probably just as upset about her distance from them as she was.

"You are right about that." She smiled, but it didn't reach her eyes.

He wanted to comfort her somehow, but he'd already sailed right over appropriate boundaries with that kiss. She looked so fragile sitting there next to him, her eyes filled with conflicting emotions as she watched Ike digging with a discarded plastic shovel in the sand. Liam made do by sliding an arm behind her shoulders along the bench, and she leaned into him, resting her shoulder against him. He caught his breath, almost afraid to move lest she move away again. She smelled of that floral scent he'd started associating with her, and he wished he could just wrap his arms around her and hold her close. But if he did, he couldn't guarantee he wouldn't sail right past appropriate again.

So he sat there with his arm on the bench, wishing for something he wouldn't do while they watched Ike. To an outside observer, they probably looked like a family. He liked that—and in a way they were a family…connected oddly, but somehow belonging together. Bernie was Ike's relative, and Liam was Ike's guardian. Sometimes a guy just had to make do with "good enough."

"You're going to be okay," he said.

"I know." She still had that Morgan self-assurance, and why shouldn't she?

He chuckled. "I really like you, Bernie."

A smile came to her lips and she tipped her head onto his shoulder. "Would you still like me without the Morgan clout?"

"Probably more," he said, and she laughed.

"That's right—you're the one person who can't stand my family. In a way, that's kind of comforting."

"I don't hate all of them," he countered. "Just your cousin."

She sighed. "I know I'll have to go back sooner or later, but I wish I could stay right here…in this moment, where it's easy and comfortable."

If only life could stay as simple as a summer morning in a park. But she was the one who'd said they couldn't freeze time. He didn't answer her, but he did rest his cheek against the top of her head. If leaning against his shoulder made her life feel a little easier, then he was glad to oblige. And deep down, he wished that her staying here in Runt River was an option, too.

CHAPTER FIFTEEN

BERNADETTE HADN'T REALIZED how much she needed comfort until she'd had this strong, quiet man next to her. Leaning against him had been a bit forward, she had to admit, but he hadn't seemed to mind. Their connections in these strange couple of weeks had made their friendship happen a little more quickly than it might have otherwise, but Liam was the one person who could understand all of it. Just sitting there on that shaded bench, watching Ike climb up the slide, had done more for her than hours of brooding on her own. Soon she'd have to head back to New York and face reality, but until then, Liam made it all a little easier.

Once Ike had played for a while, Liam called him to head back home. As they strolled toward the house, Ike scrambled between them and held up his hands.

"One, two, three?" he pleaded. "One, two, three?"

Bernadette didn't know this one, but it was hard to deny his enthusiasm.

"What's that?" she asked.

"I'm guessing he wants to be swung." Liam shrugged. "What do you say, Bunny?"

She gave him a joking glare. "Ike can get away with that. You can call me ma'am."

Liam laughed and took Ike's hand. "See, buddy? Feel special. You get away with way more than the rest of us do."

Bernadette and Liam each took one of his hands and Ike danced on the sidewalk excitedly.

"One, two, three!" Ike squealed, and they gave him a swing, his weight easy to handle between them. Bernie noticed how carefully Liam swung the boy. He was a muscular man, and he obviously was keeping his strength in check, and it softened her heart to watch.

Bernie had always wanted kids. It had been an expectation for her as a Morgan. She needed to have someone to hand the money down to after she inherited. Bernie had imagined the kids she and Calvin would have together—two boys and a girl.

She'd raise the boys to know formal manners, to shake hands, stand when a lady left the table and to make her proud. She'd raise her daughter to have a voice, to hold her head high and to accept nothing less than greatness. And after Calvin's time in the White House, they'd turn their attention to building their fortune—together as a team. They'd be the Morgan-McManns, and they'd go down in history as a family to be reckoned with.

And yet in all her daydreams of the future with Calvin, she'd never imagined a scene like this one—two people walking back from the park, swinging a squealing toddler between them. Even now, she couldn't picture Calvin like this. He'd make more of the kindly, distanced father…with a mistress on the side, apparently.

"One, two, three!" Ike squealed, and she laughed as they swung him up into the air again. It was the life—a toddler with two adults at his beck and call.

Looking at Liam, she was struck by his rugged good looks. If she needed a lawyer, Calvin was the one to call, but if she needed someone to lift a fridge or wrestle a wild animal off of her…her bet would be on Liam. She blushed at the thought.

"What?" Liam asked, shooting her a side-long look.

"Nothing."

"Okay, last swing, Ike. Make it count."

Ike got one last swing before they put him down and let him run ahead again. Liam edged closer to her, then nudged her with the side of his arm.

"Ma'am." His tone was light, but the twang in his speech and the low, gravelly timbre made him sound old-fashioned and flirtatious all at once. "You're having fun."

Was that it? Was this what fun looked like? She'd never taken the time to stroll through a Manhattan neighborhood before. She'd always been jogging with her earbuds in, or heading out to meet some friends for brunch.

"I guess so," she admitted. "This is a different pace."

A piece of dandelion fluff caught in Liam's stubble, and she reached up and plucked it off. His gaze suddenly sharpened, and she caught her breath. She shouldn't have done that—touched him so familiarly. It was making her feel things he probably never intended.

"Sorry—dandelion." She held up the fluff as proof.

"Come here." He caught her hand in his and tugged her closer as they strolled along. She couldn't help smiling. His hands were rough and strong, but he held hers gently, his fingers moving ever so slowly, and her heart sped up... Oh, she could get used to this.

"I thought you were supposed to call me ma'am," she said teasing.

"I can call you ma'am and still hold your hand. I'm gentlemanly that way." He winked, and her stomach fluttered again. He was playing, but she wasn't capable of this kind of game—not now.

"Is this smart?" she asked.

He looked down at her. "Hmm?"

"This—" She gave his hand a squeeze, not quite willing to tug her hand free, either, although she certainly could have.

He shot her a roguish smile. "Afraid for your reputation?"

No, she was afraid for her heart. He wasn't just "some cute guy." He was so much more by now—a friend, she would have said, but friends didn't kiss in the twilight or hold hands on walks.

"We said we'd be more careful," she reminded him, and her voice caught. She cleared her throat, feeling so much less polished than she normally did. He nodded, pressing his lips together.

"We did." He released her hand with one final squeeze.

The thing was, Liam taking her hand hadn't felt like a come-on. He wasn't like other men who'd tried to get her into bed or push her past her comfort zone. His gestures were tender, sweet, certainly not unwelcome... It was as though all he wanted was to connect with her—nothing more. But since when was she any judge of character?

"I'm not good at this," she said.

"At what?" he asked, humor flickering at the corners of his lips. "Letting a guy down easy?"

Why did he have to keep doing that—flirting and making her heart flutter? He was cute—no, ruggedly handsome—and he didn't seem to realize the impact he had on her.

"You don't think we have a future, either," she countered.

"No, I guess not." He sobered. "Sometimes I forget, though, and it seems like we're just a man and a woman out for a walk on a summer morning."

If only it were that simple—and everything else could melt away. But life was complicated. She watched Ike scampering on ahead of them, and she smiled sadly. She had a feeling she'd remember this particular morning for a very long time.

Ike squatted in front of a flower bed, and Liam sucked in a breath. They both saw it coming... Ike yanked a marigold out by the roots and held it up exuberantly.

"Flower!" he exclaimed.

"Oh, shoot." Liam lunged forward and caught the flower. "Can I have it, Ike?"

Ike released it, and Liam patted it back into the soil, then looked back at Bernie with a comically alarmed look on his face. Bernie couldn't help but laugh.

"He's worse than a dog!" Liam rolled his eyes and straightened again. "Ike, you can't pick flowers in other people's yards, okay?"

Ike wasn't listening. He'd trotted on ahead to grab a stick off the sidewalk. They were almost home, and Bernie felt a sinking sadness at this walk being over. She'd never felt this rush of regret when it was time to say a goodbye to Calvin. She'd chalked it up to her maturity. But maybe it had been less about age and more about—what exactly?

They stopped in front of Liam's house, and she glanced across the street toward Lucille's property. A black SUV with tinted windows was parked on the corner. She paused, squinted at it, and the motor started. It reversed out of sight, behind a hedge of lilacs.

Her heart sped up and hammered in her throat. She knew exactly what this meant— it was the Morgan security team. She wasn't alone here anymore.

LIAM MIGHT THINK better of this later, and he was sure that he would, but he didn't want to say goodbye just yet. It felt nice to have a woman at his side…*her*. Maybe it wasn't about pulling away from Bernie—that didn't seem to work anyway. Maybe he could enjoy the softness of her company while he had the chance. He'd deal with the goodbye when it came.

"I should probably get Ike inside for a snack," Liam said. "We're on borrowed time here before he gets cranky. You want to come in for an iced tea or something?"

"Yes." Her answer was almost too quick and he shot her a grin.

"Great."

Ike latched on to Liam's hand, and they headed into the house. Bernie looked over her shoulder twice before she went inside, but Liam was focused on getting Ike a snack, then putting on a DVD on the TV in the bedroom. About ten minutes later, he came back downstairs to find Bernie standing by the living room window looking out.

"Hi," he said, and she turned toward him, her face ashen.

"Hi." She laughed a little nervously.

"What's the matter?" he asked. "You looked spooked."

She paused, then said, "I saw a black SUV. Tinted windows."

"Okay." What did that mean, exactly? Sure, these parts had more dusty pickups than black SUVs, but that wasn't written in stone.

"My dad's security," she clarified. "I'd know them anywhere."

"Could have just been a neighbor who bought a new vehicle," he suggested.

"When I saw it, it backed up out of sight."

Well, that was a bit creepier. He crossed the room to the window and looked out. He couldn't see anything from here, just the street—sun-dappled, a few cars and pickups parked along the road. Nothing out of the ordinary. This was a quiet road—this was Runt River, after all. Even the main drags didn't get a lot of traffic.

"So if your father's security is in town—"

Bernie shrugged. "My vacation is over."

Vacation—this wasn't exactly a holiday for her, and he knew that. She'd run away from her family and was digging up old family secrets. Adoption didn't need to be a big deal… except that hers had been kept secret, which was strange in itself. The more Liam got to know about the Morgans, the more uneasy they made him, and the way the color had drained from her face chilled him further.

"You're a grown woman, though," he countered. "You can travel if you like."

She sank into an armchair and rubbed a hand over her eyes. "Out of the blue, Vince decides to come back to Runt River. Now my father's security team has arrived. This has nothing to do with my travel plans."

Liam's stomach sank, and he glanced out the window again. "They're here for Ike?"

"Well, Ike and me."

Anger simmered deep inside him—an emotion he was a lot more comfortable with. The thought that a man—any man—would force Bernie into something she didn't want to do... And add to that the thought of that same man taking Ike from his home—

"So this is your father at work?" he demanded. "Or is this Vince? Because I want to know exactly who I'm dealing with."

Bernie didn't answer, and the cool, collected woman who had asked him if holding hands was smart suddenly crumpled. Tears welled in her eyes, and she blinked and looked away, but he'd seen it.

"Bernie..." He softened his tone, and her chin trembled. "Shoot." He bent, took her hands in his and tugged her to her feet. Then he wrapped his arms around her, pulling her close against him, and pressed his lips to her hair. She fit in his arms perfectly, and he half expected her to pull away, steel herself again, but she didn't. Instead whatever reserve had been holding her together cracked, and her body shook with sobs.

"It's okay…" he murmured, and she wound her arms around his waist and cried into his chest. He could feel her tears soaking into his shirt, and he didn't mind a bit. If he could be her strength for a while, he was glad to do it.

"I hate this…" she said, and she pulled back, wiping her face with her palms.

"Hate what?" he asked.

"All of this." She looked around. "I hate that Ike's future is at stake, and that my father can snap his fingers and make things happen. I hate that my family's ambition overrides everything else…including me. I can't even dump a cheating loser without their permission. And when I do it anyway, the story is that I'm the problem."

"You are not the problem," Liam said, his voice low and angry. "Trust me on that."

"Well, that's not the way the country is going to see it. Shiny, pretty boy Calvin is worth more to my father than I am."

"I'm sure deep down—"

"No!" She cut him off. "I found my fiancé halfway down another woman's throat moments before the ceremony, and my parents were more concerned about the spin than about *me*. My father would rather tell the world that I'm a flighty airhead than admit the truth—Calvin wasn't the man they thought he was. I'm their *daughter*." Bernie sniffled and shook her head. "I'm sorry."

"You have nothing to be sorry for," Liam said. "You're right—none of this is fair to you, or to Ike."

"My parents always win." She pulled a tissue out of her pocket and wiped her nose. "Always."

"I don't know, Lucille seems to be holding her own," he pointed out.

"Only because she knows their secrets."

Liam hadn't realized that. How much had his matronly neighbor been hiding all these years? Still, he'd trust her over most people in his life. Her heart always seemed to be in the right place, at the very least.

"I'm sure you know a few, too," he pointed out.

Bernie looked toward the window, her brow furrowed, but she didn't say anything. This was her family, and while she probably knew a few things that would embarrass them, would it really undo her father's power? Not likely. It was too much to put onto her shoulders.

"Look, this isn't your fault," he repeated.

"I told my father about Ike, though."

"Vince already knew about Ike. You just reminded him. We'd have been facing this sooner or later."

She heaved a deep sigh. "That's probably true."

Liam moved a damp piece of hair away from her cheek, then dried the spot with the pad of his thumb. It was coming to an end—this bubble of solitude they'd been enjoying. He'd known it couldn't last forever.

"I need to find my birth mother—figure out what happened to her, and I can't do that without money and my own lawyers."

"Okay…" What was she getting at?

"If it were only about me, I might do things differently, Liam, but it isn't. She was fifteen when I was born, and whether or not she signed the papers, I know she can't have forgotten about me. Now that I know about her…" Worry crept into Bernie's expression again. There was obviously a lot more to this story than she was telling him.

"And you want to find her. I get it."

"In order to do that, I'll have to go back to New York." Her voice was stronger now. "I can do more from there. I'll make sure I get my own legal team. I've never had reason to before, but like you said, I'm a grown woman. I can probably keep what I'm really up to under wraps for a while. I'll liquidate some of my investments, and then I'll hire an investigator."

Legal teams, liquidated assets—Bernie lived in a very different world from his. He was impressed with her presence of mind in the middle of all this drama.

"Sounds like you have a plan," he said.

"I could have the lawyers look into your claim with Ike, too. If you had a top-notch legal team, you could fight this. I'd pay the legal fees, of course."

He wanted to say that it wasn't necessary, but there was no way he could pay for this on his own. Court, lawyers, intimidation… even taking the time away from work would be difficult. Chip was good, but it wasn't fair to ask him to run the place alone for more than a day or two. It would be hard for everyone—pressure on top of pressure. This was all getting very real. It was no longer about

the day-to-day challenges of taking care of
a toddler—this was now about legal rights,
parental claims. And the Morgans were not
about to back down.

"So you're leaving," he clarified. That's
what this came down to, her decisions about
the future. He didn't know what he'd been
hoping for, because heiresses didn't just settle
in backwoods towns. Runt River had nothing to offer her.

"Not immediately, but yes." She shrugged
weakly. "I still need my car fixed."

"Oh, yeah, that." Liam scrubbed a hand
through his short hair. "I'm just waiting on
the last of the parts."

She reached out and took his hand. "I'm
not forgetting about you, though."

He squeezed her hand. "You will, Bernie.
I'll be a story you tell years from now once
it's all settled out and no longer a threat to
anyone. And you'll tell about the mechanic
who was kind of sweet on you."

"So you admit to being sweet on me?" she
asked, a smile coming to her lips.

"Grudgingly." He was more than sweet on
her—he was falling for her. And that didn't
do either of them any good.

"I should get back." She nodded across the street. "Thanks for the walk."

"My pleasure."

She headed for the door, and this time he let her go.

CHAPTER SIXTEEN

BERNADETTE SHOOK HER hands at her sides as
she walked down the street. She was trying to get her emotions back under control.
She'd cried. She'd never been the type to cry
in front of other people, so to have cried *on*
Liam made it worse. She was overwhelmed,
frustrated, feeling things she shouldn't for
Ike's guardian, and now her father's security
detail had arrived… She was surprised she
hadn't broken down before this, but at the
very least she could have saved it for when
she was alone.

Except that she'd felt safe with Liam standing over her, those warm eyes focused on
her as if her feelings mattered more than
she imagined. Her feelings hadn't mattered
at her own wedding—they'd been quite low
on her family's priorities for the event. But
there in that living room with a man with
grease-stained hands, the complicated emo-

tions welling up inside her had a place to go, and his response had been to gather her in his arms and hold her close.

Heiresses didn't have futures with mechanics. That wasn't how these things worked. She needed a man who could navigate her world—the boardrooms, the country clubs, the legal teams… Attraction or personal feelings had nothing to do with it. If she could love a man who could thrive in her world, that would be best, but she certainly couldn't choose a man just because she fit perfectly under his chin.

That SUV had shaken her, but it was more than her father's security detail, it was the realization that this interlude was at an end. It would be nice if her family could respect her privacy, but the Morgans didn't work that way. They brought in the cavalry, and they stomped down fences. Morgans weren't patient people.

Bernadette wasn't terribly patient, either, and she was tired of hiding. She could sit in her aunt's house, trying to keep out of sight, but how would that help? Her father knew she was here, and knew where Aunt Lucille lived. The smart move was to march out and face it.

Which was why she was walking down the street now. She kept her eyes peeled for the SUV, but it wasn't there. What she'd have done if she found it, she wasn't sure. Walk up and slap the hood? She didn't have the chance, though, and so she walked on.

Bernie could hear a commotion as she approached Main Street. Excited voices chattered, and above it all was an amplified voice: "I know you want answers, Runt River, and I'm here as your senator to give you what information I can." Bernadette sighed. Vince. So *he* was here. Maybe that security team belonged to him—although it was funded by her father, and Milhouse wasn't the kind of man to fund something without strings attached. That was bad business.

She wandered down the street toward the crowd. Her cousin was standing on a riser, microphone in one hand, gesturing with the other to calm the crowd down. If Tabby was here, Bernie didn't see her. Two SUVs with tinted windows were parked on either side of the street, and she spotted the security detail—black suits, steely gaze—in strategic locations. It was almost laughable. What did Vince expect was going to happen to him in Runt River? He wasn't president and never would be. Perhaps it spoke more of his own sense of self-importance.

A crowd of about thirty or forty people had gathered. Bernie wasn't going to blend in. She stopped behind a small group of women in blue jeans, crossed her arms over her chest and stared at her cousin—waiting for him to notice her.

"Now, I'm not going to waste your valuable time today. You've asked for jobs, and building this new railway is going to provide them. Hiring for some temporary positions will start soon, and the pay is excellent. Your town is going to prosper because of it!"

"What about the tire factory?" someone shouted.

"I understand there is some concern about the tire factory, but you have to understand that making way for new business sometimes means there is some shifting—"

No one liked that, and while some muttered, others raised their voices, shouting their responses at their senator. Vince's gaze scanned the crowd, and he passed over her twice before recognizing her. He paused, moved the mic away from his mouth and gestured for his security officer. He murmured something, then the smile came back to his face.

"Now, I'm not some heartless politician who doesn't care about your livelihoods. I know what it's like to live paycheck to paycheck." That was a lie. He had no idea. "And I'm on your side. I'm fighting for you. This isn't over yet, and my sleeves are rolled up."

A security guard materialized at Bernie's side, latching on to her elbow with a steely grip.

"Excuse me, miss."

She tried to jerk her arm free but couldn't. "Let go of me."

"The senator wants a word with you."

"Great. But right now he's busy, isn't he?" she snapped.

"He'd like you to wait for him in his vehicle. It'll be more comfortable there."

This wasn't a request, and she looked up into the face of what she could only imagine was an ex-marine. He was well built and had the eyes of a shark.

"You do know who I am, don't you?" she

asked smoothly, keeping her tone low. "Because if you try to manhandle me into that vehicle, I will not only scream bloody murder, but I'll tell my father the story in lurid detail."

That worked, and the guard dropped his hand from her arm.

"I apologize, miss."

She shot him an icy glare. "Now leave me alone."

"The senator still needs to speak with you."

And there was no way she was getting into the SUV, even with her cousin. If she got into that vehicle, they'd whisk her back to New York in a heartbeat, and she couldn't risk that. She'd go back to New York under her own steam, and she wouldn't be fetched.

Bernadette looked farther up the street, and her gaze landed on the Runt River Christian Church. It was an old-fashioned place with white siding and a steeple. There was also a sign out front saying that the doors were open for anyone wishing to go inside to pray.

"If the senator wants to speak with me alone—which I assume is the goal here— then he can meet me inside that church. And you goons can stay outside."

The large man nodded and stepped back. He tapped an earpiece and murmured into a mic on his wrist. So dramatic.

She eased back away from the crowd and started toward the church. The back of her neck tingled, and she glanced behind her. Both security guards were watching her. The church was as private a place as any, but it was also neutral turf. Vince might not feel quite so comfortable making demands in such a setting, she was hoping, but all the same her heart hammered in her chest.

Bernadette was sick of this—the intrigue, the secrets, the ambition. She was tired of defending her decisions, and trying to guess which choices would be less damaging for her in the long run. She was tired of wondering what her family had in store for an innocent child with a broken heart. And underneath all that exhaustion she carried a secret of her own: the mother she'd never known.

If her mother had kept her, what would her life be like now? She certainly wouldn't have an Ivy League education, wear the top brand names or be part of a family plot to get a president elected. She'd have been the daughter of a teenage mother, and have grown up without money or influence. Maybe she'd have followed in her mother's footsteps and had a baby of her own much too early...but if that baby had turned out to be as sweet as little Ike, would it really be so terrible? She felt tears rise... Ike was counting on her, too.

Her life might have turned out very differently, but that didn't mean it would have been bad. If she'd been about to marry a man who was openly cheating on her, she liked to think that her biological mother would have sided with her. And if she hadn't been adopted by one of the wealthier families in America, she'd have just been a young woman making her way in the world, and a mechanic who wrapped his arms around her and soothed away her tears wouldn't be such an impossible choice.

Bernadette stopped in front of the church and looked up at the steeple. She'd chosen this church for the neutral turf, and she needed that. Because the Morgans were already on the march.

LIAM PARKED HIS truck in his spot at the garage and hopped out. This was the place he always came back to—his touchstone. Maybe he should be grateful that he found his comfort in work. But his mind was still on Bernie. She'd been through a lot, and while he was glad that she was putting together a plan for how to deal with all of this, he knew that her plan wouldn't involve him. Or this town. Not that he blamed her—she was better than this place.

A delivery truck pulled in behind him, and he nodded at the driver. He'd gone to high school with Dave Thorner. In a place this small, everyone knew pretty much everyone else. Normally, he and Dave would stop for a chat—catch up on some local gossip—but Liam wasn't in the mood today.

Dave pulled to a stop and lowered his window. "Liam! Hard at work, or hardly working?"

Liam smiled at the worn joke and accepted the box that Dave handed him, and when he looked down at the label, he felt his smile falter. Rolls-Royce.

"Thanks. Been waiting on this."

He signed the tablet and handed it back.

"So how's it going?" Dave asked, tossing the tablet onto the passenger seat.

"Not too bad. Keeping busy." Even if he

wanted to talk about all of this, he wouldn't know where to start. "Taking care of a toddler is more work than I thought."

"Oh, tell me about it." Dave had three kids of his own. "If you think a two-year-old is hard, wait until Ike turns three. They're obstinate and have a vocabulary."

Liam smiled at that. Ike already knew how he liked things, but he wasn't sure he'd see the kid turn three. Or five. Or fifteen. The Morgans were already mobilizing.

"I'd better get to work, Dave," Liam said—more as an excuse to end the conversation than anything. He was knotted up inside, and he needed to find a way to untie it all.

"Have a good one," Dave said with a nod. "Mark my words—three-year-olds are worse!"

Dave gave a salute and laughed, then pulled out. Liam attempted to look congenial, and turned toward the door. Dave had no idea how much Liam longed to have those kinds of chats—the in-the-trenches dad jokes. He looked down at the box in his hands. These were the last of the parts he'd ordered for Bernadette's car, and while he normally felt elated at having a project so close to completion, he didn't this time. All of it was ending—he could sense it.

When her car was ready, Bernie would have no more reason to stick around. This was it—three more days and then her car would be good to go. Job complete.

He headed into the garage, the box under his arm, then tossed it onto the workbench. Chip was reading a newspaper, which he dropped guiltily.

"Sorry about that, boss. I'm on lunch. Sal Vieni is bringing his wife's car by—engine light."

"Great." Liam nodded. "And those are the parts for the Rolls-Royce."

"Okay, so we've got something to do." Chip brightened.

"Yeah—we do."

What was with him? He'd known all along that this was short-term, and he'd known better than to get attached. But apparently he was drawn to the women who wanted to get out of his town.

"Did you see that paper?" Chip asked.

Liam picked it up and scanned the column that Chip had been reading. It was an old society column—the cancelation of the wedding between Senator McMann and Bunny Morgan.

"That's Bunny Morgan who's here in town, isn't it?" Chip asked.

"Yeah…" There was no use hiding it. Her father's security detail was here, and it looked like it was all out of the bag now anyway.

Chip let out a low whistle. "Jessica was the one who pointed out the story. She loves celebrity weddings. Turns out Bunny left him at the altar."

Liam scanned the article.

"Bunny wasn't ready for a lifelong commitment," McMann told reporters. "It was my fault for not realizing earlier that we needed different things. My only regret was that I put her into that position to begin with. I loved her—and love is blind. I think most people can identify with that. I know there is a stigma surrounding mental illness, but there shouldn't be. Bunny is valiant, brilliant, beautiful. I wish her only the best."

When asked about the reference to mental illness, Senator McMann deferred, saying it was a slip of the tongue.

Liam shook his head. Smooth—McMann looked like the long-suffering romantic and Bernadette was the mentally unstable heiress. Would this affect their stocks if Bernie took over more of the business? Doubtlessly, the Morgans had already considered all of that.

He slapped the paper against his hand. "This is garbage."

Chip's eyes widened in surprise, then he nodded quickly. "Sure. Of course."

Out the window, Liam saw Sal Vieni pull in. "Can you take care of Sal, Chip? I'm going to make a call."

Chip nodded but gave him a curious look. Liam didn't particularly care, and he pulled out his cell phone and headed through the reception area to his office, dialing as he walked. He put the phone to his ear as it started to ring.

"Is that you Liam?" Lucille said cheerily, no doubt seeing his number on her call display.

"Sure is. Hi, Lucille."

"Ike is doing just fine," she said. "He's watching some TV while I make him some scrambled eggs."

"Great." He swallowed. "Have you talked to Bernie?"

"No, why?"

"She saw her dad's security detail in town."

Lucille heaved a sigh. "So my brother is going to meddle, is he?"

"What am I dealing with? Bernie's told me her version, but I need to hear yours."

She lowered her voice. "Ike is a scandal waiting to happen," she said quietly. "They'll want to hush that up. You are Ike's legal father because you were married to his mother, but the Morgans always think ahead. If at some later date the Democrats offered you a large sum of money, you could declare Ike to be Vince's son and demand a paternity test. It could ruin Vince, especially right around an election. He's going to be thinking about future damage control. This is how it's done— sweep it up before it becomes a problem. And with Ike in your care, he's a potential problem. Plus, Bernadette did the unthinkable— she walked out on the family. I have no doubt that it's a hornet's nest."

"And what about Ike?" Liam pressed. "Will they take him?"

"Keeping Ike in their control means they

can hide him more effectively. So they'll try," Lucille replied, and somehow she sounded more optimistic than he felt right now.

"Meaning?"

"Meaning, even a Morgan has an Achilles' heel."

"Do you know theirs?" he pressed.

"Bernie knows theirs," she replied. "But it would ruin her, as well."

That was what he was scared of—that the price of helping him would be too high.

"She's offered to pay the legal fees for me to fight this," Liam said.

"That sounds good," Lucille said softly. "Are you willing to take on one of the wealthiest families in America?"

Liam wasn't entirely sure. He'd have to be pretty convinced that he was a better dad for Ike than his own biological father would be... and that was a tough call to make. Who was he to decide that? He heaved a sigh.

"You'll need to have your eyes open for this, Liam," Lucille went on. "Milhouse doesn't stop when someone is in his way. He'll take your business and leave you bankrupt. He'll ruin your reputation. He takes opposition personally."

"And Vince Morgan?" Liam asked.

"He's not as smart as Milhouse, but he's the same breed. I'd advise you to step carefully, Liam. If the Morgan security team is in town, then the family means business."

Liam knew all of this from Bernie, but he needed to have it confirmed by his friend. In this mess, he trusted Lucille more than the others. Was he really willing to play some David and Goliath game with the Morgans?

"Liam?"

"Yeah, I'm here."

"She was raised by my brother, and he taught her everything he knows. Bernie knows how to fight just as dirty as he does. You don't need to rescue her."

"Who says I'm—"

"You don't need to rescue her," she repeated firmly. "In fact, you can't. You are very much out of your depth."

How obvious had he been about his feelings for Bernadette? He shut his eyes and sighed. He should have kept his distance—wasn't that what he'd said all along? But he couldn't undo it all now. He had his life here in Runt River, and that was worth protecting.

"Thanks, Lucille."

"My pleasure, Liam." Her tone became almost motherly. "You'll be careful, won't you?"

"I'll definitely try to be."

And that was all he could promise, because he'd already been tossed into the middle of this mess when Ike had been deposited on his doorstep. He was well past getting his heart out in one piece.

CHAPTER SEVENTEEN

BERNADETTE STOOD IN the foyer of the little church and looked around. This was a heritage building—over a hundred years old—according to a plaque on the wall. There were some framed photos of the congregation in the early 1900s, standing solemnly in front of the building.

"Hello."

She startled and whipped around to see an elderly man regarding her with a smile. His hair was silvery and thin, and he wore a saggy pair of dress pants and a short-sleeve button-up shirt.

"You scared me," she said with a breathy laugh. "Hello. How are you?"

"I'm Reverend Phipps." He held out his hand.

Bernadette drew in a deep breath. "Nice to meet you. I'm actually… I hope it isn't inappropriate, Reverend, but I asked someone to meet me here. My cousin."

"Oh?" He shook his head. "I don't see a problem with that. I have often said that we'd do better if we kept the church at the center of our lives."

Bernadette blushed at that. Other than for weddings, she couldn't remember the last time she'd so much as stepped foot in a church. "Thank you. I appreciate that."

As if on cue, the front doors opened, and a suited security guard came inside first, followed by her cousin.

"Without the goons, Vince," she said curtly, then glanced sheepishly at the reverend. "Please," she added, moderating her tone.

The reverend headed off down a hallway, leaving them in relative privacy. Vince nodded at his security guard, who retreated outside. Her cousin's forehead was dewy, and he pulled out a handkerchief and mopped his face.

"There is air conditioning in the car," he said drily. "What's this about? It's all Shakespearean."

"What's with all your security?" she countered. "You aren't president, you know."

Vince scowled, then smoothed his expression. "The security is courtesy of your dad. He likes the optics."

Bernie had to admit that it lent an air of success to Vince that he hadn't achieved yet. Still, it made an impression, and considering her father's dedication to Calvin's political career right now, she was suspicious.

"Did Dad send you to take me home?" she asked.

"What?" Vince shook his head, then stepped closer and lowered his voice. "I'm here to clean up my own mess, Bunny. You're the one who told your dad about it. Thanks for that, by the way. You could have called me personally, you know."

So now Vince, the philandering politician, was wounded that she'd sidestepped him. She'd be amused if she weren't so irritated right now.

"So you're here for Ike."

"Yes." He looked toward the door. "You sure you wouldn't be more comfortable discussing this in the SUV?"

"Perfectly." She gave him a cool smile.

"So here's the thing," Vince said, lowering his voice even further. "I understand that you and Calvin are through."

"Obviously."

"But you won't be taking him back," he pressed. "Your father did ask me to talk to you about the reality of marriage these days. It is possible to have a highly successful arrangement that takes the bigger picture into account. I mean, look at me and Tabby. We make it work because we have the same goal."

"No offense, Vince," she replied, "but you and Tabby aren't my relationship goal."

"Fine." Vince sighed. "That's all I have to say about that. So this is really it between you."

"Yes, Vince. It's over. He was cheating, and unlike other members of this family, I'm not willing to put up with that."

That was a dig at his wife, but Vince didn't react. After a beat he shrugged. "And how do you feel about the official story—Calvin as the brokenhearted victim, soldiering on after your immature and possibly mentally unstable choices?"

She shot her cousin a baleful look. "I hate it, and I never agreed to it. What do you think?"

"Because I don't like seeing you dragged

through the mud over something you didn't do. You're better than that, and I don't think it's fair that your reputation gets tarnished to protect some political upstart."

Calvin was a senator—not exactly an upstart—but Bernie let that one go. "And what do you recommend?"

"Telling the truth." He spread his hands. "Is it so ridiculous?"

Bernie smothered a laugh. "Kind of, yes. I mean, I've been suggesting it from the beginning, but that isn't actually an option if my father is going to groom Calvin for the White House, is it?"

Vince muttered an oath. "*I'm* family. I'm the one who is supposed to have the family endorsement, not some political unknown."

"He's a senator. He didn't exactly drop from the sky," Bernadette quipped.

"Are you actually saying that you support making a president out of your cheating ex?" he demanded.

"No, of course not." She just couldn't resist poking holes in her cousin's flawed logic. Vince was the same kind of man that Calvin was—just slightly older and with a little more bulge.

"Well, neither am I. We're on the same team here, Bunny. Morgans first. I still have a chance to get the nomination, and if your father pulls his support early, it will signal failure to the voters."

Vince had never had a chance, and even Bernie could see that. She dug her sandal into the carpet. "I don't exactly have my father's ear right now."

"No, but you're sitting on a gold mine of information." He met her eye—in the same way she'd seen him do with voters. "We can do this together, Bunny."

A gold mine of information—he had no idea! She could drive more than one political future into the dust if she put her back into it.

"Do *what* together, exactly?" she asked.

"Take down Calvin McMann. He might have a gleaming reputation right now, but if his ex-fiancée were to tell the shocking story of how he cheated on her on the very day of her wedding…how he'd been cheating on her from day one—"

"From day one—how did you know that, Vince?" she interrupted.

Vince shrugged. "Anyone close enough knew it. He didn't hide it very well. She was the blonde—right? Some girlfriend he was told to dump in order to marry you."

Anger simmered up. Vince had known? They'd all known? No one had thought to clue her in to that fact early enough to end this without embarrassment?

"Anyway," Vince went on, "if you were to have some well-timed interviews—tap into the female voter—and tell them exactly why you ran out on your wedding, it would not only polish up your public image, but it would also knock Calvin down to earth. I can deal with him on a level playing field."

She eyed her cousin—honestly tempted. Calvin had broken her heart and embarrassed her publicly. Now he was spreading the rumor that she was mentally unstable. Revenge would feel good, but she knew better than to react emotionally. Vince wasn't here because he cared about her so much. He had his own motives.

"And you want me to do this for you," she clarified.

"For us." Vince shot her a grin. "Come on—a president in the family. You know you want *that*!"

"Your reputation isn't exactly stellar, either," she said.

Vince's expression soured. "I have a beautiful, poised wife who will stand by me and tell the world that I'm trustworthy. Besides, like I said, I'm here to clean up my mess. It'll be fine. You don't need to worry about it."

"But I am worried about it, Vince," she said quietly. "That little boy isn't a pawn in a presidential run. He's a child with a broken heart."

"Yeah, yeah…" Vince sighed. "Look, I obviously knew about him. I had no idea that Leanne would up and leave her husband. It was supposed to be a bit of fun, nothing else. I've done this before, and there was no problem. I may have other kids out there, but the husbands never knew any better. No harm, no foul. So when she showed up on my doorstep, you can imagine how angry I was."

Bernadette pitied Leanne for that eye-opening first visit. She'd have seen exactly how important she was to the senator…but she hadn't gone home, either. Had her cousin kept up some sort of relationship with her?

"Did you ever see the baby?" she asked.

"A few times. But after she signed the nondisclosure agreement and received her payment, she went away. Her death was tragic and untimely, and seriously inconvenient for me, too."

Inconvenience—that spoke volumes about how much he cared for her.

"Does Tabby know about your son?" she pressed.

"Tabby knows everything." Vince shot her an incredulous look. "If she didn't, I wouldn't be this calm. She and I are dealing with this together. We're a team."

A team. Yes, that was what marriage had always been in their family—a team sport.

"And what do you mean when you say you're going to clean up your mess?" she asked.

Vince shook his head. "Don't worry about that."

That wasn't reassuring in the least. Bernie wasn't worried about the Morgan reputation or about Vince's political future. She was worried about Ike.

"The child is already in a loving and stable home," she said. "I told my father that this wasn't a problem. The guardian doesn't want anything from you."

"Yet." Vince smiled indulgently. "This isn't my first rodeo."

"This isn't a threat." She tried to keep her voice calm, but she wasn't sure she succeeded.

"Then you're more naive than I thought." He sighed. "This isn't about Ike, it's about my campaign. If anyone discovers that kid, they'll use him to discredit me. I'll look like a monster—a man who not only cheated on his wife, but then abandoned the kid. Leaving him here in Back Woods, Ohio, isn't an option, Bunny. You should know that."

Bernadette's heart seemed to be lodged in her throat. "And what will you do with him?"

Vince shrugged. "Does it matter?"

She bit back a curse. "It matters *to me*."

"Boarding school. A nanny. A generous allowance. It wouldn't exactly be agony for him."

"It would be cheaper to just leave him where he is," she countered. "You could deal with the story if it ever came up, and paint a picture of how you financially supported him in a home where he was loved."

Vince paused, seemed to consider, then shook his head. "Too risky. I'm guessing he's with Leanne's ex. Am I right? Of course, I am. This whole situation is messy. It would open a whole new can of worms for the press."

But if Vince had his way with the nannies and boarding school, there would be no one who loved Ike for himself. Everyone in his life would be paid to be there. An idea leaped to mind. If Vince didn't trust Liam, what about her?

"What if I took him?" Bernadette asked. "What if I raised him?"

Vince shook his head. "You aren't exactly an old maid yet, Bunny. Your father would never allow it. I'll take care of my responsibilities, and you'll go home to your parents." Vince's expression turned stony. "Your father's patience has run out."

Bernadette's stomach turned. She was a grown woman with some funds to her name, but not enough to support her search for her mother and live on. Everyone knew what happened when Milhouse Morgan was crossed, and it wasn't pretty.

"My security guard can drive you back," Vince said, turning toward the door. "Give some thought to my idea about putting the truth out there."

One small sliver of truth. It wasn't much.

"I'm waiting on the Rolls-Royce," Bernie said. "I'm driving it back myself. I'm not going anywhere with your security team."

Vince shrugged, then pushed open the outer door and disappeared outside. Bernie stood there in the dim church, her heart hammering. The ironic part was, if she looked at this objectively, Vince's solution was probably the most attractive. She got revenge on her cheating ex, and put an end to those horrible rumors. She'd already angered her father, and at least she'd be siding with a Morgan.

But what about Ike? There was a curly-haired little boy with big, sad eyes who needed more than biological family—he needed love.

It was a busy afternoon, and Liam had gotten a good amount of work done on Bernie's Rolls-Royce, but even that didn't soothe his mind. He could hear the angry, raised voices, the echo of an amplified voice coming through the open garage door. Senator

Morgan was in town—there was no denying it. Bile rose in his stomach.

Three years ago, the town had clapped and cheered for the same man—and Leanne had come home with eyes sparkling. If he'd tried a little harder, would she still have cheated?

Maybe it was only a matter of who she chose. Maybe if it hadn't been Vince, she might have chosen someone closer to home.

The afternoon bled away, and Liam locked up the shop five minutes early. He saw the black SUV as soon as he turned onto his street, hunkered in his driveway, the motor running. Liam knew who it was, and while his chest ached at the thought, he wasn't surprised. Liam had someone Vince Morgan wanted.

Liam looked across the street—was Ike with Lucille still? He could only hope. He parked on the street and got out, and as soon as he was out of his truck, the back door of the SUV opened and the suit-clad senator joined him on the pavement.

Liam's hands balled into fists before he could think better of it, and he glared at the man who stood on his property with the casual stance of someone who could take whatever he liked. He tried to will away the anger—they needed to be able to talk if Liam was to have a chance of keeping Ike. He needed to have a civilized conversation with the man, but hadn't banked on feeling this level of rage.

Vince had aged since Liam had last seen him. There was a smattering of gray in his hair now, and he looked a little broader, a little rounder. A smile spread over the senator's face, but didn't reach his eyes.

"Mr. Wilson," Vince said, stepping forward and putting out his hand. Liam crossed his arms, ignoring the handshake. He'd shaken this man's hand before, just before his wife left him. He should shake it now—he knew that—but he couldn't bring himself to do it.

Vince dropped his hand. "Okay, I see how it is."

"And how is it, exactly?" Liam snapped. "Last I saw you, you asked for my vote."

"Yes, I did." Vince put on an expression of contrition, but it didn't ring true.

"You were also sleeping with my wife."

"Three years ago," Vince said. "And it was a mistake."

Yeah, no kidding.

"Can we go inside, Mr. Wilson?" Vince nodded earnestly. "Please? I know I disrespected your home the last time I was in town, but I can promise you that I will not do that again."

But the damage was already done, so that promise was worthless.

"You aren't coming inside my home."

"Then perhaps we could talk in my vehicle?" He pulled out a handkerchief and ran it over his forehead. "It's a hot day out, sir."

"You can stop the misters and sirs," Liam said. They both knew who held the power here, and it wasn't Liam. "And, no, I'm not getting into your car. If you want to talk to me, you do it here."

The senator sighed, then nodded. "Can we at least get out of the sun?"

Liam walked over to the shade of an old elm tree, and the senator followed. "You're here for your son, aren't you?"

Vince chewed the side of his cheek. "First of all, I came to apologize to you, man to man."

"Yeah?" That was hard to believe.

"I took advantage. Your wife was beautiful, and she was interested in me—"

"Shut up!" Liam grit his teeth. "Do you think I want to hear about this again?"

"I'm saying I was in the wrong," Vince said, keeping his voice low and calm. "I should never have done what I did, and I want to make that up to you."

"I don't think you can, Senator. Not where it comes to Leanne. Ike, on the other hand—"

"Hear me out, Mr. Wilson. I think I can at least make a start on mending things between us."

Mending things… It was like Vince still had some tiny hope that Liam would vote for him…or was he trying to seem vulnerable? Liam knew enough about this family to know better than that.

"How would you do that?" Liam asked. "Because Leanne's gone. There's no fixing dead, Mr. Senator."

"Life is expensive," Vince said, furrowing his brow just a bit too much. He seemed to be avoiding the mention of Leanne's death altogether. "Things come up, and a working man has a lot of bills. I know I can't undo the wrong I've done to you, but I can try to make the next few years a little easier on you. That's something that I can control."

Liam glanced across the street toward Lucille's house, and he thought he saw some movement through the living room window, but it was hard to tell.

"I understand you know my aunt," the senator went on.

"I do. She's a good woman."

"She'd want you to live more comfortably, too. I know that. She'd also want me to hurt a little because of what I did. So let's look at this as something that will make my aunt happier, as well." Vince pulled an envelope out of his suit jacket. "I have a check for you—"

"No."

"You haven't looked at it yet." The senator tapped the envelope. "It has enough zeroes to make me really squirm."

Did Senator Morgan buy off all the people he'd hammered down over the years? This little presentation looked awfully polished.

"And what do you want in return?" Liam demanded. "My forgiveness? A handshake? Maybe a manly hug? Do you want me to let bygones be bygones?"

Vince's composure faltered for a moment, and Liam felt a surge of satisfaction. He wasn't about to be handled, especially not by this smarmy politician.

"I want you to sign an agreement not to speak about this to anyone." The senator's voice had changed—he seemed to have abandoned his political drawl. "And I want you to take the money. Then I want you to live your life and never look back."

"I'd be willing to do that, Senator," Liam said, "if that meant you'd leave Ike alone, too."

"Well, now…" The smoothness was back. "That little boy is my son. And I can't just walk away from him now, can I?"

"You didn't care about him before."

Vince shook his head. Tears came to his eyes, and he cleared his throat twice. "I tried. Leanne was angry. I was married, and I wouldn't leave my wife the way Leanne left you. She wouldn't let me near my son, and I didn't fight her. I asked, though. Repeatedly. But it broke my heart. I have five children—four with my wife and Ike. I know you don't think too much of me, Mr. Wilson, and I don't blame you. But I'm a father, and I love my kids. I'm truly sorry for your loss, but I need to bring my son home."

Liam stared at him, stunned. Was it possible that the senator would be a true father to Ike after all? He hated the jealousy he felt at the thought. Did Liam even have a right to feel territorial of another man's child? Or was this his gut warning him that something here wasn't right?

"I'd like to bring him home today," the senator said. "With your blessing."

Liam caught his gaze flicker over Liam's shoulder toward Lucille's house. Vince knew exactly where his son was, and Liam chilled. He was being handled.

"I'm Ike's legal guardian," Liam said. "If you take him out of my care, that would be kidnapping. A felony. Think of how that will play in the media."

Vince chewed the side of his cheek, then nodded slowly. "I understand that this is overwhelming. Take a day and think it through. Talk to my aunt. Think about your finances. Think about what's best for Ike. And then we can talk again." Vince smiled and put a hand on Liam's shoulder. "Would that be okay with you, Mr. Wilson?"

Liam had to hold myself back from driving a fist straight into the senator's smug face. Vince gave Liam's shoulder a squeeze, then he turned and walked back to his SUV. He got inside, and the door slammed, shielding Vince behind a tinted window.

Liam hated him, but the senator had a point. He was Ike's father, and who was Liam to stand between them? Liam stood there and watched as the SUV pulled out and slipped away down the street. He had no idea what to think, but he knew what he felt—and for the first time in a long time, he was scared.

CHAPTER EIGHTEEN

BERNADETTE WATCHED AS the SUV pulled away and Liam stood in the shade of his large elm tree, hands in his pockets and his face unreadable. He was motionless for a moment, then he looked over at the window where Bernie stood with Ike in her arms, and her heart broke. Liam was a good man, and he didn't deserve to be pulverized in the Morgan machine, but he would be.

Lucille came over and gave Bernie a wary look. "You know your cousin better than I do—what was that?"

Bernadette shook her head. "I don't know."

But she'd find out. Bernadette handed Ike to Lucille.

"Bunny?" Ike reached for her again.

"I'll just be on the porch, sweetie." She hoped she sounded reassuring. Lucille nodded, and Bernie pulled open the front door. Liam was already heading across the street, and she met him at the bottom of the steps.

"Is Ike inside?" Liam asked.

She nodded. "He's with Lucille."

Liam rubbed his hands over his face. "Your cousin wants to give me a check and have me sign some papers—"

That was how this worked, and Bernie's stomach sank. She led the way to the stairs and sat down. It took a moment, but eventually Liam sank down onto the step next to her.

"And you said?" she asked.

"I said no." Liam shook his head. "I'm not for sale. He wanted to take Ike with him today, and I told him that he'd be kidnapping. So he left."

Bernie was mildly impressed. "That was a smart answer. The thing is, Vince is only interested in Ike because of the way it would look if the media got hold of this. He's interested in his career—nothing more. So you made the right threat there."

"Are you sure about that?" Liam leaned forward, his elbows on his knees. "He seemed pretty sincere about loving his kids and all that."

Bernie laughed softly. So Vince had put up a convincing act, had he? "He told me that if he gets custody of Ike, he'll be setting him up with boarding schools and a nanny."

"Not exactly hell on earth," Liam said.

Bernadette knew the truth behind the code words. And she'd attended boarding schools herself, but her mother had never handed her over to a nanny. Kitty was nothing if not an attentive mother.

"No, you don't get it." Bernie swallowed hard. "He'd be shunted off into hiding. No family, no support, no love. Just a bunch of strangers and a school system. Vince has no interest in being a father to Ike. He only wants to keep him under wraps."

Liam's face paled, and he looked over at Bernie, meeting her eye. "When did you discuss this?"

"A couple of hours ago. He met up with me after his big speech downtown."

Liam nodded. "So what will happen now?"

That was the problem. Bernie knew exactly what would happen now, and she hated to be the one to tell him. But he deserved to know the dangers.

"My cousin won't want to bring this to court, because he'll then have to acknowledge his son publicly. If he's intent upon getting Ike safely tucked away in some summer house with a nanny, then he'll focus on you."

"Me?" Liam barked out a low laugh. "Like he'll come and beat me up?"

"Har har." She smiled wryly. "No, he'll find ways to pressure you financially until you have no choice but to sign his papers and accept his money."

"My garage?"

Bernie nodded. She didn't know exactly what Vince would do, but he'd likely concentrate on ruining the business. Damage to the building, perhaps, or rumors about poor service and fraud. If Vince cared enough, he might even suggest a big chain of auto shops set up a garage in Runt River. She'd seen her family at work before, and Vince wouldn't simply walk away because a small fish had stood up to him.

"So what are my options here?" Liam asked. "That legal team you mentioned— would it help?"

"It couldn't hurt." She nodded. "And I'm good for it. When I get back to New York, that's top of my agenda."

"But it doesn't sound like Vince's plans would be entirely legal anyway." Liam looked gutted, his eyes hollow. Bernie slipped an arm through his and leaned her head against his strong shoulder. He'd been her strength for the last few days, but now he needed some support in return. She knew what was coming, and for a man with Liam's pride and determination, the blow would be agony.

"If Vince does get guardianship of Ike, I'll keep tabs on him. I'll visit him at school, bring him presents, keep in touch with him."

Liam leaned his cheek against Bernie's head. "Thanks."

"He'll never be alone, I can promise you that," she whispered. But it still wouldn't be the same as being raised in a loving home.

"So you're going back?" he asked quietly.

"When the car is finished, yes."

"Okay."

He straightened slightly, and she did, too. If she'd never come to Runt River, Ike would have stayed under the Morgan radar. If Bernie had never come looking for her aunt, Lucille could have continued to keep an eye on Ike and made sure he had everything he needed. That was the thing—Bernadette hadn't actually been needed here. She'd blown into town and demolished everything by her very presence.

And now she had to do her best to help put things back together again.

The door behind them opened, and Ike came clattering out onto the porch.

"I got goldfish!" he declared, holding out a bag of orange crackers.

Bernie glanced back at her aunt, and they exchanged a hollow look. Then Bernie held out her arms to Ike. "Come here, kiddo. Share with me?"

Ike was only too happy to oblige. After a few minutes of playing, Liam took Ike back across the street for supper, and Lucille sank down onto the step next to Bernie.

"Vince won't stop until he has his way," Bernie said quietly.

Lucille nodded slowly. "He's a Morgan through and through."

"What am I supposed to do?" Bernie asked, with tears in her eyes. "I want to help, but I'm a Morgan, too… All I know is how to fight fire with fire."

Lucille handed her something small and plastic, and when Bernie looked closer, her breath caught. It was a tiny hospital bracelet.

"Is this—" She couldn't finish the sentence.

"When you were released from the hospital after you were born, I took this."

"But why?" Bernie whispered.

"Information is power." Lucille smiled sadly. "I thought it might come in handy one day."

The information had been typed into a slip of paper and then slid into the plastic covering. Her birthday was recorded, some numbers that didn't mean anything to her, but above all of that was a name: Lynn Warren.

"Is that my name?" Bernie asked.

"Your mother's. In hospitals, babies are identified by their mother's name. Your mother is Lynn Warren. It's a place to start."

Bernadette swallowed hard, her hands shaking. She had a name—it was more than she'd even allowed herself to hope for.

"Do you know where she lives?" Bernie asked.

Lucille shook her head. "No. I did try to find her—I told you that before. I searched and searched, but I didn't have the same resources available to me anymore. And if I found her, what would I say? What could I even offer her?"

"But from New York, with the right people, I might be able to," Bernie said.

"That was my thought." Lucille smoothed her hands over her thighs. "It's different at the bottom, Bernie. I might pretend that I haven't stepped down, but I have. I need to be honest about that, because I don't want you to do something you'll regret, and then live to blame me for it."

"Like what?" she asked.

"Like give it all up." Lucille licked her lips. "If you make that choice, you have to know what you're walking into. I've had a good life. I've loved a man dearly and been a part of this town…but I gave up power, privilege, travel and a reach long enough to make a serious difference."

"You have made a difference," Bernie said quietly. "You were here for me."

"But there was a time when I would have been able to snap my fingers and hand you your mother's address." Lucille's voice was soft, but strong. "And that's the kind of convenience you can start to take for granted. Life might be simpler down here, but it's also harder. Money matters—and people work hard to keep enough of it in the bank to keep body and soul together. They don't have any clout, and if someone bullies them, they don't get the last word. You need to know the reality of the situation, Bernie."

"Okay." Bernie sucked in a breath. "I've already decided to go back to New York, liquidate some assets in my name, and hire my own private eye and legal team."

"Good." Lucille nodded. "I'm glad to hear it. Use the privilege to work for you, Bernadette, because once you let it go, you can't get it back. Take it from someone who's been there."

Bernadette pushed herself to her feet and looked down at the tiny hospital bracelet in her hand. It was a start, and God willing, she'd be able to track down her birth mother and make up for some of the damage her parents had done.

"Auntie, you have no idea what this means to me."

"I have some idea," Lucille said with a sad smile. "Good luck finding your mother, Bernadette. I have a feeling she's missed you something fierce."

LIAM SAT ON the side of his bed, a storybook on his lap. He'd pulled the blinds to block out the evening sunlight, and Ike sat up in bed, his little legs splayed in front of him.

"Are you tired yet, Ike?" Liam asked. He always asked—he didn't know what he expected, but he asked.

"No," said Ike. "I wanna play."

"Well, it's very late."

"It's day!" Ike pointed to a crack in the blinds, letting in a shaft of sunlight.

"It's summer, Ike," Liam said. "It's always like that in summer."

"Can Bunny come?" Ike smiled angelically up into Liam's face. "Can Bunny come for stories?"

Liam chuckled. "No, Ike. Bunny is at Aunt Lucille's. She has to go to bed, too. Everybody has to go to bed. It's nighttime."

A lie, but Liam had found that it worked to keep Ike thinking bedtime thoughts when he'd rather play. He had Ike here for—what was it?—six weeks now, and he'd picked up a few tricks of his own.

"Bunny's in bed?" Ike asked doubtfully.

"Yep. She's in her jammies, and she's had a glass of milk, and she's brushed her teeth, and she's yawning so big…"

Ike yawned in response, and Liam smiled.

He shouldn't be thinking about Bernadette and beds, because he'd been realizing lately that he'd love to share one with her. Three years of sleeping alone had gotten him used to spreading out in the center of his—until Ike arrived, at least—but spending time with Bernie reminded him of all the parts of marriage that he missed...the soft scent of a woman around his home, spooning at night, waking up to hair in his face. Okay, he'd never been keen on that last one, but if he had the chance to share his life with a woman, he'd never complain about it again.

Except that Bernie wasn't a candidate if he wanted to settle down. She might have helped him to see what he missed in having a partner, but she wasn't a woman he could trust. She came from the wrong family for that. And his feelings for her...he'd just have to get those under control.

"Okay, so let's read the story, Ike," Liam said, opening the book. "Once upon a time there was a little boy named Ike."

"Ike?" Ike's eyes widened. "That's me!"

"Is it?" Liam looked at the page closer, flipped back to the cover in an exaggerated display, then shrugged. "Well, look at that."

Ike scooted closer and looked at the page, enthralled. How many more bedtimes would they have together? Liam didn't exactly like sleeping on a twin mattress on the floor, but he'd be willing to continue in order to keep this little guy around. Bernadette may have shown him what he missed in marriage, but Ike was showing him what he was missing out on as a father.

"So once upon a time there was a little boy named Ike who lived in a forest…"

The story was really about a racoon who lived in a forest and went to the city on a vacation, but Ike loved having his name in stories so much that Liam put his name in every single one. So far, Ike was amazed every night. This was fun, finding ways to bring delight to that little face. And it was easy enough—Ike wasn't a hard kid to please.

Ike cuddled up to Liam's arm, his breath warm against his biceps. The story went on, about a little raccoon who packed a bag and went to the city to visit his auntie. He rummaged through garbage and watched the cars from the roofs of buildings, but he started to get homesick after a while.

"Daddy?" Ike said, tapping his arm. "Ikey misses Mommy."

Liam held out his arms, and Ike crawled into them. "I know, buddy," he said huskily. "I'm so sorry about that. I should have chosen a different book."

How was he supposed to fix this? How was he supposed to make any of this easier? If Vince managed to get custody of Ike, then Bernie could look in on him, but Liam had been a kid in a system before. Granted, foster homes weren't quite the same thing as summer homes with nannies, but Ike would learn some similar life lessons there. Take care of yourself. Don't let anyone see what you're feeling. Don't get attached. Liam didn't want that life for Ike. He'd taken the boy in to save him from the foster system, but it would be terrible to have him dumped into an equally sterile situation if Vince sent him off to some nanny whose loyalty was to the family, not to Ike.

Ike needed his mother still. He needed her protection, her love. And Liam was doing his best to stand in, but he wasn't going to pass muster, either. Not if he couldn't make this arrangement permanent.

"Bunny?" Ike pleaded.

In some respects, everything had improved once Bernadette arrived. Ike had settled down, he'd softened up, he'd started smiling. Before Bernie arrived, Ike hadn't seemed to like Liam too much—maybe sensing that he was the disappointing replacement for Leanne. And here Liam was, hoping he could keep raising Ike, but would it even work once Bernadette was gone?

Except all of this drama had descended upon them because of Bernie's arrival. If she'd gone anywhere else, Vince would have kept ignoring Ike for a while longer, at least. It was possible that he'd have left him alone indefinitely. Bernie's presence had both healed and exploded everything he'd been trying to build. That included his heart.

"Close your eyes a little bit, Ike," Liam said quietly, and he patted Ike's back. It felt good to cradle this boy in his arms. "Let me think about it while you close your eyes…"

That was another trick he'd discovered a couple of nights ago—putting Ike off for long enough that either Ike forgot, or the moment passed.

Should he call Bernie? It might be wise

to encourage Ike to bond with her as much as possible if she'd be the one checking in on him when Vince cloistered the kid away somewhere. But Ike's breathing was coming more slowly now, and Liam kept rubbing the boy's back in slow circles the way he'd seen Bernie do it that first night she'd arrived. He still wanted to be able to do this on his own. He didn't want to rely on Bernie too much, either, because he was still Ike's legal guardian, and she wasn't sticking around.

Whenever Liam thought about raising Ike lately, he'd pictured Bernie there, too. Stupid—he knew that! Not only was she a Morgan, but she had a life and a massive inheritance in New York. She wouldn't have anything here for her in Runt River. So if he was able to keep Ike, he'd better adjust his expectations to something more realistic. Bernie wouldn't be going along for trips to the park, and she wouldn't sit with him on the step after a long day. She wouldn't be there for fevers or for birthdays. It would just be him and Ike, and maybe one day he'd meet someone else, but the thought of someone else seemed murky and distant.

What was he doing to himself here? This

had never been the plan. Except he'd gotten attached, and this little boy didn't know that Liam wasn't supposed to love him… Somehow, Liam's heart hadn't figured that out, either.

Ike's hand hung limp down Liam's chest, and he lifted the little arm and let it drop—his test to see if Ike was sleeping. Ike's hand plunked back against his chest, and he didn't move.

"All right, buddy," Liam said softly as he tipped Ike down onto his pillow. "Sleep tight."

Ike curled up into a little ball as his head hit the cool cotton, and Liam pulled the sheet over his shoulders. Ike used up about one percent of the bed—the center one percent—and that was all it took for him to own it. Hearts seemed to work the same way. Liam looked down at Ike's sleeping face for a moment, then stood.

Ike didn't know what was coming, and neither did Liam, but he knew one thing for sure—he'd never forget this boy. If Vince took his son back, Liam hoped that a small part of Ike's heart held on to these memories, and that one day he'd come back to visit. A lump rose in Liam's throat.

Why was it that he always loved the people most capable of breaking his heart?

CHAPTER NINETEEN

THE MOON WAS full that night, the light illuminating the front yard. Bernadette sat in the living room, an untouched cup of tea beside her. Lucille had gone to bed hours ago, but Bernie's mind wouldn't stop spinning. Everything she trusted had been turned upside down in the past two weeks, and she felt as if she'd been torn down and somehow it was up to her to rebuild.

It was hardly fair. She hadn't asked for any of this, but here she was.

Her cell phone felt heavy in her hand, and she stared down into the glowing screen. She needed to talk to her mom—Kitty. She'd heard Aunt Lucille's side of things, and she needed to hear her mother's side, too. It was late—past ten—but her mother tended to stay up and read at night. She'd be awake, as she always was, propped against a pillow with her bedside lamp on... Her father would be snoring already—he was the "early to bed, early to rise" kind of businessman, and he slept with both earplugs and an eye mask.

Bernie's finger hovered over her mother's cell phone number for a moment, and she wondered if she was ready for this. She'd been avoiding her mom, afraid of her reaction to the wedding, but with the newest revelations, that felt strangely distant—like it had already slipped into the past. Maybe her mom was thinking about her tonight, too.

Bernie pressed the button and put the phone to her ear.

"Bernie?" Kitty's voice sounded alarmed.

"Hi, Mom."

Silence, then some rustling, as if her mother was getting out of bed.

"Look, Mom, I know you said you didn't want to talk unless I came back, but—"

"Never mind that." Her mother's voice was thick with emotion. "But when *are* you coming back? You need to come home."

"When the car is fixed. Don't tell Dad, but the engine gave out on me, and I'm having it taken care of out here. I'll bring it back in good shape."

"We aren't worried about the car, Bunny."

"Okay…well, that's good."

She had a feeling her father might have something else to say about that, which was why she was asking for the secrecy. "I saw the news story—that I'm mentally unstable."

"I didn't agree with that," her mother interjected. "I wanted Calvin to say that it had been a mutual decision, but he was embarrassed…"

"So Calvin went rogue on that?" Bernadette sighed. "So why is Dad still backing him?"

"Because he has a real chance of being president." Her mother's voice firmed. "He might not follow orders terribly well, but he's a good candidate and if he owes us…"

She knew the drill, the goal, the hopeful payoff. She knew all this, and she listened as her mother went through it again. The Morgans knew what they were after, and they didn't get derailed over something as small as an insult to their daughter. They talked for a few minutes about the wedding fallout, the pile of gifts that needed to be returned to guests, the constant barrage of questions from friends and acquaintances, the stress of it all… As if finding her fiancée cheating hadn't been stressful for Bernadette.

"Mom, I didn't really want to talk about Calvin," Bernadette said after they'd exhausted the topic. "Lucille told me something…and I needed to hear it from you."

Silence.

"Mom?"

"What did she tell you?" Her mother's voice had tightened.

"That I'm adopted."

"Your aunt is a lunatic. You know that."

"So I'm not adopted, then?" Bernadette leaned her head onto her hand. She had the hospital bracelet—was that proof? There was silence on the other end, and all Bernie could hear was her mother's breathing.

"It's—" Her mother sighed. "Oh… I didn't ever think the time was right to tell you about it, but… Bernie, I couldn't conceive. We tried every treatment, hired every doctor, and it just wasn't happening for us."

"Mom, lots of people adopt. I don't get why you wouldn't tell me."

"It was…" Her mother paused. "Mercy House had all those girls having babies when they were too young to take care of them, no money to raise them, no hope for their futures and… Well, so many of those girls were looking to give their babies up. Can you imagine how that tore at my heart? There I was longing for a baby of my own, and those girls were just giving their children away!"

"I'm sure it was more complicated than that." Bernadette sighed. "No one just gives up a baby without a struggle."

"Anyway, we adopted you. End of story."

End of story. That was not the end of Bernie's story, and certainly not the end of her biological mother's.

"What about my birth mother?" Bernie asked.

"She didn't want you. I did. I wanted you more than anything."

Tears welled in Bernadette's eyes. "I know you love me, Mom, but I need to know about her."

"There is nothing to know." Her mother's voice wavered. "She was a teenager who had nothing to offer."

"Where did she go after I was born?"

"I don't know. I don't care."

At least the story was confirmed. That was something. Bernadette leaned back in the chair and let out a long sigh. "If I wanted to find her?"

"You won't."

"Why are you so certain?"

"Because she didn't want you!" Her mother's voice rose. "Bunny, you have to let this go. This is why I never told you about it. You are a Morgan—do you hear me? You are *mine.*"

"You keep saying she didn't want me, but Lucille says otherwise." Bernie swallowed against a lump rising in her throat. "She said my mother changed her mind—"

"Your mother…" Tears were in Kitty's voice now. "*I'm* your mother."

Bernadette's heart was torn. She knew that—Kitty was the mom who'd raised her and adored her. Nothing would undo that. As Liam had said, adoption counted. She was most certainly a Morgan, but this was no ordinary adoption, either. There was a shady side to this, and Bernadette couldn't let that go.

"But did she change her mind at the last minute?" Bernie pressed.

"No." Kitty's voice turned hard. "No!"

Someone was lying, and in her heart, Bernie suspected that Kitty was covering up her deepest shame right now. She'd never admit to having intimidated a teenager into giving up a baby. If she'd kept her secret this long, she wouldn't give it up that easily.

"Your aunt Lucille is a sick and vengeful woman," her mother said. "This is all about an engagement ring…stupid! She's angry and bitter. That's all. I can't believe she'd stoop to trying to turn you against us. We're your *parents*."

Bernadette knew her mother was lying. Her mom's version of things didn't make sense. Why would she hide an adoption if it was all aboveboard? Why hide away birth certificates and insist that hospital pictures with newborns were somehow crass and low-class? She'd gone to great lengths to hide this adoption…for no reason? It didn't ring true, but more than that, she could hear the lie in her mother's voice. And in spite of it all, her heart ached for the only mother she'd ever known.

"I'm coming home, Mom." She wanted to reassure her mother somehow, make this better. She wanted to start on her plan to get some cash pulled together and hire her own legal team. She had so much to do, and she couldn't hide from her real life any longer.

"When?" her mother pressed.

"In a couple of days. As soon as the car is fixed, I'm coming back."

"Good…" Her mother sighed. "Leave the car. Come now."

"No, Mom." She sighed. "I'm coming with the car. Don't worry. I'm perfectly safe, and I'll be back soon enough."

They talked for a few more minutes, and then said their goodbyes. After she'd hung up, Bernie tossed her phone onto the table next to her untouched tea and heaved a sigh. Everything was different, and yet it wasn't. No matter what happened all those years ago, Kitty Morgan was her mother—and her love for her mom wasn't going to evaporate because Kitty had done something wrong. Parents didn't stop loving their children, even when they did horrible things…and Bernie couldn't stop loving her mother, either. That was part of the deal—that was family. But how did her birth mother fit into that?

Guilt wormed up in the back of her mind. Maybe more should change now that she knew the truth, and yet, if her love for her mom changed, she'd feel guiltier still. Bernie had no choice in any of this, and yet here she sat feeling guilty and angry.

She pulled a hand through her hair and stood. She needed fresh air—something to clear her mind. She left her cell phone where it was. She didn't want to talk to anyone right now. Well, not just anyone.

Bernie went out onto the porch and closed the front door softly behind her. She was barefoot, and her summer dress felt a little flimsy against the breeze. As she looked across the street, she saw a form sitting on Liam's front steps. She'd know him anywhere, and she felt a sudden wave of relief.

What was it about that man that made her want to run straight into his arms every time her own world turned on her? Liam rose when he saw her, and she picked her way across the lush lawn, then crossed the street, pebbles digging into the soles of her feet. When she reached him, she stopped short and looked up into his face. His eyes were soft, and he gave her a funny look.

"You okay?"

"Not really." She felt tears burn her eyes and tried to blink them back. She hadn't come here for that—not for pity and not for comfort.

"What happened?" he asked, his voice rumbling deep in his chest. Liam brushed her hair away from her face, and her words evaporated. Was she using him as an escape? No, it was more than that, even though she knew better. She should be strong. She should be dealing with this alone—because getting used to Liam's support wasn't sensible. When she didn't answer, he added, "Ike's asleep upstairs. You want to sit with me for a bit?"

That was the best suggestion she'd heard yet—to be together in the quiet, let it all melt away. She wanted to sit with him and lean her head against the comforting warmth of his shoulder. She wanted to listen to the rumble of his voice in the cool evening air, and she wanted to let everything else disappear. But nothing *would* disappear.

"Liam, how long until my car is done?" She rubbed a hand over her eyes.

"I'll finish it up tomorrow at best. Probably the day after. Why?"

His dark eyes glimmered in the low light, and she drank in the sight of him—the stubble on his chin, the way his hair was rumpled, and she was willing to bet he had no idea…

"Because I have to go home," she said, her voice catching. "I need to go back to New York."

LIAM BLINKED. HE HADN'T exactly expected *that*. Her cousin was here demanding Ike, and she was leaving? He'd known she would go eventually, but why couldn't she wait until that was settled? He cleared his throat.

"Now?"

"When the car is done."

Yeah, that didn't make it easier—he'd be done with it soon. He'd known this moment was coming, but the way his heart had constricted had caught him off guard.

"Okay." He took a step back.

"Liam, you knew I had to go back." She looked toward her aunt's house and then back at him. "And you need a legal team. I can provide that. But liquidating investments takes time, and the longer I stay here, the longer I'm putting off the representation you're going to need to hold off my cousin—"

Is that what she thought—that he needed her to rescue him? Was he just some project for her—a glimpse into the life of the lower-middle class? Anger slid over the more complicated feelings, and he shook his head.

"I don't need your help, Bernie."

She stared at him incredulously. "Yes, you do."

"I need—" But his mind wouldn't pull it all together. He didn't need her to swoop in with all the help *money* could buy. He needed her to be here—to understand him…to *stay*. Was that what he really wanted from her? He hadn't put it all together until now, but he realized that it was—he wanted her to stay here, make a life with him, raise Ike with him. Was it logical? Maybe not… His heart was saying something that went against every logical thought in his head…

He needed some time to sort that out, but he wasn't going to get it. He wanted her with him, not dashing off to the city, because he knew exactly what that meant—whatever had been building between them was about to end.

"You need a legal team," she said, her voice low. "And I can get that for you."

"I need *you*." His voice sounded rough in

his own ears, and he hated that. He wasn't trying to bark at her.

Bernadette froze, her lips parting ever so slightly as she met his gaze, and he had to hold himself back from kissing her.

"I just ended an engagement, Liam, and—"

"I know." He swallowed hard. "I know…" He scrubbed his hand through his hair. "You've been betrayed and hurt and people don't just bounce back from that. And I knew that from the first minute I met you. So you don't have to explain anything or—"

Liam stepped closer—why did the twelve or so inches separating them feel like too much?

"You need legal counsel—"

"Would you stop with that?" He looked away, frustrated, then back down into her face. She wasn't shocked, and she didn't back up, either. He was a big man, and he knew he could intimidate, but she hadn't even flinched. "Bernie, I never meant to feel anything more for you, it's just…"

"More than what?" she whispered.

"More than friendship, more than—" How was he supposed to put it into words? He couldn't—it was too tangled, too complicated—so he did the next best thing and slid a hand into her hair and tugged her closer, then he dropped his lips down to hers. She inhaled sharply through her nose, but she didn't pull away, and as he moved over her mouth, he felt her soften in his hands, leaning into him. He slipped his arms around her, pulling her as close as he dared, and yet it still didn't feel close enough. He'd go too far if he weren't careful, and he broke off the kiss with a shaky breath.

"That," he said huskily.

"Oh…"

He hadn't released her, and she didn't pull away. Why did she have to fit so perfectly in his arms? Why did she have to kiss him back in a way that melted his inhibitions? He'd be wise to have a few. Her family chewed up people like him and spat them out—they had already. And here he was, kissing the enemy in his own front yard.

"I know I shouldn't. I know the timing is awful," he murmured, letting his arms slide down her sides as he released her. "But I'm in love with you."

She blinked, opened her mouth as if to say something, then closed it again. Yeah, he was equally shocked, but as the words came out, he knew them to be true.

"Me, too." Her voice was barely louder than a whisper, and he felt a surge of elation. She loved him, too? A woman like her—beautiful, smart, from a world beyond his greasy shop—could fall for a guy like him? "But I can't, Liam. I've been lied to so many times… I'm having trouble trusting anyone right now."

He'd known it all along. Falling for her had been a mistake, and there was no way around that.

"Do you have to leave?" he asked quietly.

She nodded and dropped her gaze. "I know my birth mother's name now. I can sidestep Mercy House and hire an investigator. My family would never need to know what I was doing. But I still need them—without their money and their clout, I'd have no hope of finding her. Lucille already tried."

"You couldn't do that from here?"

"If I stayed, Liam, I'd infuriate my father. I might come from money, but very little of it is actually in my name. I'm an heiress, not an actual money-holder. If I stay here, it's the equivalent of walking away from my family, and that would have consequences—financial consequences."

"A price too big to pay." He heard the bitterness in his own voice.

"If I stayed, I'd be giving up any chance of finding my mother."

"And the life of an heiress." Because that had to factor in—the clothes, the car, the lifestyle that he couldn't even fathom... He could never offer that.

"It isn't about the money, Liam! This is about safety, security. Damn it, Liam, this is about Ike! I have...options...right now. I can help him. I can help you. But I can't do that from here, and I can't do it if I'm cut off from the family money. That's just reality. I have to go back! Can you see that?"

"Yes." And he could, but he didn't have to like it. She was silent for a moment, and then she looked up into his face hopefully.

"You could come with me."

He frowned. "To New York?"

She nodded, her eyes brightening in the moonlight. She put a cool hand on his forearm. "My father owns an entire garage filled with antique cars. He's always acquiring more and fixing them up. Sometimes he sells a few…but there are a lot of employees to maintain all of them. I could ask him to give you a job. He'd pay you well—I'd see to that. It's a dream job for a car lover. And we'd be closer together, at least. My family might even feel more comfortable with Ike nearby. It might be the solution."

Moving to New York, working for the money man behind the politicians, keeping Ike under their noses… No, that wasn't a solution. That was some sort of purgatory. He wasn't about to settle for some heart-wrenching secret relationship with Berna-dette, a poor man in a rich woman's world. He knew where he belonged—right here in Runt River—no matter how much it hurt.

"Bernie," he said quietly. "I can't do that. I own my business here. I'm my own man. I can't just go be some car lackey for your dad. I'm sure the pay is good, but…my life is here. I've built something—I'm not a kid starting out—and while it might not look like much to you, it means a whole lot to me."

"I know," she said quietly. "I was grasp-ing at straws. I just want… I need my fam-ily, Liam. And I'm trying to find a way to have it all."

But he wasn't a Morgan, and their interests weren't aligned with his. He'd be a bump in their road.

"I don't trust your family," he admitted.

"We aren't monsters." But her voice quavered as she said it. She knew the family she came from—she'd just spent the last few days warning him of exactly what they were capable of. Now she was defending them?

"Some of you are," he retorted. "Vince, for example."

"Vince is a jerk, but he's—"

He was a cheater, a liar, a manipulator and he would do anything to get political power. She could call it what she wanted, but that combination was chilling.

"If you're a regular person, Bernie," he said, trying to keep his tone low, but irritation simmered nonetheless, "then your family is incredibly dangerous. I can't fight them. I can't demand their respect. I can't offer them anything. I'm nothing to them, and as a result, they'd eat me alive. You know that."

"So you're asking me to stay, but for what?" Tears sparkled in her eyes. "I'm a Morgan. You can't change it. I come with a family you can't trust. What would I be staying for?"

"This is my fault." He felt his eyes well up, and he cleared his throat. "I knew I needed to keep my distance, and I didn't."

"I'm not some weak little mouse who gets swept along."

"I know...and that's what I love about you." He swallowed hard. "It's not going to work, Bernie. My loving you isn't going to be enough...it never seems to be."

"I'm not Leanne." Her lips trembled. "Whatever happens between us, Liam, don't lump me in with her."

"I know." She'd stabbed right down to the heart of it. "But I'm still the same guy. Let's do what we can for Ike, Bernie. It's supposed to be about him, right?"

A family of his own would be very good for Ike, but Liam couldn't make that happen, either. All of this was bigger than he was. He didn't have the money or the influence that her family wielded, but he wouldn't pull his forelock for Milhouse Morgan, either. Not even for Bernie. He was man enough to love a woman with his whole heart, but he was also man enough to let her go, and to deal with the pain on his own.

He nodded across the street where a light

had flicked on in an upstairs window. "You should probably get back." His throat was tight.

She wiped an errant tear from her cheek. "Goodbye, Liam."

"Bye." The word choked off in his throat, and he didn't trust himself to say more. She turned and made her way across the street, and it took every ounce of willpower he had to keep himself from striding after her, and pulling her into his arms. But there was no point—one night wouldn't change the future. He waited until she was safely back inside Lucille's house, the door closed behind her, and then he slowly climbed the steps to his own.

He'd lost a wife, and he'd thought that was the worst pain possible—a woman walking out on him because she didn't love him anymore. But tonight, he'd lost a woman who loved him, too, who felt the same yearning to close that distance between them that he did. Somehow, that made it worse. But it had been doomed from the start.

CHAPTER TWENTY

BERNADETTE FOLDED A T-shirt and tossed it into her suitcase. She wasn't leaving today, but it couldn't hurt to be ready. She sighed, then sank onto the edge of her bed. She should have known better than to let herself fall for some guy in Runt River. How had this happened? He was strong, sweet, rugged…everything that Calvin wasn't. Maybe that was all this was…a rebound.

She grabbed a pair of jeans and shook them out, tears welling in her eyes. She'd cried for Calvin, but not like this… Calvin had been a smart choice, a logical decision. Liam was neither of those things, and it made this hurt so much more, because she'd fallen for him against her better judgment.

She crumpled the jeans in her hands and pushed them against her eyes. She was helping him. She sniffled and shook the jeans out again. She could do something useful if she went back to New York—she could help him fight her snake of a cousin, but he didn't want it that way.

But staying was impossible. If she stayed, she'd give up too much, and even Lucille had warned her against that. She'd never before imagined what it would be like to live without the money and family influence, but Lucille had done it, and Bernadette didn't want to live in a little house with threadbare furniture and nothing to do but tend a garden. Unless she put that Harvard degree to work and started a business of her own... This was a town desperate for jobs, and she could make a difference here, except in order to do that, she'd have to give up a chance of making a difference elsewhere.

She'd been raised for better than Runt River, for more. She'd been raised a Morgan, and she'd inherit a fortune. She could do good things with that money—help people. One day when the money was hers, she could fund charities that would help single parents in Liam's situation. She could back politicians who made a difference. And if Vince got his hands on Ike, then she'd need to be in this position of power if she were to be in the boy's life.

What was so wrong with privilege?

But this mental argument helped nothing, because it didn't solve the problem. Liam didn't want that life, and he didn't trust her family. She could understand that all too well. And she'd been lied to and cheated on—she couldn't just follow her heart. That would be foolish.

"I'm a Morgan," she said aloud, and she folded the jeans, finally, and tossed them into the suitcase. She couldn't apologize for who she was.

There was a tap on the bedroom door, and Bernie turned to see her aunt poke her head in. She held a folded towel in front of her like a shield.

"Packing?" she asked quietly.

"I'm not leaving today," she said. "But the car is almost done, and I have to—"

The tears welled again, and she swallowed hard. This hadn't been the plan—falling for Liam, or letting it show. She was supposed to be stronger than this. This little town was supposed to be nothing more than a pit stop... But it had become more than that. Everything had broadened, deepened and grown so much more complicated.

"Ah." Lucille came into the room, depositing the towel on the top of the scratched dresser. "I see."

Bernadette picked up another T-shirt, then let it drop to her lap. "If you'd stayed in the family's good graces," she said, "you could have done more."

"More." Lucille looked around the room. "Maybe."

"Do you regret it?"

Lucille smiled sadly. "I miss them. They might have been flawed and frustrating, but they were my family."

Bernadette nodded. "I can't stay, Lucille. I have too much to do. I can't help Ike from here, and I can't find my mother, either."

"And Liam wants you to stay."

How had she guessed? Bernadette smoothed the T-shirt against her legs. If she kept busy, kept focused, she could keep moving in the right direction.

"He loves me," she said woodenly. "But it's impossible. I have to go back, and he won't come with me. He wants me to stay, and I can't."

Lucille was silent, her gaze leveled on Bernadette with the familiar Morgan intensity. After a moment, she said, "You could help Ike here."

"I need lawyers. I can't bully Vince."

"Knowledge is power, dear."

"What knowledge?" she asked, shaking her head. "I don't know how to make things happen at this level, Lucille. I'm a fish out of water. I need to get back to what I know!"

"Your parents had significant help in your unethical adoption."

Bernadette frowned, pieces starting to fall into place. "Aunt Ellen?"

"Of course. It wasn't only your parents. Ellen had to convince the girl that your parents were good people. And if it hadn't been for her constant pressure, Lynn might not have caved. Vince's mother was a big part of that deception."

"And you want me to use that," Bernadette clarified, rolling the information over in her mind. She paused, considering. "If I made that information public, it would humiliate my parents. It would irreparably tarnish Vince's political career by association, that's true, but my family would spit me out.

It would be the end of everything. There's no going back from that. No apology is enough. What good does digging up the past do now, anyway?"

"I'm not telling you what to do, Bernie." Lucille heaved a sigh. "I can't tell you what will make you happy. You're right—there are lasting consequences, and if you thwart the family, you'll end up like me. You might see that as a threat or a warning, I don't know."

"I'm trying to be logical here," Bernie said. The price was too high—it would cost more than just her, it would cost her family, too. They were single-minded, tough and obsessed with power, but they were still her family.

"From what I understand, you've always been the clearheaded type," her aunt said. "And the first time you followed your heart was when you ran out on your wedding."

"And look what that got me!" Bernadette laughed bitterly. "I need to think. I need to make a smart choice here—"

"Agreed." Lucille nodded. "But sometimes the smart choice is marrying the senator who would bring you to the White House."

Was Lucille seriously advising her to go

back to Calvin? She stared at her aunt in shock. Had her parents gotten to Lucille, too?

"Even the White House couldn't make up for a cheating louse of a husband," Bernie said softly.

Lucille shrugged with exaggerated innocence. "If you're going to make the smart choice and ignore your heart, then you might as well come out with the biggest payoff. You could feasibly be First Lady and an heiress. Think of all the good you could do then. Power. Influence. The nation's love. Couple that to your inheritance, and you'd be the most influential woman in the West."

Bernie saw what her aunt was doing, and she smiled wryly. "I get it."

"Do you?" her aunt asked quietly. "Because life doesn't give very many chances to follow your heart, and the rest of your life is an awfully long time to go without the man you love."

"It isn't only me," Bernie admitted. "This all happened so fast, and he isn't ready to commit to anything either. I'm a Morgan—and I can't change that. He's been hurt by our family, and he isn't about to make nice with Dad, or…" She sighed. "It won't work, Auntie. You don't just marry a person. You marry a family. And he can't do that. He loves me, but I'm a Morgan, and he can't get past that."

Lucille nodded. "I do know how hard it's been on him."

And Lucille probably understood better than anyone. She'd seen what Liam had gone through.

"Love was enough for you," Bernie said, her voice tight, "but it isn't enough here. You were lucky."

Lucille went back to the door and put a hand on the knob. "You're determined, and I respect that. But don't leave without giving me a hug, okay?"

Bernie nodded, and her aunt closed the door behind her. The tears that had been threatening all morning finally pushed their way to the surface, and Bernadette put her face into her hands.

Love wasn't always enough. Her birth mother's love for her hadn't been enough to keep them together, and what deeper love was there than a mother for her child? Even if she was willing to give up the life she'd been raised to expect, Liam couldn't accept her family. Love was the goal that everyone chased—a hope for a union that surpassed money or influence, but that didn't mean it always worked. Love sometimes failed...

LIAM HANDED IKE another wedge of toast. The boy wouldn't eat it from a plate on the table, but he'd eat it if Liam handed it to him one triangle at a time. It was both frustrating and kind of cute—a weird mix that Liam was starting to appreciate.

Ike had been calling Liam "Daddy" lately, but that didn't make Liam Ike's biological father. It only made it harder to let go.

"Let's go see Lucille," Liam said, wiping his hands on his jeans, and then opening the front door. He'd finish Bernie's car, and then come back to spend the rest of the day with Ike. Chip could take care of the rest of the work—a full-time employee wasn't such a bad idea after all, it seemed.

As he opened the door, his stomach sank. A black SUV had just pulled up, and the back door opened. Except it wasn't Vince who got out, it was a slim, blonde woman in an immaculate red suit. She stood to the side and waited until Vince emerged after her. They didn't touch each other but moved in tandem as if connected by an invisible string. This was Vince's wife—he'd seen her in enough pictures with her husband to recognize her.

They waited while Liam closed the front door and took Ike's hand. Vince gave Ike a quick once-over with a calculating eye, then turned his attention to Liam, a practiced smile coming to his lips.

"Good morning," Vince said. "Meet my wife, Tabby."

Liam nodded, and the woman stared back at him, her expression granite. Vince was making a statement here—his wife was part of this. Should Liam be nervous?

"What can I do for you?" Liam asked curtly.

Tabby bent down and regarded Ike solemnly.

"Hello, Ike," she said softly.

"While Tabby gets to know my son," Vince said, "why don't you and I talk business?"

"Ike isn't business," Liam retorted.

Vince nodded slowly. "But you do own a garage."

Here it came. Bernie had warned him about this, but instead of fear or reluctance, Liam felt a surge of defiance. Across the street, Bernie came outside wearing the colorful dress she'd worn a few days ago—red and pink swirled together. Her hair hung around her shoulders, and her makeup was done today—she was no longer trying to blend in. She paused on the step, looking at them. Then she started toward them.

"Thing is," Vince went on, stepping closer, "if you don't quietly sign Ike over to me, I'll make sure you're audited every single year from now until I die. Terrible things can happen to property—things that insurance might blame on you. There are countless ways that a business fails, and I know most of them—"

"So you're threatening to ruin my business if I don't give you Ike."

"Threat is a nasty word." Vince smiled cordially. "I'm just…okay, yeah. It's a threat."

Tabby reached for Ike, and the toddler pulled back.

"Daddy!" Ike wailed, and Vince raised an eyebrow.

"That would be me," Vince said, and Liam clenched his fists. Punching the senator would be a bad idea, but it would feel so good to connect a fist with that smug face.

Tabby tried to pick up Ike again, but Bernie arrived at that moment, and she slid between them, scooping Ike into her arms in one smooth movement.

"Hi, sweetie," she crooned, then turned to Vince, her voice hardening. "So what's going on here?"

"I'm bringing my son home."

Bernie met Liam's gaze for a moment, and he saw something different in her today—she was almost regal, undaunted. This must be what she was like when she was in control, he realized, and she was amazing.

"I don't think that's a good idea." Bernie shook her head.

"Liam and I have talked it over." Vince planted a hand on Liam's shoulder. "Haven't we, Liam?"

"You see…" Bernie didn't even acknowledge her cousin's words. "I know things, Vince, things you don't want to come out."

"An affair?" Vince asked, his lips turning up in a sneer. "A love child?"

He'd be able to cover that up easily enough if Ike were hidden away, Liam realized. There was already a rumor about Bernadette's mental instability, and he recognized the genius of Calvin's move. What better way to control a potential liability than to erode her credibility before she even opened her mouth? The realization curdled his stomach.

"I'm adopted." She said it blithely enough, and Vince startled.

"What? No, you aren't."

"I am. My birth mother was a teenager in Mercy House." She looked toward Liam, and he saw some of that confidence slip. Her cheeks paled, and she licked her lips, but she kept talking. "My parents forced her to give me up. The whole thing was very ugly."

"And you're telling me this because…?" Vince looked confused.

"Because your mother set it all up." Bernie shot him a dazzling smile. "And if Senator Morgan's mother was involved in forced adoptions… I mean, it might not be technically illegal, but it's very distasteful. People tend to get awfully riled up about that sort of thing. Can you imagine what it would do to your career? What a wonderful photo op, your mother being confronted by the women she'd taken advantage of at their most vulnerable."

"Don't be stupid, Bernie." Vince's tone turned dark. "Those are some very dangerous claims."

"Not claims. I'm not just making up stories here." She met her cousin's eye. "I have proof."

"What, Lucille?"

"A woman with nothing more to lose." Her eyes snapped fire.

Vince swallowed and looked away for a moment, then shot Bernie an ugly glare. "You'd suffer, too. There would go your nice little inheritance. Your father might even decide to make me his heir."

Bernie shrugged. "You don't know what lengths I'm willing to go to."

"For what?" he demanded.

"For Ike." She pulled the toddler a bit closer. "He belongs here with Liam, and if Liam's business should suffer in any way, if he should suddenly fall upon hard times or terrible luck, I'll know exactly who is to blame."

"You're threatening *me*?" Vince was incredulous.

"Yes." She smiled sweetly. "Your political career would be over. We both know your mother wouldn't hold up very well in prison if we could tie those forced adoptions to child trafficking, and the Morgan name would go down in the papers as mud. It would be front page news for months. Think it over."

Vince turned to Tabby, and for the first time, he looked daunted. The cocky smile had been replaced by a twitch in his cheek. Then he nodded slowly.

"Point made," he said quietly. "And if Ike stays here?"

"I keep my mouth shut," she replied.

Liam had never seen Bernadette in action like this before. But was she willing to give up everything to keep him and Ike together? Or was this one magnificent bluff?

"Fine." Vince seemed to believe her. "But if Ike hits the news—if reporters start asking questions…"

He didn't finish. The words hung there in the morning air, and then he turned toward the SUV. Tabby followed him, and they got back into the vehicle, the door slamming behind them. Liam moved closer to Bernie and slid a hand along her waist. They stood together watching as the SUV drove off, and when he turned the corner out of sight, he felt her start to shake.

"You were amazing," he said as she turned to face him.

"I was terrified," Bernie whispered, and she gave Ike a squeeze. "But that should do it. He'll stay away now. He can't risk my story coming out, and he doesn't know how angry I am. He won't take the chance."

Liam leaned forward and kissed her forehead. He stayed there for a moment longer than he needed to, just breathing in the scent of her. She'd just tipped her hand to her cousin—and that might be the most dangerous thing she'd done yet. How long would it take for word to get back to her father?

"Thank you," he said, emotion catching in his throat. And as he looked at her, he could see exactly why she didn't fit in here in Runt River. She was so much—so much beauty, so much heart, so much bravery—she overflowed. And this place couldn't contain her.

"I'll take him over to Lucille's, if you want," she said.

Liam ruffled Ike's curls. "You ready to play at Auntie's house, Ike?"

Ike nodded. "Toast?"

"I'm sure she can make you more." His head was still catching up to all of this, and he felt a belated wave of relief. Was it really over? Could he actually call himself Ike's dad?

"I'll have your car done by four today," Liam said. "If you wanted to come by and pick it up."

"Okay."

They paused, and he wished he could kiss her, pull her against him, find his balance in her arms, but he couldn't.

"Was it a bluff?" he asked after a moment.

"No." Her voice was barely louder than a whisper. "And I'll follow through if I have to."

Then she turned and carried Ike toward Lucille's house, and Liam watched her until she'd disappeared inside. She'd just risked everything for him today, and his heart squeezed almost painfully.

He had a car he had to finish—a deal was a deal.

CHAPTER TWENTY-ONE

BERNADETTE DRAINED THE last of her latte and picked up her bags from the floor of the coffee shop. She'd gone to a few stores that afternoon as she tried to sort out her thoughts. Lucille had nudged her out of the house while Ike napped.

"Go," Lucille had insisted. "Shop. Walk. Think. But you promise me that you'll come back and say a proper goodbye after you pick up your car, do you hear me?"

Bernie had carefully prepared before marching out there to face her cousin, and she didn't regret it one bit. Her aunt was right—if she was going to follow her heart, she needed to stop making excuses and do just that. This wasn't a halfway, caution-taped life. This was her chance to live with integrity and pride—and she was proud of what she'd done today. Liam and Ike deserved to stay together; they'd both be happier for it.

She would pick up the Rolls-Royce, say goodbye to her aunt and she'd drive back to New York where nothing would ever be the same again. She couldn't go back to being a dutiful daughter—not in the way her parents expected—but she wasn't walking away from her family. She'd quietly start the search for her birth mother and see if her father could respect this new, independent Bernadette. Frankly, she thought she'd be a bigger asset to the business this way. She wasn't anybody's little girl anymore.

Bernie looked at her watch. It was nearly four. Her heart sped up, and she felt a wave of sadness. She'd been anxious to see Liam again, but at the same time she dreaded their final goodbye. She pushed open the coffee shop door, stepped out into the fresh air and started up Main Street toward Anderson Avenue—now a familiar walk.

She'd miss this town, she realized, but not as much as she'd miss Liam and Ike. She paused at Anderson Avenue, then turned toward the garage. The doors were open, and she could see her car parked out front waiting for her. Had it really only been a couple of weeks since she'd arrived in that soiled wedding dress?

"Bunny!" Ike came scampering out of the garage as she approached, a bag of crackers in one hand, and a half-eaten cracker in the other. She felt tears gather in her eyes when she saw him, and she bent down to scoop him up as he flew into her arms.

"Hi, Ike," she said, kissing his cheek. He squirmed to be put down again, and she complied, but as she looked up, she saw Liam standing in the doorway, wiping his hands on a rag. He smiled, tossed the rag aside and sauntered out of the garage to meet her.

"So you're here to pick up your car," he said, warm eyes meeting hers.

"Yes." She blinked back her tears. "And to say goodbye."

Liam didn't answer, but he took her hand in his strong, calloused grip and tugged her gently closer. He smelled good—musky and warm—and she wished with all her heart she could just slip into his arms and stay there.

"I don't want to say goodbye," he said gruffly.

"I don't think we have much choice."

"Thing is," he said, "I've been thinking. I

hated Vince for years, and I blamed all the Morgans for what he did. But I have a son to raise now, and that's because of you. You were willing to sacrifice everything to keep him with me, and I—" He brushed her hair away from her face and let his hand drop. "I can't offer much. I've got this garage, and I have Ike. But I love you...*we* love you."

"I love you, too," she whispered.

"And I wouldn't ask you to settle for less than you're worth, Bernie," he said quietly. "Your cousin hasn't called your bluff, and you're in the clear. You can go back to your life in New York and do all the things you wanted to..." His voice caught. "Or you could stay."

"Stay?" She'd been willing to put it on the line to keep Ike with Liam, but was she willing to join them here in Runt River, to be the family that was wrapped up together with love instead of with money? There wouldn't be privilege here, or status. She would lose the Morgan influence, the ability to snap her fingers and have a team of lawyers jump. And if she stayed, would she be able to find her mother?

She smiled and wound her fingers through

his. "If I don't go back, finding my mom will be a whole lot harder. But if I walk away from you…"

Her heart ached at the prospect, and with Liam looking down at her like this, asking her to stay, asking her to be his… She'd fallen in love with him, and she liked to think that her birth mother would want her to follow her heart—the one life lesson the Morgans had never taught her.

"We'll save up," he promised. "We'll hire an investigator. We'll find a way. She's out there somewhere, and maybe she's looking for you, too. This is my last chance before you go, and I'd never forgive myself if I didn't at least ask. Runt River might not be much, but it's home. I can offer a simple life…with me and Ike. I'll never be president, but I'll be faithful."

"Oh, Liam." She sucked in a breath and a tear finally escaped and trickled down her cheek.

"Bunny?" Ike stood at her knees, and she looked down at those big brown eyes. He still clutched a cracker in one hand. And when she looked back up to Liam, he held a diamond ring between two grease-stained fingers. She gasped—it was antique, and at least three carats.

"Where did you get that?" she whispered.

"Lucille said to tell you that you'd never be without family," he said. "And she volunteered the ring."

This was home—she could see that clearly enough. Her heart was leading her now, and she couldn't go back to practical plans when she'd experienced so much more.

"I'd have said yes without it," she said, wiping the tear from her cheek.

Liam slipped the ring onto her finger, then wrapped his arms around her and his lips came down on hers. Her eyes fluttered shut, and she leaned into his kiss, feeling his heart pounding against her chest. Ike squirmed at their knees, and she started to laugh, then broke off their kiss to look down at Ike.

"What do you want, Ike?" Liam asked with a low laugh. "I was busy kissing your new mom."

Bernie bent down and scooped him up, snuggling him close. Liam wrapped his arms around both of them, and she looked up into the face of the man she'd just agreed to marry. No politics, no grandeur, just love.

"Share?" Ike held up the cracker in his chubby fist, and Bernie laughed, then pretended to take a bite.

"Forever and ever, Ike," she whispered.

EPILOGUE

BERNADETTE POKED A large green candle in the shape of the number three into the top of the homemade birthday cake. It wasn't perfect—two layers of vanilla cake frosted with store-bought chocolate icing. She'd even added some colorful sprinkles on top because she knew Ike would love them.

Bernie was staying home with Ike for another year until he was old enough for preschool, and she was working on some plans to start her own marketing company to help a few local operations move some of their business online. She could start local and then broaden her scope as Ike got older. Her Harvard degree would come in useful yet. Bernie still had a few investments in her name—they were saving those for a rainy day. Liam was a big budgeter, and he'd been showing her the ropes. It was actually kind of fun—a bizarre challenge when she hit the grocery store with some cash, a list and a week's worth of eating to do.

Liam came up behind her and slid a hand around her waist. She still liked to look at his work-roughened hand and see the shine of his wedding ring. They'd had a quiet ceremony at the courthouse, and Lucille had hosted a barbecue in her backyard. It had been simple, but perfect.

Her parents hadn't come to her wedding—they were still angry at her decision to stay in Runt River. They knew that *she* knew about her adoption now, and while that had been tense, she could at least talk about it with her mother. Vince had gone straight to her father and told him that she was threatening to expose them all to the press, and Milhouse was still enraged about that. Kitty was the one who kept in contact with her daughter, but Kitty had told her how much her father missed her. Bernie had no idea if she would ever inherit. Her father had threatened to leave everything to Vince, and he might do just that. Time would tell.

But Kitty had sent a birthday present for Ike—a tricycle. It arrived by courier that morning with a birthday card, and while

Milhouse hadn't signed the card, Kitty did confess that he had picked out the gift. That had meant a lot to Bernie. It wasn't about the money anymore, although she wouldn't turn it down. She wanted a relationship with her dad.

"Time for cake!" Ike sang in the background. He'd grown up a lot over the last several months. He was taller and more rambunctious. He talked a lot more, too. He'd turned into a regular chatterbox.

Bernie leaned her head against her husband's shoulder, enjoying his warm strength. "I need matches, Liam."

"Oh." Liam released her, and he started opening drawers. "They're here somewhere."

The doorbell rang, and Bernie laughed softly. "I'll get that. You find the matches."

She headed to the front door—*their* front door. She wasn't entirely used to this yet, but she was now a wife and a mother. It wasn't the life she'd had in New York, but it was sweeter. She pulled open the door to see a woman in her mid-forties. The woman had dark hair pulled back. She was dressed in jeans and light jacket, a scarf around her neck to fend off the April chill, and there was something strangely familiar in those dark, almond-shaped eyes.

"Hi," Bernie said. "Can I help you?"

"Are you Bernadette Morgan?" the woman asked hesitantly.

"I used to be," Bernie said. "I'm Bernadette Wilson now."

Tears sparkled in the woman's eyes, and she nodded quickly. "Oh…that's really nice. So you're married."

"Uh—" Bernie stood a step back. "Yes. Who are you?"

"I'm Lynn Warren."

The room spun, and Bernie clutched at the doorjamb to steady herself.

"I imagine that your parents told you that you were adopted at some point," Lynn went on. "It was a long time ago, I wasn't very old, but—"

"You're my mom?" she whispered. Had this really happened? She'd started her search just after her wedding, but she hadn't gotten too far. She'd tried to keep her expectations low so as not to be disappointed, but…

Lynn blinked back tears. "I was afraid to tell you who I was, but I followed your life from the papers, and when you canceled your wedding a few months back, I thought it might be the right time to say something… I can't believe I—"

And Bernadette flung herself forward and wrapped her arms around her mother's neck; Lynn hugged her back just as tightly. They stood there in the doorway, the cold air from outside winding around them until she heard her husband's voice behind her.

"Bernie? What's going on?"

Bernadette pulled back and looked from her mother to her husband. "Meet my mom, Liam."

Liam's jaw dropped, but even so he put out an instinctive hand to stop Ike who was careening past in his birthday excitement.

"You'd better come inside," Liam said with a grin as he recovered. He swung the door shut behind them. "You two have a lot of catching up to do."

And as Ike bounced at his seat, waiting for his birthday cake, as Liam struck the match to light that candle in the shape of the number three, as Bernie stared into that strangely familiar face of the birth mother she'd longed to meet, she felt a wave of such gratitude that she could have drowned in the happiness of that moment.

"Happy birthday to you... Happy birthday to you..."

"Time for cake!" Ike squealed, and Bernie looked up into Liam's face with a smile.

To think she'd ever been afraid to follow her heart.

* * * * *

*If you enjoyed this story, look for
Patricia Johns's first Heartwarming book,
A BAXTER'S REDEMPTION.
And pick up her next story,
coming in November 2017!*

Get 2 Free Books,
Plus 2 Free Gifts—
just for trying the Reader Service!

Love Inspired®

LI17R

Get 2 Free Books,
<u>Plus</u> 2 Free Gifts—
just for trying the Reader Service!

HOMETOWN HEARTS ♥

YES! Please send me **The Hometown Hearts Collection** in Larger Print. This collection begins with 3 FREE books and 2 FREE gifts in the first shipment. Along with my 3 free books, I'll also get the next 4 books from the Hometown Hearts Collection, in LARGER PRINT, which I may either return and owe nothing, or keep for the low price of $4.99 U.S./ $5.89 CDN each plus $2.99 for shipping and handling per shipment*. If I decide to continue, about once a month for 8 months I will get 6 or 7 more books, but will only need to pay for 4. That means 2 or 3 books in every shipment will be FREE! If I decide to keep the entire collection, I'll have paid for only 32 books because 19 books are FREE! I understand that accepting the 3 free books and gifts places me under no obligation to buy anything. I can always return a shipment and cancel at any time. My free books and gifts are mine to keep no matter what I decide.

262 HCN 3432 462 HCN 3432

Name	(PLEASE PRINT)	
Address		Apt. #
City	State/Prov.	Zip/Postal Code

Signature (if under 18, a parent or guardian must sign)

Mail to the **Reader Service:**
IN U.S.A.: P.O. Box 1867, Buffalo, NY. 14240-1867
IN CANADA: P.O. Box 609, Fort Erie, Ontario L2A 5X3

* Terms and prices subject to change without notice. Prices do not include applicable taxes. Sales tax applicable in NY. Canadian residents will be charged applicable taxes. This offer is limited to one order per household. All orders subject to approval. Credit or debit balances in a customer's account(s) may be offset by any other outstanding balance owed by or to the customer. Please allow 4 to 6 weeks for delivery. Offer available while quantities last. Offer not available to Quebec residents.

Your Privacy—The Reader Service is committed to protecting your privacy. Our Privacy Policy is available online at www.ReaderService.com or upon request from the Reader Service.

We make a portion of our mailing list available to reputable third parties that offer products we believe may interest you. If you prefer that we not exchange your name with third parties, or if you wish to clarify or modify your communication preferences, please visit us at www.ReaderService.com/consumerschoice or write to us at Reader Service Preference Service, P.O. Box 9062, Buffalo, NY. 14240-9062. Include your complete name and address.

Get 2 Free Books,
Plus 2 Free Gifts—
Just for trying the Reader Service!

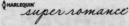

Get 2 Free Books,

Plus 2 Free Gifts—

just for trying the Reader Service!

Love Inspired. HISTORICAL

Get 2 Free Books,
Plus 2 Free Gifts —
just for trying the Reader Service!